Praise for Traveler

"A complex thriller that will literally keep you on the edge of your feet. I honestly could not step away from this book until the very end! 5 Stars!" - *Terry's Book Addiction.*

"I can't wait to read the next one! - *Book Lover's Life.*

"What if Law & Order, Harry Dresden and Sliders had a baby? A fantastic page burner!" - David Adam Suski, author of *The Wired Man.*

"...intriguing, roller-coaster ride of a thriller that was action packed and engaging throughout." - *Avid Book Collector.*

"The traveling between parallel universes is neatly explained and the plot draws you in. Mystery lovers and science fiction fans should get a kick out of the novel. Traveler gets a solid thumbs up." - *Second Run Reviews.*

"...a fun novel that fans of either sci-fi or crime fiction can see themselves shifting into." - *Iowa City Press-Citizen.*

"Dennis Green has written a very entertaining book in "Traveler," one that appeals beyond the science fiction genre where it started." - *Cedar Rapids Gazette.*

"Phillip Marlowe meets Philip K Dick in an intriguing mystery that crosses shifting planes of reality." - Denny Lynch, ICON.

"Plenty of thrills await readers as they journey with the traveler." -Rob Cline, author of *Murder by the Slice.*

"Traveler succeeds with surprises at every turn." -Lennox Randon, author of *Friends Dogs Bullets Lovers.*

TRAVELER

Dennis W. Green

ISBN: 978-0-9977452-0-7

LOCN: 2013949217

Editing by Elizabeth Humphrey

www.bookwormediting.com Littleton, Colorado USA

Cover art and design by Drew Morton

www.drewmadestuff.com Iowa City, Iowa USA

HAPPY HOUR
PUBLISHING

www.happyhourpublishing.com

To my parents, for…well, birth and everything.

To Jack, for bringing the magic to our house as well as this book; to Alex, whose writing continues to inspire mine (and whose edits really improved Traveler);

and always to Debbie, who never allowed me to give up.

The Traveler Chronicles

Traveler
Prisoner
Traitor

PREFACE

H E'D ALWAYS THOUGHT it was stupid to call it "eating your gun." Even with the barrel in his mouth. Which tasted, by the way, like an engine.

Not that he had ever eaten one of those, either.

He might not have found this last thought as funny before the vodka, but it was either laugh or cry, and there were no more tears left. And now that he thought of it, going out with a laugh actually seemed like a good idea. So, he pulled the trigger mid-chuckle.

Well, hell. That was unexpected.

You stupid SOB. Now, I have to start all over.

1

B EFORE THIS MOMENT, if you had asked me what color pain was, I probably would have replied "red."

Red is the color of blood, after all. Pretty much all the wounds I've had, or seen (and there have been a bunch), started out some shade of red.

But as my mind swam back to consciousness through the muck of last night's alcohol, cigarettes and general nausea, the agony lancing past my eyelids was definitely yellow.

Yellow like the sunlight that poured in through the dirty window. It speared my head even worse as I forced a gummy eyelid open. This allowed me to look around the room, and the floor swam blearily into view. My piece lay on the floor near my right hand. I'd fallen asleep holding it again.

The safety was off.

Christ, what a rookie. I safed the gun, trying to ignore how the room started to spin as soon as I moved.

Of course, adding to the pain behind my eyeballs was the ache in my neck and back from sleeping sprawled across the recliner that had been my bed more nights than not lately. I thought about standing up to stretch the kinks out, but even the slightest change in position caused the alcohol still in my stomach to try and force its way back out again. It seemed smart to wait till my stomach settled a little more.

The pounding in my head was like a relentless bass beat. *Wom Wom Wom.*

But after a few seconds I realized the noise wasn't solely from my sluggish blood trying to redistribute itself amidst the alcohol. It was pounding on the door, and it had been going on a while.

Locking my jaws, I gingerly pushed myself upright, kicked the vodka bottle aside and made my way across the small living room of my apartment.

It was a measure of how flimsy the door was that even a pounding from Sam would make it rattle as much as it did. I'm slim and a little shorter than average. But next to Sam I look like a bodybuilder.

Sam Markus couldn't have been more than five-five or five-six and may have barely tipped the scales at one hundred-forty pounds. He looked up at me through the forest of spiky red hair that sprang out from his head in uneven clumps—the mark of a scientist, particle physicist actually, whose journey from bed to lab only occasionally included a stop at the shower.

Which should have made the look of disgust *he* gave *me* amusing, had I been inclined to see humor in anything this morning.

"Christ, Trav, it smells like a tomb in here. What happened to you last night? I turned around and you were gone. You were going to come to my lab. I wanted to show you my new stuff." He picked his way across the room and tried to open the lone window, through which the offending sun shone.

"Doesn't open," I said quietly, returning to the recliner. I sat down heavily, leaned back and closed my eyes. When I opened them again, I saw that Sam had given up on the window and turned around. He was looking at my gun.

"What the hell is this?"

"I'm a cop. I have a gun."

"You're suspended. Even I know you're supposed to turn in your weapon when they tell you to leave."

I shrugged.

"And what's it doing in the middle of the floor?"

I closed my eyes again.

"Trav. *Trav.*"

I opened one eye.

"Don't even pretend you weren't playing Russian roulette with that."

"You can't play Russian roulette with an automatic. Chamber doesn't spin."

4

"You know what I mean."

I shrugged again.

Sam didn't need to know what I'd been considering last night before I'd passed out.

Instead I said, "This is where you tell me how much I have to live for? How I can't do this to my friends, my family? Explain to me who that might be. Mary? *Adam?*"

"Yes, Mary. You think she doesn't still care what happens to you? And… Adam. I've already told you how sorry I am. How sorry everyone is."

"Yeah, we're all sorry. And that makes it all better."

I closed my eyes again as, unbidden, the scene replayed itself in my mind for the thousandth time.

The radio call sending us to the apartment complex.

Seeing one male chasing another male across the parking lot, practically smacking into our front grille. Grabbing the one, handing him off to Adam and taking off after the other one.

Turning around just in time to see the man pull a gun and put four shots into my partner.

Facing Mr. and Mrs. Yount at the funeral, and having to endure their resolute refusal to blame me. But no amount of therapy, sympathy or alcohol could erase the fact that I'd fucked up and Adam had paid the price.

I stood up. I had to *move*.

Which was a mistake.

My head started to swim, not to mention pound like the bass in a jacked-up Monte Carlo.

"Geez, Trav. You're white as a sheet. Sit down."

Sam dug into the messenger bag that always rode his right hip. He shook a couple of tablets out of a mint case. "Here. I'll get you some water."

He returned a moment later with a cloudy glass. "Take 'em. Doctor's orders."

"You're a PhD, not an MD. What are they?"

"Advanced B complex vitamins with ginger, prickly pear extract and a secret ingredient that elevates them from herbal supplement to actual *gen-you-ine* medicine. Testing phase. The lab rats say guaranteed hangover cure."

"You have talking lab rats?"

"T.A.s. Grad students. They make extra money participating in drug trials. They always know the good shit. C'mon. Bottoms up."

I washed the tablets down. The first sip made me realize how dehydrated I was, and I quickly downed the remainder of the glass.

"Better?"

I shrugged.

Sam looked at me expectantly. "Well? You gonna get ready?"

"Ready?"

"For your hearing. Don't you remember? Before you left last night? You asked me to swing by and make sure you were up and got to the station on time."

I had no memory of seeing Sam the previous night, let alone asking him for a wake-up call, but most of last night was a blank, as was much of the last two weeks, so I didn't feel that surprised. What did surprise me was that I had even mentioned the hearing to Sam at all. I'd been planning to blow it off. The outcome was a forgone conclusion. Calling my suspension "administrative leave" was just to satisfy the union. The official ruling would be negligence in an officer-involved shooting.

Not for the first time, I found myself wishing it had been me instead of Adam taking the dirt nap. The kid had everything ahead of him, and the life that had been traded for it was not amounting to much.

Lost in this cheerful train of thought, I realized Sam was still speaking.

"C'mon, Trav. It's not like you to give up. Even if everything has already been decided, don't let the bastards sweep it under the rug. Go down there and make 'em fire you to your face."

He slid his phone out of a side pocket of his bag. "You got time to shower. By the time you're done, the Anacol will have kicked in, and

6

you'll feel better. Besides, my car's in the shop. I could use a lift downtown."

I held up my hands. "All right. You win. I'll be back."

Whether it was Sam's miracle pills or the scalding hot shower, as I toweled my hair dry a few minutes later, I was starting to feel almost human again.

I wiped the steam from the mirror and brushed a thatch of black hair out of my eyes, still bloodshot even though my head had stopped pounding. A narrow, almost pinched face stared back at me. My nose was a little too long, my eyes a little too small to be called handsome. Remember in *Star Wars*, (the first trilogy, the real ones), the other X-Wing pilot? The one who got away with Luke when the Death Star blew up?

Yeah, nobody else ever does either. But people (okay, geeks like Sam) say I look kind of like that actor.

Or perhaps this morning, not so much.

Dark circles rimmed either side of my nose, and my complexion in general would have needed time in a tanning booth to get *up* to sallow. On the whole, I probably looked older than the thirty-one I was.

I certainly felt older. And tired. And I was wishing that Sam hadn't shown up. Then maybe I could have stayed home and not had to face this day.

I knew I should have been grateful to him for sticking with me. Over the last few months, most of my friends had started avoiding me. They didn't understand. Kept saying I needed to move on, get back to normal. I wish I knew how to explain that I didn't know what normal was any more.

Finally, even Mary had given up, helped by a particularly nasty fight I had to honestly admit I had started.

But not Sam.

Like a yappy little dog, he was relentless once his mind was set. Easier just to go along. Be nice to get things over and done with anyway.

I found a black t-shirt on the floor that looked wearable and slipped it on. Yesterday's jeans were still fairly clean as well. My shoulder rig came next. A St. Louis Cardinals jacket completed my normal ensemble.

Back in the living room, Sam had cleared a pizza box off the couch and made himself at home, idly swiping a finger up and down the touchscreen of his phone.

Which reminded me that my phone wasn't in my pocket.

"You see my phone?"

Sam looked around. He moved the pizza box off the coffee table. "Here it... Aww, God, Trav. Haven't you gotten rid of this yet? Why do you keep torturing yourself?"

My phone lay next to an LP. An honest-to-goodness vinyl record. Actually, two records, since it was broken almost exactly in half. The two pieces lay on top of the album's jacket, obscuring the lower half of the face of Miles Davis.

"Trav."

I bent to pick up my phone, not looking at Sam.

"Trav," he said. "Mary is gone. Adam is dead. The record is broken. I understand it's not easy, but you have got to find a way to move on. Otherwise, you're going to find yourself sitting in this room night after night, staring at your gun."

I glared at him until he turned away.

"Look, it's getting late," he said. "Let's go."

I grabbed my keys from a bowl next to the door and locked the apartment behind us. We didn't speak as we walked down the stairs and outside where my Mustang was parked on the street. It's the current model, not a classic. I'd always wanted something like the early seventies Cobra, but had never had the money and opportunity at the same time.

And it was probably just as well. Like everything in my life these days, the car had been nice at one time, but now looked the worse for wear. It was covered with dust. A collection of fast food wrappers, half-empty water bottles and loose papers littered the passenger and back seats.

"Sorry," I said. "Been meaning to clean it out."

I started the car and pulled into traffic, still silent. Sam reached over to turn on the radio, obviously unnerved by the quiet. He arched an eyebrow at me. I shrugged.

"It doesn't work. There's a CD jammed in there. I haven't had time to try and pry it out."

"You can't even listen to the radio? Man, The Axe's ratings will never be the same."

I ignored his attempt to lighten the mood.

So we rode in silence downtown, where Sam's office at the university and Central Station were a few blocks apart.

"Trav."

"Yeah?"

"Um…" Sam obviously was re-thinking the wisdom of blurting out whatever it was he was about to say. He had pulled out his phone and seemed to be studying the screen intently. "Uh, nothing."

I was about to tell Sam to spit it out, whatever it was, when I was wracked by a wave of nausea.

My stomach started to try to claw its way up my esophagus. My vision swam. The street ahead exploded into a rainbow of colors.

…Dark brownstone now stucco…

…red coupe now blue…

…Woman in raincoat…tan…now red…now black…

I slammed on the brakes and squeezed my eyes shut. A moment later, the stomach ache passed.

I opened my eyes. Everything looked normal again.

Except the look on Sam's face. He was white as stone. He turned to me, eyes wide.

"What the hell, Trav? Are you all right?"

I nodded slowly. "I don't know what happened. My stomach got twisted up. Are you okay?"

"Yeah, yeah. That stop was a little abrupt is all. You all right to keep driving?"

"Yeah." We had halted mid-block, and horns blared. I gave the Mustang some gas and we pulled back into traffic.

"You may have had a reaction to the Anacol," Sam said. "Maybe it's not ready for prime time after all."

"I think you need some new lab rats."

My knees were still a little weak a few minutes later as I pulled into a fenced lot, which served as a combination impound/motor pool area and staff parking. Sam had gone back to studying his phone, frowning and grunting.

"Not far enough," he muttered.

"What?"

"Huh? Oh, nothing. Trying to level up on this game."

"Good to see you're using your time wisely, buddy."

I'm afraid I don't see the point of computer games. Sam had suckered me into joining him in some rounds of *Myst* when we were in college, and I actually kind of enjoyed the combination of strategy with the randomness of the cards. But anything where you have to memorize a bunch of keypad or controller sequences to open a door or lift your sword, let alone kill the troll?

I don't get the point.

We got out of the car, Sam still fussing with his phone.

As soon as I stood up, I was rocked by another bout of nausea.

This one was not quite as bad as the first, but I still had to lean against the side of the car to keep from sinking to my knees.

My vision went in and out of focus again, and the dusty car seemed to become shiny and clean, then back to dingy.

"Trav! My God. Did it happen again?"

Sam was at my side—I hadn't even noticed him coming around the car.

I took a couple of deep breaths. Fortunately, there wasn't anything in my stomach, or it might have come up all over the Mustang's hood. But after a few seconds, it passed.

Sam was peering up at me with a worried look on his face.

"Maybe we need to take you to the emergency room."

I shook my head. "Better now."

I held very still, waiting for the last wave of dizziness to dissipate. When I was sure I wasn't going to be sick, I hit the lock button on my key fob and ran a hand through my hair, trying not to think about what was to come.

"You need a ride home?" I said, trying for nonchalant. "I can swing by. Probably won't have anything else to do."

"No, I'll catch a ride with Pete." Pete had the office next door to Sam. "You sure you're going to be okay?" he continued with concern in his voice. "I can come in with you."

"No, it's fine. Go smash some quarks, make some mesons or whatever it is you do."

"All right," he chuckled. "If I discover a new particle today I'll name it after you. Seriously, call me if you need anything."

I nodded. He studied me a moment, then nodded, and turned to go.

"Sam?"

"Yeah?"

"You were right. I needed to see this through to the end. Thanks."

"*De nada*, bro."

I gave him a wave and crossed the parking lot, where the employee entrance was. I entered and slowly climbed the stairs.

The top of the stairs led right into the squad room, which could have doubled as a TV set, as it fit about every cop show cliché you've ever seen. Beat-up desks, most of them pushed together in facing pairs, crowded the floor space, leaving only the narrowest of paths in between. Not exactly ADA compliant, although that point was moot. The elevator didn't work anyway.

Somehow, the air seemed cloudy, even though smoking had been banned indoors for years. It did smell, though. Of burnt coffee and too many, mostly male bodies in too close quarters for too many hours of the day.

But there was one incongruity. A little girl sat at a small conference table in the center of the room, wearing navy blue tights, a Hello Kitty jumper and a pair of Ugg knockoff boots.

She had frizzy red hair, a dusting of freckles on each cheek and a nose just begging to be tweaked. Her face was screwed up in concentration as she focused on the game she was playing on her iPod. My entrance caught her eye, and she looked up.

"Hi, Trav."

"Hi, Holli."

Holli Benjamin was nine. Her mom worked in records one floor up. Most mornings Anne brought Holli to work with her so she didn't have to pay for a sitter for the hour between the time she had to report and the arrival of the school bus, which happened to pass right by the station house.

Technically, Holli was supposed to stay upstairs with her mom, but if there were no suspects being actively booked, she pretty much had the run of the station.

"Got a trick for me?"

Somehow, Holli had heard I used to do magic. But doing card tricks for children in the police station was a Mike Becker thing, not a Trav Becker thing. At least not anymore.

"Told you, kid, I don't know any tricks."

"Yes, you do," Holli replied firmly. "Tomorrow I'm bringing a deck of cards for you."

"Suit yourself."

I felt a little bad that her mom would get the unpleasant duty of telling the girl that after today, I wouldn't be coming back. But on the ever-growing list of people I'd disappointed, Holli would be pretty far down. I managed a smile and ruffled her head as I passed her.

I passed by my own desk—empty, of course. It faced the equally empty desk that had been Adam's, whose personal items were still scattered across the desktop. Apparently, no one had thought to box them up for his parents.

The captain's office was at the far end of the room. A couple of detectives called out a cheerful greeting to me as I passed.

I waved back, but was a little puzzled. Everyone knew I was under suspension and about to be terminated, but people were nodding and greeting me like it was a normal beginning of shift.

No quick glances both at or away from me, none of the nervous chatter you tried to exchange with a cop who you knew was going down. No trying to act normal while at the same time hoping the unlucky-cop mojo wouldn't rub off on you.

Maybe these guys were all better actors than I had ever thought they were.

Two chairs sat outside the captain's closed door. I stopped by the desk nearest the office, occupied by a detective named Anderson.

"He in?"

Anderson sighed. He didn't waste a smile on me. Acting as Captain Martin's unofficial receptionist pained him to no end.

"Yeah, he was waiting for you, but then Monroe had to see him."

I nodded and grabbed the chair nearest the office door—which, as it turned out, wasn't shut after all. It gapped open five or six inches, and I could see Alex Monroe's wide ass taking up most of the space in front of the captain.

I wasn't trying to eavesdrop, but Monroe's voice easily carried to where I was sitting.

"It was dumb luck, Leon. We got to the scene, he was already dead. Shot close range, looked like someone came up to him on the dance floor and jammed the gun right into his abdomen. Between the loud music and the vic's clothes, noise of the shots pretty much muffled. Got off three shots even. Couple of hundred people in the bar, no one saw anything, of course.

"Then we caught a break. Our CI was behind the bar. I know better than to go up and talk to him, of course, but he caught my eye. Everyone is craning their necks to see the body, buncha people are snapping cell phone pictures. CI makes sure I see the one guy who doesn't appear to be interested in the commotion at all, he's just inching toward the door. Not in a hurry or anything, just making sure he's not looking at any of us. I intercept him right before he gets to the door.

"But he's cool as can be. 'What is the problem, officer?' in that accent they all got. Why can't they learn to use contractions?

"Anyway, 'You're the only one leaving,' I say. About this time, I recognize him as one of Kaaro's chief goons. He says, 'I don't like looking at blood.' Then I happen to look down. He's wearing white leather shoes, like glow-in-the-dark bright. Except for three little red drops on the left one. I tell him I got a few questions, and that's when he tries to bolt. Uniforms were right outside the door, of course, so he didn't get far. We searched him and came up with a gun. Smelled like it had been fired recently. Bagged his hands. Tech will be here in a few minutes to test for powder residue, but I think we got this nailed down."

"I agree," said Captain Martin. "Do you think Kaaro had anything to do with it?"

"If it happened in The Kremlin, Anton Kaaro is involved somehow."

"What's your next move?"

"Gonna sit on our suspect a while. Might bring Kaaro or one of his stooges around. And…"

"The CI?"

"Yeah."

"You can contact him, but for God's sake be careful," Martin warned. "It's taken months to get someone that close to the action in Kaaro's club. And we don't want him to disappear."

"Right," said Monroe. "I'll keep you posted."

He lumbered out past where I was sitting. "Hey, Trav," he said pleasantly.

I stared after Monroe's departing bulk. Part of me was chewing over the conversation I had heard, putting it together with investigations that had been ongoing when I'd last been here.

But then I realized I was wasting brain cells. This was none of my business. Leave the crime fighting to actual cops. Of which I would only be one for about another minute.

Captain Martin's voice interrupted my reverie.

"Hi, Trav, thanks for coming in. Sorry to make you wait."

"S'all right."

"You hear any of that?"

"Some."

"Nothing good ever happens at The Kremlin. Kaaro lets his thugs drink at the bar, then some preppie and his date go slumming, the wise guy hits on the girl, the preppie objects and the next thing you know, we're carrying pieces of college boy out in a bucket."

The captain sighed and ran a hand through his hair. "Well, never mind that. It's no concern of yours. Sit."

He didn't mention the CI—the confidential informant. I'm sure he was hoping I hadn't heard that part. Letting a soon-to-be-fired officer know you had a source inside a crime boss's inner circle was definitely a no-no.

I shut the door behind me and took the lone chair in front of the captain's desk.

Leon Martin was in his early fifties, but looked ten years younger. His gray hair was cropped astronaut-close. There was only the barest hint of a middle-aged paunch at his waist. He wore black chinos, a royal blue oxford shirt with the sleeves rolled past his wrists, and a yellow tie, loosened at the neck.

A pair of glasses, rimless to the point of invisibility, were one of very few concessions the captain made to his age.

A nationally-ranked Masters swimmer, he was tan pretty much year-round, a result of hours of lap swimming in the sun. It paid off. He routinely crushed athletes half his age in the pool. Ribbons and trophies from a variety of regional and national meets lined a shelf behind his head, right next to a half dozen marksmanship awards.

"Trav, I don't really know where to start."

Martin paused, and looked down at his cluttered desk.

"Look, Leon. It's all right. Let's get it over with."

"Good idea. Detective Becker, as a result of the events of 19 August and the subsequent investigation, it is the opinion of the review board..."

Here it comes.

It was funny. I had thought that I was prepared for this moment, but now that it was actually here, I didn't know what to do.

I fought to keep a neutral expression on my face. I couldn't look at Martin, so I studied a spot on his desk, which almost caused me to miss what he actually was saying.

"...That your quick thinking and bravery during the shooting prevented loss of life and certainly saved that of your partner. So, it's my pleasure to tell you that in a unanimous decision, the board is recommending you to receive the Award for Valor in the performance of duty. There will be a presentation ceremony next month. Congratulations, Trav."

What the hell?

"I...I don't understand."

Now I did look up at the captain, searching his face for some explanation.

"Is this some kind of a joke?" I finally managed to say.

"I'll say," came a voice from behind me. "I get shot, you get a medal."

Still trying to make sense of this insane turn of events, I hadn't heard the door open behind me.

Now, I turned and saw half the squad crowded into the doorway, huge grins on their faces. They gathered behind the young man who had just spoken.

Right arm in a sling, crooked grin on his face and not looking at all dead, Adam Yount leaned against the doorjamb.

INTERLUDE

*T*HE SMALL GROUP *worked its way up the side of the hill. A stiff breeze blew out of the north, carrying the scent of pine, last night's cookfires and old rodents' nests as the group labored through the dense brush.*

The wind whipped through the furs they wore wrapped as tightly as a culture that had not yet invented the knot could get, but barely stirred their bushy hair, which was matted down effectively by dirt, leaves and small insects. If the cold bothered them, none showed it.

There were five in all. All but the leader carried both their weapon—a short spear with a fire-hardened tip—and a hide gathered at four corners to form a carrying bag. Each bag bulged with tubers, grain, charred meat and even several pieces of wood burned down to black-gray charcoal.

The Leader carried only his spear, which was about half again as long as those carried by the others. He was a giant among his people, nearly five feet tall.

He didn't really have a name, none of The People did. Their small language was mostly common nouns, as succeeding generations had agreed and passed on to their children sounds that had come to signify tree, cave, wolf, mammoth, etc.

The People were such a small group that the need to create references to others beyond—Him, Her and That One—had not come about yet. Other tribes were simply thought of as Others.

The Leader was the exception. He did have a name of sorts, the click and grunt that might loosely translate as "The One Who Can Kick All of

Our Asses." *Actually, it was probably more of a title since, should he be defeated in combat, whoever beat him would then be known by that appellation.*

Not today, though. If any other members of the party were pondering rebellion, those thoughts would have been suppressed by the need to focus on the uphill toil, not to mention empty bellies.

Finally, The Leader grunted, calling a halt in front of a shallow cave. He paused, looking back at his crew, who stopped in place, not coming forward to join him at the cave's mouth. Their expressions said it all.

"You wanted to be the boss. Here's why we pay you the big bucks."

The Leader turned back around, not willing to let trepidation show on his face, although he knew they could smell his nervousness.

He planted his staff firmly on the rocky ground and pushed off into the cave. Almost immediately, he was presented with a wall of solid rock in front of his wide nose. But he'd been here before, although not often, and knew to turn to his left. The wall did not signify the back of the cave, but rather the bend of a tunnel.

He made his way through the passageway, and could hear the rest of the band following him. As he pressed forward, the smells of the outside dropped away and were replaced by scents of smoke, mildew, and decaying meat.

Presently, the tunnel opened into a large oblong room, maybe twelve feet across. A small fire burned in the center, smoke curled up to some natural vent invisible in the darkness above. The vent had to be there, even though you couldn't see it, or the room's occupant would have suffocated long ago.

And in fact, at first glance it appeared the room was empty, and that the rotting smell came from a corpse, but as the group entered, a pile of fur near the fire started to move.

The small band halted and watched as the pile rose and revealed itself to be an old man. Ancient. He had to be nearly forty years old. Skin hung loosely from his arms and legs. Much of the hair on his head had fallen out, along with many of his teeth. His beard was mostly gray, with the remnants of his last several meals making a slow descent down the tangled hair. He blinked at them, his eyes large and watery.

The Leader beckoned to his men, who brought forth the carry-skins, carefully spilling their contents onto the floor beside the fire.

When they were done, a substantial pile of goods was revealed. There were tubers not unlike a potato or maybe a yam, various grains, and some cooked squirrel and rabbit meat, along with some charred pieces of wood. It was these the old man was the most interested in. In fact, he ignored the food altogether, picking up the charcoal and rubbing several pieces across the palm of his hand until he finally found a few pieces that satisfied him.

After he'd finished this examination, he looked up at The Leader, who had been rummaging through the pile himself. When he saw that he had the old man's attention, The Leader showed him what he had found.

It was a small, smooth, flat rock, about eight inches in diameter. There were several scratches on the rock's surface, which upon closer examination, were revealed to be marks made from charred wood pieces not unlike what the old man held. In the light of the fire, the scratches resolved themselves into an inverted triangle, with several curved lines coming out of the figure's bottom point. Two short lines, dashes really, sat parallel to the top of the triangle.

Maybe no one but the artist would have recognized the triangle as the representation of the head of a wooly mammoth—dashes for eyes and curved lines below the head the trunk and tusks—but since the old man was in fact the person who had made the drawing, he nodded.

The negotiations were conducted in grunts, gestures, and physical actions that would have reminded a modern human a little of charades. Rendered into English, the conversation might have sounded something like this:

<They say you're the guy who can help us find a mammoth.>

<Maybe.>

<What's it going to cost?>

<Well, this stuff should just about cover it, even though the meat is overdone.>

<We can always take everything back to our village.>

<No!> The old man licked his lips, eyes darting to a rabbit leg, still warm from The People's fire. It smelled delicious.

<No, that won't be necessary, But....>

<But what, old man?>

<After you catch it, bring me its eyes.>

<Its eyes? Why? You can't eat those.>

<You do the hunting, I'll take care of the miracles. Do we have a deal?>

<Yes, but get on with it. You and your cave stink.>

<You guys don't exactly smell like a forest flower either. Now, stand back while I make the magic.>

Despite his bravado in conversation, The Leader was only too happy to step back to stay out of the way of whatever supernatural forces the old man was calling up.

But if The People were expecting lightning, noise, or the appearance of spirits, they were disappointed.

The old man stared off into space for a long time, then grabbed a piece of charcoal. With his other hand, he motioned for the leader to throw more wood on the fire from a convenient pile nearby. As he did so, the old man now shifted his gaze to The Leader and held his eyes for what seemed like an eternity. Finally, the old man looked at The Leader's spear, and the piece of wood stuck in the belt of his furs which served as a cudgel for close-in encounters.

Then, the old man began drawing.

For quite a while, the other men watched in silence as the old man completed his first set of shapes and then began another set. After a moment, one of The Leader's crew pointed to some etchings that were of a familiar shape.

The Leader narrowed his eyes. Yes, it was a hill he knew well, a short walk from the village. With that clue, he was also able to identify another series of scratched lines as a stand of trees at the base of the hill, and...

The old man had drawn a group of stick figures near the stand of trees. The figure at the front was a little taller than the others, and sprouting from each of the lines representing its arms were two other lines—one long, one short. Weapons held in each hand. The Leader looked at his spear and the club hanging from his waist. Then he looked back at the drawing on the wall.

The old man was putting the finishing touches on another figure which each man in the party could immediately identify. An enormous mammoth. The old man drew some spears embedded in the animals hide, then stepped back to admire his work. He turned to look at the group.

The Leader gestured to the drawing. <It will happen like that?>

The old man shrugged. <Will happen, could happen, might happen, has already happened.>

<It's all the same.>

2

I WALKED SLOWLY back to my desk, trying not to stare at Adam, who was now seated across from me. I could feel his eyes on me as I went through the motions of getting settled in for the day, unclipping my weapon and putting it in the top side drawer, turning on the computer. I pretended to study the blank screen intently.

"Is everything okay, Trav?" He asked finally.

I forced myself to look at him, trying to keep a somewhat-composed expression on my face.

Adam Yount was twenty-three, average height, but skinny, almost gangly. His blond hair was long but tightly curled, with hooded blue eyes, giving him something of a surfer-dude look. Although I knew for a fact that the closest he had ever come to catching a wave was buying Ron Jon flip-flops on a spring break trip he refused to talk much about.

He wore khakis in a military olive green and a lightweight V-neck sweater.

Adam had been jumped from uniform to detective pretty fast out of the academy, unusual—but he was very bright. And then assigned to me.

For the first few months, it had felt like I had been given a Labrador puppy—all curiosity and energy, tripping over paws he hadn't grown into yet. But he was a quick study, and had just finished his probationary period when the fateful call to the Spring Green apartments had come in.

The call that had ended with me desperately pressing with one hand and both knees on his armpit, failing to staunch the spurting arterial blood, while the blue eyes lost focus and finally went blank and gray.

But those eyes were back to their normal color now, and they watched me closely, with an inquisitive look that was about to edge over into concern.

I knew I had to say something. He was beginning to sense something wasn't right. And there were a thousand things I wanted to say to him.

Unfortunately, they all began with, *Why aren't you dead?*

Finally, I cleared my throat and tried the only thing I could think of.

"You're...uh, looking good."

He smiled and ducked his eyes—I swear he started to blush. "Well, it's been a long time coming. I'll still have physical therapy for a few more weeks. Not like you, out of the hospital the next day."

"I was, uh, not in nearly as bad a shape as you."

Again, I searched for something innocuous to say. "So, the arm is better, then?"

Now, a hint of a smile tugged at the corners of his mouth. "Well, the bruising from you practically sitting on it to keep me from bleeding out is almost faded."

Adam had only recently felt comfortable enough to start flipping a little of the shit back at me that I, and the rest of the squad, routinely threw in the direction of a new plainclothes officer. I was glad to see his, well, *apparently* near-death experience hadn't drained the vinegar out of him.

"Next time I'll try to be more gentle."

He cast his eyes down, losing the nerve to keep up his cheekiness, and continued talking in a low voice.

"You know, I don't remember much about that night after I caught the bullet, but I do remember you giving me First Aid with one hand, all the while keeping a gun on those two morons with your one free hand. I never had the chance to say thanks."

The view of Adam bleeding to death underneath me was still all too real in my memory. I pushed it out of my mind.

"Better than the...uh, the alternative."

"Too right." Adam checked the time on his phone. "My desk shift doesn't start for another hour, and you're good till three. Breakfast?"

I seemed to remember I'd been too nauseated to eat earlier, but my stomach had settled down. Did it have something to do with Sam, with drinking too much last night? This morning seemed a long time ago already, and the details were now kind of foggy.

Regardless, I realized now that I was ravenous. And desperately in need of coffee.

"Sounds good," I said. "I'll drive."

Getting out of the building took some time, as we had to stop several times for congratulations, hearty slaps on the back for me, gingerly handshakes for Adam. Finally, we achieved the parking lot and crossed to the Mustang. I brushed an imaginary fleck of dust from the shiny hood and slid in as Adam did the same.

As I turned the key, the sound of the engine turning over was drowned out by the dueling horns of Miles and Cannonball.

I quickly hit the CD player's eject button.

"Geez, Trav!" Adam shouted, then modulating his volume in the sudden silence. "Bad enough you make me listen to fifty-year-old jazz all the time. But at this volume, I think I have an OSHA grievance."

I frowned and slid the CD from its slot and stared at it. It was a homemade disc. Instead of the usual title and artist, or date of recording jotted on the top, however, were several lines in neat, feminine script.

Sorry again about the LP. Know how you feel about digital, but I hope this will do till we can find another vinyl copy. —M.

I turned the CD over in my fingers. Mary had given me this. Why was I surprised to see it?

"Earth to Trav."

"What?"

"Are we going to breakfast or not?"

"Yeah, sure."

I stuck the CD in the sun visor and pulled out of the lot. "Where to?"

"Oh, Dinah's would be okay," replied Adam, a little too casually.

I raised an eyebrow, but didn't reply, simply aimed the Mustang at our usual spot.

"Someone's in the Kitchen with Dinah" was a restored dining railcar from the Twenties, parked atop tracks which used to be a part of a spur that went right through downtown.

It was small but cheery. Railroad memorabilia festooned about every square inch of wall space, much of it playing on the theme of the old work song Dinah had appropriated for her restaurant's name. There was a counter with stools along one side, cash register on the end nearest the door.

There was enough room for two people to work behind the counter (if they were friendly), and a pass-through to the cramped grill just behind. Six cozy booths lined the window side.

"Hey, guys," Dinah called to us as we grabbed our regular booth, then went back to making change for the customer at the register with her.

The only other employee, a young woman, slid cups of coffee in front of each us before we even had a chance to ask. The mugs were different sizes and colors.

Dinah had never purchased a coffee mug in the entire history of her store, relying on customers to provide castoffs and logo mugs to promote their business. It was one of the most successful recycling strategies ever. I had never sipped from the same mug twice.

The waitress gave me a quick smile, but focused on Adam. Her name was Kim, and she was a senior at the U. She was also Dinah's niece, staying with her aunt and working at the diner part-time.

She was trim, but carried the right amount of body fat in exactly the right places. Comfortable-looking but very snug faded jeans framed her attractive bottom, and the top two buttons of her Henley top had long ago given up on ever closing. Her hair was dirty blonde, and gathered in a tight pony tail.

"Do you need menus?"

"No thanks, Kim," I replied. "Two Number 7s." I glanced at Adam for confirmation, but he had suddenly become fascinated with his mug, intently studying the font of the letters reading, *You don't have to be crazy to work here, but it sure helps!*

"So, have you decided what you're doing after you graduate?" I asked her.

She shrugged, frowning prettily. "I've got resumes out everywhere, and am networking with every warm body that comes in. But the job market is pretty tight. Looks like I'll be working here for the foreseeable future."

"Well, that's lucky for us."

She dimpled and looked at Adam. "So, a Number 7, then, Adam?" Trying to draw him into the conversation.

"Sure, sure," said Adam, glancing quickly up at her, with a pleasant, if vacant, smile before turning his attention back to his cup.

Kim continued to study Adam for a beat longer than you might have thought normal, then jotted our order on her pad.

"All righty then. I'll put this in."

She stuck her pencil behind one ear and called the order out to Dinah, who had moved to the kitchen.

"What is it with you and her?" I murmured to Adam. "We come in here four times a week. You never suggest eating anyplace else. She's obviously interested. But you become Mr. Caveman when we come in here, communicating with clicks and grunts."

"Geez, Trav, can you keep your voice down?" Adam whispered.

"Six words. *Do. You. Want. To. Go. Out.* Is it that hard? You're not usually this shy with women. You get dates at crime scenes. What gives?"

Adam started to say something, then stopped and shook his head. "Maybe I have *your* best interests at heart."

"My best interests?"

"Of course." Adam put down his mug, glanced over to make sure Kim was out of earshot and leaned slightly over the table so he could speak softly and still be heard.

"Because I know how this will go. I'll ask her out, she will, of course, jump at the chance to date a classically-handsome, wounded-in-the-line-of-duty hero cop. It'll end after four dates, because we either go to bed too fast or not fast enough. Then, you and I will never be able to show our faces in here again. And Dinah's Number 7 is God's primary reason for creating eggs. So, I dial down the magnetism I naturally exude to allow her to keep her distance and not deprive you of one of the few genuine pleasures in your miserable life."

26

"I don't think so," I countered.

I kept my tone light, even though for some reason, the phrase *miserable life* caused the hair to stand up on the back of my neck. "A shipwreck breakfast is a shipwreck breakfast. I think you actually like her, and are trying to figure out a way to approach her with a line she hasn't heard on 'Jersey Shore'."

"Get stuffed, Trav. Like you should be giving anyone love advice. She's just a girl."

Adam went back to his coffee, and I didn't push him any farther. Still, one didn't have to be a trained investigator to notice that Adam tracked the progress of Kim's delightful hips with laser-like focus as they swayed to avoid obstacles between the booths and counter.

After breakfast, I dropped Adam off back at the station. He was working the day-shift during his convalescence, while I had several hours to kill before I went on shift, so I pointed the Mustang toward home.

I remembered the Miles CD and poked it back into the player, warbling along in a counterpoint to the melody, whistling on the off beats of Miles' changes, while my hands tapped the steering wheel in perfect duplication of Jimmy Cobb's drumbeats. The tune was "Freddie the Freeloader."

For a while, I was lost in the music. That's the thing about jazz—no matter how many times you hear a particular tune, and I had literally been listening to "Kind of Blue" since birth—a great tune always shows you something new each time you listen.

My cell phone rang.

I flipped the volume knob down with a practiced wrist flick and worked the phone out of the pocket of my jeans.

The screen said "Mary."

Why was she calling me? Hadn't she sworn never to speak to me again?

"Hello?"

"Hey." Mary's voice was like a warm breeze, even though it held a nervous tone.

"Hey."

"Is this a bad time?" I was expecting to hear resentment in her voice. But if anything, it was just tentative.

"No, just heading back from the station. Listening to the CD you gave me. Thanks."

"It was the least I could do after breaking your LP. Actually, that's what I was calling about."

"Yeah?"

"I told you I'd replace it. I found one on eBay. It came yesterday."

"You didn't have to do that."

"I know." She paused. "Trav, I, uh..."

"What?"

"Oh, Trav." She sighed. A very long sigh. "I...I miss you."

"I miss you, too."

It was an effort to keep my voice steady.

"But...oh, why is this so hard? Trav, we could get back together. And it would be great. For a month, or maybe six. But, you know eventually we'd end up right where we were last week."

That did ring true.

"Let's not be the kind of exes who keep circling each other so neither of us can move on. This isn't a TV show. I'll leave you alone. But, I did want to give you your record. I'll be rehearsing till late tonight, but can I come over tomorrow and leave it at the station?"

"Sure."

"Okay, then."

Neither of us spoke for a long time.

"G'bye, Trav."

"Bye."

I snapped the phone shut.

Crap.

I had thought I had adjusted to not being with Mary, but it only took the sound of her voice to bring the flood of memory and emotion back.

I didn't have time to even lay the phone on the seat, let alone shove it back into my pocket when it went off again. I glanced at the caller ID.

"Sam."

"Man, what's wrong? You sound like you lost your best friend. And I'm right here."

"Not in the mood."

"All right, all right. Sorry. Hey, I wanted to check in and make sure you were okay."

"Why wouldn't I be?"

"Well, you were pretty green around the gills when you left me this morning, and I wanted to make sure you are feeling all right."

"Yeah, fine."

"And, I wanted to let you know that you don't need to come by the lab later to pick me up. I can get a ride home with Pete."

"Yeah, I know. Didn't you already tell me that?"

"Did I? Maybe I did."

"Whatever you say, bu — — Ahhh!"

The buildings and cars visible through the windshield suddenly began to swim and shimmer in my field of vision. The Plymouth that was coming toward me—I swear—actually changed color twice, from blue to grey back to blue again. My stomach dropped, like on a roller coaster ride.

"Trav, what's wrong?"

"God."

But the dizziness passed as quickly as it had come on. A cold sweat was all that remained.

I suppressed a shiver. "Uh, nothing. Just got lightheaded for a minute."

"Have you eaten anything lately?"

"Yeah. Big breakfast a few minutes ago."

"Well, maybe it's indigestion. I told you that you eat too fast. You should listen to me, I'm a doctor."

"We've been through that," I snorted. "Your PhD does not qualify you to dispense medical advice."

29

"See? You're doing better already. You gonna be okay?"

"Yeah, I'll talk to you later."

At home, I puttered around my apartment for a while, tidying up, although the place really didn't need it. I wasn't there enough for it to ever really get too cluttered, and while Mary and I had been dating, I had gotten into the habit of keeping it presentable so it was decent if she had happened to stop by.

By the time I finished, my emotions and stomach had settled, so I pulled on some sweats, laced up my Sauconys and went out for a run.

The myths about fat cops and donuts are pretty much just that, at least if you're smart. True, an irregular schedule and extra shifts can make it easy to self-medicate with sugar and caffeine, but as Adam and I had found out a few weeks ago, a cop can be called on at any time to launch himself out of the car and take off running like an Olympic athlete. And you wanted to make sure your heart was ready for the strain.

Smart cops like Captain Martin found ways to stay in shape, which was probably why he was still on the force. Not to mention alive. I was trying to follow his example. And since running after someone was what would most likely be required of me at work, that was also what I did to train.

I was feeling pretty energetic when I hit the street, but for some reason, got tired quicker than I expected. Still, I trudged out five miles, and ended with a nice long walk to cool down. A quick shower and I was back in the Mustang, headed to work.

I didn't plug the CD back in. It made me think of Mary, so I settled for the radio.

Our town may not be much to get excited about, but it does have something very few cities have these days—a decent radio station.

Axe 106.9 is that very rare thing in modern media, a truly local music station. One with DJs who actually get to pick the music they play. The guy on at this time of day mixed old rock, folk, and jazz in a daily playlist that might as well have been called "Trav's Favorites, Nonstop."

I turned the radio up as they segued from John Hiatt's "Buffalo River Home" into Weather Report's "Birdland."

Awesome.

30

I stopped at Subway for a sandwich and ice tea to go, then headed into work.

I unwrapped the sandwich at my desk and chewed thoughtfully as I started to make my way through the pile of paperwork that had accumulated while I was on administrative leave, required after being involved in a shooting.

And while Adam was on desk duty for medical reasons, I would probably end up spending much of the next several shifts at my own desk for lack of other work. Most of our cases had been re-assigned during our time off.

However, there were enough old reports and follow-up to the shooting to keep me busy for several hours.

I was coming to the bottom of the pile when Alex Monroe, seated a few desks over, slammed his desk phone down into its cradle. We all looked up from what we were doing. A short call ending with a noisy hang-up usually meant action.

"Shots fired at The Kremlin," Monroe said tersely. "At least one person down."

Again? What is it with that place?

Monroe was looking around the room, mentally tallying up the available workforce to respond. In addition to him and me, there were four other detectives present. Protocol required him to take no more than half, so as not to deplete the shift.

"Trav, Stevens, let's go." I nodded, grabbing my weapon and jacket.

Stevens, a wiry black guy a few years older than me, did the same, adding a ball cap to cover his shaved head. He grabbed a set of keys off a pegboard on the wall. We hit the stairway at precisely the same time, following Monroe quickly down the stairs. Even though Alex trended more toward the *yes, please* side of the donuts and coffee equation, he moved pretty fast for a big guy. We had to hustle to stay with him.

We burst out of the door together. A part of my mind wondered if we looked like the final shot in the opening title sequence of a cop show. But I refrained from asking the others to walk in slow motion to complete the effect.

Stevens and I piled into one unmarked car, Monroe into another. We didn't speak on the drive, instead listening carefully to the radio chatter from the officers on the scene.

It was a short trip. We passed east through Campus Town and approached the river, home to a warehouse district, where the skeletons of heavy equipment manufacturing centers were gradually being remade into industrial-styled condos and lofts, with funky shops, galleries, small restaurants, and lounges on the ground floors.

We pulled up to one such building. Nondescript from the outside (except for the half-dozen squad cars and big bunch of people milling around that some uniforms were trying to keep corralled), the bar sat on the first floor of a former button factory.

The building pretty much sat square on the border between the gentrified, neo-Bohemian style of the reclaimed neighborhood and the decaying structures that had gone unclaimed by urban developers.

As Leon had said earlier, the location of the bar was problematic. Prosperous, white-collar kids wandered in from their nearby urban lofts, not realizing they were crossing a Mason-Dixon Line to an area that was home to a rough clientele.

There was no name on the door. The only indication the building wasn't empty was a single neon sign right above the door, a square that pulsed in scarlet.

Like the building that housed it, the owner straddled the line between reputable and disreputable, although I knew which side of that line he spent most of his time on.

Anton Kaaro had started out as a penniless refugee from some former Soviet satellite whose name was all Ks and Xs. Using superb street smarts, and an army of fellow refugees who followed his orders like an infantry battalion, he was able to take over most of the criminal ventures in the city in a couple of years.

Normally, this was done leaving a bloody trail of discarded predecessors, which helped us cops keep any one goombah from getting too powerful.

But in Kaaro's case, there was no trail explicitly linking him to any illegal activity. People who complicated Kaaro's life tended to disappear. Whether from flight or murder, no one had ever been able to figure out.

From this bar, his seat of power, Kaaro controlled the lucrative drug trade common to most college towns, and a healthy prostitution market as well, largely staffed by girls imported from Eastern Europe. The organized crime unit suspected dozens of merchants in the warehouse district were paying Kaaro protection money as well, but of course no one was talking.

The uniforms had already put up some barricades and strung crime-scene tape between them to keep people away from the door. One officer nudged a barricade aside to let us through.

"Who's inside?" Monroe asked her.

"McCoy, Boyle, and Vega," the officer, whose name was Amy Harper, replied.

"They don't need you in there?" I asked.

Harper frowned at me, and looked at Monroe.

"She can't go in there, Trav," he said in a tone that was really saying, *you should know that.*

But I didn't have time to ponder this exchange, because a few more steps and we were through the door.

The neon theme from the sign outside was repeated throughout the club. Dozens of long tubes of light, all red, provided the majority of the illumination, punctuated by pinpricks of white light from small lamps at tables and booths. More lights, multicolored on those revolving stalks that rotate in synch with music, spun without guidance above a dance floor, empty of both music and patrons, to our left.

A huge mirror backed the bar, which took up most of the entire rear wall of the room. Dozens of bottles of liquor lined three shelves under the mirror.

The patrons were gathered into a clump near the doorway that led to the dance floor. Three officers stood nearby, each one talking to a person cut out of the herd. As we watched, one of the officers jotted some information onto her notepad, and nodded to the young woman she was interviewing.

Released, the girl headed in our direction. She had come dressed for battle—a silver mini-dress that hung at mid-thigh shivered across her hips as she crossed the room, platform sandals clacking on the floor. Her hair was carefully arranged in a "freshly fucked" muss. Her makeup, striking earlier in the evening, was now smudged, and contrasted with her ashen face and frightened eyes. She hurried past us, looking at the floor.

A young man, all low-riding pants and too-small t-shirt, took her place. Monroe went over to that duo, Stevens and I moved toward the others.

I arrived at the same time as the officer, a recruit named Caleb Vega, was deep in conversation with his witness, another young woman. A cloud of blonde hair framed wide-set, inquisitive eyes. She also looked a little shook up by what she had seen, but seemed to handling it okay.

As she spoke, Vega scribbled furiously on his notepad, flipping to the next page. It looked like he'd already done this a couple of times. He looked up as I approached.

He asked the woman to excuse him for a minute and turned to me.

"Hey, Trav. Ms. Foster, here…" he inclined his head toward the woman he'd been interviewing, then paused.

"Yeah?" I prompted.

"Well, she says she's a psychic."

"Okay…"

Vega held up a hand. "No, she's not giving me any mind-reading bullshit." He showed me the multiple pages of notes on his pad. "Most observant wit I've ever interviewed. Look at all this."

We turned back toward her. I stepped forward. She was watching me intently, a strange expression on her face. She extended her hand. I took it, although social conventions like handshakes are not real common at crime scenes.

I tried to reconcile my mental image of a psychic—crystal ball, head scarf, long skirt and peasant blouse—with the perky blonde in skinny jeans and camisole top before me, although the sexy effect was spoiled a little bit by the sparkly silver Chuck Taylors on her feet. Her head was cocked to one side as she examined me right back.

I met her eyes for a minute, then looked away, uncomfortable for some reason with the depth of her gaze. At a loss for words, I finally fell back on crime scene convention.

"Ms. Foster."

"Morgan."

"Morgan. You've given Officer Vega a very complete statement. Thank you very much."

"My pleasure," she said with an open, innocent smile. Then, as my words seemed to sink in, she frowned.

"Oh! I've been rambling on and on while you have more important things to do and so many other people to talk to. That is JUST like me, talking nonstop when you have a CRIME to investigate! There are so many other people here who want to go home and forget about everything they've seen and here I am talking and talking to poor Officer Caleb here, who is being SO nice and taking down everything I say into his little notebook, while I prattle on..."

She stopped. Good thing, too. I hadn't seen her take a breath during all this. Unless she'd mastered circular breath like a jazz saxophonist, she would be in danger of passing out.

But she just looked chagrined. "Oh, NO. There I go, doing it again. It's what happens when I'm nervous or under stress, you know? I feel like I have to fill up all that empty space with something..."

She stopped again, holding up a hand while she closed her eyes and took a deep breath.

"Okay. I'm better now, I promise. I am SO sorry, Officer..."

"Uh, Becker. Detective Becker. Travis. Trav."

She was still holding onto my hand, and pulled on it to draw me closer. She looked from side to side, then back at me.

"What does it feel like?"

"Pardon me?"

"Being... you know. I've always wondered."

What the hell? "Ma'am, I'm sorry, I'm not sure what you mean."

She put a hand to her mouth.

"You don't know."

"Don't know what?"

She looked at me again for what seemed like a long time, then shook her head, rolling her eyes in self-mockery.

"Never mind. I know you guys aren't interested in any of my mumbo jumbo."

Now it was my turn to look at her, trying to ferret out what had just happened. But she turned two guileless eyes on me, and gave me a bright, innocent smile. Whatever it had been was now passed.

I turned to Vega. He'd been looking through his notes, oblivious to our conversation.

"You got any more questions for Ms. Foster?"

He shook his head. "Thank you, ma'am."

She looked at the crowd yet to be questioned, still corralled near the dance floor. Her gaze crossed mine, but so briefly I didn't have the opportunity to continue my own line of questioning.

She gave me an impish smile. "Nice to meet you Detective Becker-Travis-Trav. I'll see you again."

She turned to leave. It didn't seem like her cryptic comments had anything to do with the shooting, but I sure wanted to ask what the hell she was talking about. I started after her, but I was suddenly distracted by some movement out of the corner of my eye.

The center area where we'd herded all the people was brightly lit by big lights left over from the room's original industrial purposes, usually used during the day for cleaning and maintenance, but now illuminating every crack in the upholstery of the furniture and stain on the carpet.

However, the periphery of the room remained in shadow. It was hard to make out, but it looked like someone was picking their way around the edge of the room.

I didn't know why this had attracted my attention. Something in the back of mind was saying it had to do with Monroe.

I glanced over at the big man, but his back was to me, deep in conversation with one of the uniforms. Or was it to do with the bartender? I looked in that direction.

The bartender was keeping busy washing the huge number of glasses that had gotten stacked up around him when the club had gone from busy night spot to crime scene. He'd stacked some clean ones behind him, and was in the process of grabbing four more to swish in his dishwater, but he wasn't really looking at what he was doing. His eyes sought out mine, and as he ran the glasses through the cleaning ritual, he looked at me, then pointedly shifted his gaze to the area where I'd seen the movement.

36

He raised an eyebrow. I looked over at Monroe, but he was still talking, not paying attention to either of us.

I pushed my way through the crowd, and as I got nearer to the source of the movement, the shadow resolved itself into the figure of a large man.

"Excuse me, sir." But he didn't stop.

"Sir, please stop." By now, I'd reached him and I was able to grab him by the shoulder.

He whirled around and glared at me belligerently.

"What do you want?" He demanded, his voice thick with the accent of some Baltic country.

Now that he'd turned to face me, I got a good look at him. He was a couple inches taller than me, thick and muscular, about as wide as he was tall. His greasy, black hair had started to recede, although he was compensating by letting what hair remained droop down well past his collar. But if he was hoping that somehow the long hair in back would balance the several inches of shiny scalp on the front, it wasn't working.

A single eyebrow topped his close set eyes and wide nose, which featured a cross-hatching of tiny blood vessels. He wore a light gray suit, with a rather dingy white shirt open at the collar.

"Have you checked out with one of our officers?" I asked calmly, trying not to let the situation escalate.

"Yes. I need to go now." He turned to leave.

"Wait." My grip tightened on his shoulder. His eyes darted side to side. I could sense, as much as see, him shifting his weight to the balls of his feet.

Before he could run, or take a swing at me, I reached into my jacket and put one hand on my weapon.

I didn't have to say anything, he knew exactly where my hand had gone. He watched me with narrowed eyes, taking my measure. I looked calmly back at him.

"Problem, Trav?"

Alex Monroe had trundled up behind me, breaking our stare-down. The man looked from one of us to the other.

"No," I replied, "I was checking to see if Mr...." I looked at the swarthy man, but he continued to glare at me, not offering his name. "...uh, this gentleman had been checked out by anyone."

"And have you?" Monroe asked him.

"Yes." It sounded more like *chess*.

"By who?"

The man waved an arm vaguely in the direction of the uniforms.

"One of them, I don't remember which. Uh, the spic."

Vega, the subject of this delightful slur, was right in the man's field of vision, so he was an obvious choice to single out.

But even without his shifty behavior, there was something, something else that had drawn me over to him. What was it? The bartender had quietly pointed the way...but there was something I was missing. What the hell was it?

Monroe was watching me. "Trav?"

And as I looked at him, it clicked into place. Tightening my grip on the man's shoulder, I forced him forward a few steps, into better light. Monroe followed us, looking at me curiously.

"What are you doing, Trav?"

I looked at the floor, then at Monroe. He followed my gaze to the man's shoes.

There were two things uncommon about them. First off, they were white. Not white tennis or running shoes, but white leather dress shoes. The only other pair of white dress shoes I'd ever seen like that had been at a college football game. Only then they poked out from the bottom of a pair of red polyester slacks worn by a drunken fan the year we played Nebraska. I didn't even think they made shoes like that anymore.

But like the Cornhusker's outfit, there was red here as well.

Three bright red bloodstains, one on the left shoe and two on the right, shone in the stark light.

3

Had it just been me, the suspect (whose name was Bilol Grymzin, according to his driver's license) might have put up a fight. But when Monroe appeared beside me, hand also on his weapon, Grymzin allowed us to put the cuffs on him. He stared blankly at the wall while we read him his rights.

We bundled him into the unit Monroe had driven to the scene and left Stevens behind to supervise what questioning was left.

After Monroe put his hand on Grymzin's head to keep him from bumping it on the doorframe top (yeah, we really do that), he slammed the door shut and turned to me.

"That was a good catch, Trav. With everything that was going on, he might have been able to slip out. What tipped you off?"

I thought for a minute. What had made me go over to him? He'd been in a position in the room that made it look like he'd already been interviewed, and his conduct after I'd braced him had shown him to be a pretty cool customer. There had been *something* that had drawn my attention to him, then I had looked over at...

"The bartender," I said. "He was looking over at Grymzin, then at me, and I thought that was kind of weird."

Monroe looked stricken.

"Jesus Christ!" he whispered fiercely. "Keep your voice down. Why didn't you tell me it was Lennox?" He looked around, checking to see if anyone was listening to us. A concerned frown creased his face. He leaned over to me.

"See that chick over there?" he whispered.

He gave his head a tiny jerk to my right. Knowing better than to telegraph my glance, I slowly turned my head and swept the crowd, as if I was trying to decide if there was anything else I needed to do before leaving. My gaze caught a woman smoking a cigarette. Like most of the women at the club, she was dressed to attract attention, but her skirt was a little shorter, heels a little higher, breasts a little more exposed than the amateurs. The scarlet gash of her mouth stood in stark relief to her pale skin, and hard eyes watched us with suspicion.

"Yeah," I confirmed, not moving my lips.

"She close enough to hear us?"

"I dunno. Maybe."

"Damn. Well, we'll need to report to the Cap that our CI may be compromised. What's the matter with you? You of all people should know better than to open your mouth around here."

He jerked his head toward the passenger side of the car. "Let's go."

I walked around the car and got in. Monroe shoved the key into the ignition and pulled out. His mouth was set in a hard line, and with the suspect in the back, I knew better than to try to continue our discussion.

I took advantage of the silence to review what had just happened.

I had gone from hero to goat in pretty short order. I didn't know the bartender, although when Monroe mentioned a CI that had seemed familiar somehow. I thought hard, but couldn't dredge up where I may have heard about it.

But Monroe seemed to think that was something I did know and was pretty pissed off that I had referred to him in public.

Well, even with what little I knew about Kaaro, I couldn't blame him. Kaaro's inner circle was small, mostly composed of men who hailed from the same former Baltic state Kaaro had emigrated from. Getting a source into such a tight-knit group would be really hard. And potentially hard on the source.

We arrived at the station, pulled Grymzin out of the car and headed up into the squad to start processing him.

It didn't take long, as every time I asked him a question, the only response was a sullen stare. Fortunately, I could fill in most of what was needed from the ID in his wallet. When I was done, I called down for a uniform to have him printed and complete his intake.

By this time, it was almost eleven, and time to go off shift. I looked over at Monroe, whose desk was a couple of yards away from mine. He was standing, and throwing his wrinkled suit jacket over one shoulder.

I pulled my own coat on and we walked down the stairs together.

"I hope this sticks," Monroe muttered.

"What?"

"Aw, you know guys like Kaaro. Probably have him out before we come on-shift tomorrow."

I shrugged. "Watcha gonna do? At the very least, he gets a free night in our plush lockup."

That brightened Monroe up a little. "Yeah, maybe when his boss lets him spend the night curled up on a bench, breathing piss and vomit, he'll think twice about his loyalty."

"I'm not sure I'd go that far, but at least he'll be in for the whole night. I'm in early tomorrow. I'll let you know if anything pops."

Monroe nodded. By now, we were in the parking lot.

I got in the Mustang, yawning. The scene in the bar must have taken more out of me than I had thought. I was exhausted.

The Axe was in the midst of a Poco retrospective as I drove home. I turned the radio up loud, but did it with a twinge of sadness. This was one of the many groups Dad had turned me on to.

If ever there was a band with multiple personality disorder, it was Poco. Over its history, it changed personnel a dozen times and morphed from a proto-bluegrass band formed from the ashes of Buffalo Springfield to believe it or not, a kind of British funk, then back to country. Along the way, it had sent not only one, but two of its members to make it big with the Eagles. The band finally had a couple of pop hits late in their career.

And I loved every incarnation. I was warbling along in a dangerous falsetto to the Spanish lyrics of my favorite tune from the band, "Too Many Nights Too Long," when I arrived at home.

Definitely a driveway song. I sat in the car till it finished, acoustic refrain fading into the distance like *El Hombre Escondido*, The Hidden Man who is hunting the song's narrator.

I trudged inside, tossed my keys into the bowl by the door and went into the spare bedroom I used as an office. I locked my gun up in the safe I had made for it, and went into the kitchen for a drink.

I drained two big glasses of water. I hadn't realized how thirsty I was. I pulled off my t-shirt as I walked into the bedroom, tossing it and the rest of my clothes on the bedroom floor.

I pulled open the top drawer of my dresser, but instead of the sweatpants I normally wore to bed, I pulled out a women's nightshirt. It was gray, with *Angel* stenciled on the front in glittery script.

I looked into the drawer.

It was full of girl stuff. T-shirts for working out in, some underwear, couple of pair of socks. There *were* sweats at the bottom of the pile, but not black like mine. These were pink with the university logo across the butt. Definitely not the pair I was looking for.

These were Mary's things. And in fact, this was the drawer she had used when she stayed over. But I had cleaned it out weeks ago, and re-appropriated it for myself.

I stared at the drawer like a pervert in the lingerie department.

It smelled like her. And as scents often do, immediately brought back the memories of Sunday afternoons spent on my couch, her doing the Sunday crossword ("Why is the Sunday one so much *harder?*"), me reading or watching football.

The violinist and the cop.

If this were a movie, I would now tell the story of how we met on a case, and I had ended up saving her from the murdering cellist knocking off other players in the orchestra, but the reality is we were fixed up at a dinner party by the wife of Gene Palmer, my first partner.

We weren't even booby-trapped into a blind date. Kate simply said, "There's this nice girl at the health club. You're coming to dinner tomorrow night."

I looked over at Gene to save me, but he shrugged. "Surrender now, bub. You will anyway. No sense wasting time."

"She's into music, like you," Kate continued, as if that sealed the deal.

Of course, there's a little bit of difference between a guy who likes Miles Davis and a woman with her masters in violin performance. I did not have high hopes.

So of course, we hit it off immediately. Gene said it was months before Kate lost the smug smile she wore whenever she saw us together.

Continuing the movie motif, had this been a film, we would have broken up because one or the other of us didn't want to get married, or was caught in a compromising position with an ex-flame, a hooker, or both.

However, we were comfortable as we were. We both knew marriage would happen sometime, but neither of us was in a hurry.

But even though Mary wasn't my wife, she felt the same stress found in the families of a lot of cops—and increasing since 9/11, firefighters. She wouldn't ever say it, but I knew she hoped I'd get tired of The Job. And when I went on administrative leave after the shooting, it came to a head.

She told me not to be in a rush to get back, I accused her of wanting me to quit.

I was totally out of line, but we both ended up saying things we shouldn't have and I stomped out.

All that was left was a drawer full of her stuff.

A drawer that I distinctly remembered emptying. Just as I remembered re-filling the drawer with the items I had previously kept there.

I pulled open the next drawer down.

Yep. Sweats, t-shirts, athletic socks, right where I had stuffed them when it became obvious Mary was going to need a spot. At the time, I remembered feeling lucky it was only one drawer.

I went into the bathroom, wondering if it also would be different than I remembered.

Sure enough, there was an extra toothbrush in the cup next to mine, and an examination of the drawers revealed more feminine accoutrements that I could have sworn I had removed.

So, either I had imagined removing all traces of Mary from my living space, and had been unconsciously fingering her stuff all this time, or I had bagged everything up, stuck it in the closet as I remembered, then *put it all back*.

Either scenario was way closer to nuts than I really wanted to be.

"Trav, buddy," I said to myself. "It is possible that this whole mess has affected you more than you want to admit."

I went over my behavior during the last several days. Was there anything that could be considered erratic? The last thing I needed was being recommended for a psych eval.

But nothing came to mind. I wandered back into the bedroom. I still had her night shirt in one hand.

I breathed her smell in, cursing myself again for driving her away. I thought about bagging everything up and putting it in the closet, but finally just stuffed the clothing back into the drawer where I had found it and finished getting ready for bed.

I turned the radio on softly, but fell asleep almost immediately, and dreamed.

"You must find the Hidden Man," Mike Becker told me sternly. He was making an ace of spades appear from thin air, again and again.

"How can I do that from here?" I complained. My elbows rested on the bars of a squirrel cage cell right out of Mayberry, and I was on the wrong side of them.

"Talk to the man." Dad jerked his head toward a doorway across the room.

I looked up, following his gaze, expecting to see Leon Martin. Instead, it was Sam who strode into the room, wearing Andy Griffith's sheriff uniform.

"Where's Barney?" I asked him.

"I did not shoot the deputy," Sam replied solemnly.

Suddenly, there was a gun in my hand. The jail cell and my dad had disappeared. Now it was just Sam and me, standing in one of those foggy, indistinct scenes that only appear in dreams.

"You going to shoot me?" asked Sam.

"I only have one bullet," I said.

"It'll have to be enough," Sam said.

BLAM BLAM BLAM BLAM.

Sam jerked, as bullets made a line across his chest.

"No!" I screamed. *"I didn't fire! I only have one bullet!"*

I sat up in bed, still feeling the panic of watching my friend collapse. I was sweating, and my hand was reaching across my chest, in the place where my shoulder rig would have been if I was dressed.

The radio was playing "I Shot the Sheriff," which explained one thing about the dream. Although the Mayberry thing was kind of a mystery. I didn't hate the show, but I wasn't what you'd call a fan. Old music is my thing, not old TV shows.

But I now realized that the banging that had penetrated my dream as gunshots was also real.

It was someone banging on the door.

I stumbled out, and opened it.

Sam Markus (wearing a t-shirt, not a sheriff's badge) squinted up at me.

"I'd ask if you were ready, but my keen mind, trained in the intricacies of observation and the scientific method, reveals to me that you are not."

I didn't say anything, just stared at him, frowning. Sam standing in my doorway, waking me up, was giving me a distinct feeling of *déjà vu*. But why?

"What? Do I have something on my face?" He reached a hand up to his face and rubbed his mouth.

"No, no," I said. "C'mon in."

I swung the door open, and Sam entered. We stared at each other for a few minutes, me still trying to figure out why this scene looked so familiar.

Finally Sam said, "Well? Are you going to get ready?"

"Uh, yeah... Are we doing something today?"

He sighed and said patiently, "I asked you for a ride to work, because my car is in the shop. You didn't have to be in till eleven, but you said you wanted to see the lab. Remember?"

"I didn't give you a ride yesterday?"

"No-o-o," he replied, stretching out the word. "You weren't around yesterday. Trav, are you all right?"

"Yeah. You, uh, woke me out of a pretty sound sleep, I guess."

"Sorry, buddy. I probably should have called or texted last night to remind you."

"It's okay. Gimme ten minutes. Make yourself some coffee if you want."

"I will."

We headed off, him to my small kitchen, me to the shower.

45

I couldn't shake the feeling that something was odd about Sam being here, but finally shrugged it off. I cleaned up, got dressed, and was combing my hair with my fingers as I entered the kitchen.

Sam had, as promised, made coffee, and helped himself to some toast while he was at it. I wolfed down a piece as well and drank a few swallows of coffee.

Sam studied the screen on his phone, reading the news.

"Anything interesting?"

"Eh." He shrugged. "Everybody's pissed about the new version of Windows...Which director is going to screw up the next *Star Wars* movie...Oh! Wow!"

His voice went up in an excited squeak.

"What?"

"New intel chip! Twice as fast as the ones we have now."

I sighed.

"When I asked, I meant the *real* news."

He looked at me blankly. "That is the real news."

"Right. I forgot who I was dealing with."

I rinsed our cups in the sink and went back to the spare bedroom to unlock my gun. I returned a moment later, shoulder rig and jacket in place, grabbed my phone and keys and, a few minutes later, we were in the car.

Central Station and the university are only a few blocks apart, but the town changes character pretty quickly. Not far past my shop, the office buildings give way to the cluster of funky shops, bars, and coffee houses that form the buffer between town and gown in about every college town in the country.

I parked in the fire lane in front of Sam's building, flipping down my sun visor, to which a POLICE tag was attached. Even campus meter readers, the ultimate parking Nazis, would think twice before ticketing a car with that sign.

Sam shook his head in disgust as we climbed out.

"As a taxpayer, I am shocked at how public employees take advantage of their positions for personal gain."

"Even though I'm off duty, I might have to respond to a call. And if I'm parked in the next county, that would be bad."

"So, if I went to the city council with a picture of your car parked here, and invited the media, that would be okay?"

Lazy Public Servant and Outraged Community Watchdog is one of our favorite games.

"The city council *wants* me to park there," I replied patiently. "No, they *demand* it."

"Well, don't blame me when you're saying 'no comment' as they hustle you down the courthouse steps."

"At least my car will be parked at the bottom."

And with that, we entered that shining beacon of academia, Building 231.

Building 231 (someone important was going to have to die for it to get a name, Sam said) was one of the taller buildings on campus, with the tall, narrow windows that had been the architectural rage for institutional design in the early 1970s. Inside, if the honey-colored wood trim wouldn't have given away the building's vintage, the long, dimly-lit halls lined with narrow doors leading to tiny offices bespoke the pre-cubicle era.

From this angle, I couldn't see the second, newer wing of the building, which had been added during the time Sam and I had been students together. The lab wing was as horizontal as the original building was vertical, jutting out from the north side like a glassy knife blade, and LEED certified.

We went up a flight of stairs to Sam's office.

"Hang on, let me dump my bag," he said, unlocking the door. He pushed inside, leaving me to see if anything new had been added to the door.

Sam's office door was typical—the light wood darkened by six decades of hands, along with the occasional knee, elbow or butt, pushing it open. Most of the original finish was obscured by a veritable architectural dig of science cartoons.

The top layer were all printouts of online comics, recent vintage. Two titles, *PC Weenies* and *Lab Bratz*, neither of which I was familiar with, seemed to dominate. Real newsprint formed the next layer down, mainly the *Dilbert* stratum. And I knew that deeper still was the Precambrian, *Far Side* layer.

Portions of a detailed poster depicting the home stars of the Twelve Colonies from *Battlestar Galactica* were visible beneath some of the later comics.

The door opened back up as Sam returned. I had known better than to try to follow him into his office. It was tiny, and the lone guest chair was hidden under a pile of papers and journals. How a man whose scientific discipline exchanged most of its information online could collect so much paper was beyond me.

As Sam shut the door, I also caught a glimpse of his work station. His laptop was propped up on a tilted stand which in turn sat atop a couple of thick books on a small desk pushed against the far wall to my right. I hoped the force of the door closing didn't cause the whole tower to fall.

"Okay," Sam said as he locked the door back up. "Let's go check out the site of my future Nobel Prize."

"Lead on."

He led me out a fire door and down two flights of stairs that hadn't seen a broom since the Reagan administration. Then we spilled out into another, much newer-looking hallway. This was the passage into the new wing, which was as airy as the old building was cramped.

We zigged and zagged to avoid several grad students, until we came to a set of double glass doors. Sam pulled his phone from its belt case, made a series of inscrutable gestures on it and then waved the device in the direction of a sensor mounted on the right side of the doors. The phone beeped at the same moment a small red LED on the sensor turned green.

There was an audible click as the door unlatched. Sam opened it and led me through the cubicle nest that formed the outer office of what was called, simply, the New Lab.

Someone slightly less important would probably have to die for *it* to get a name.

Sam used his phone again to access a second set of locked doors. Now the hallways got narrower, and the open areas broken up into workstations became small offices once again—the desire of a scientist to be able to work behind closed doors trumping design aesthetics which decreed that the best work was done collaboratively in a hive of low cubicles.

Eventually, we turned down a narrow hallway that looked remarkably like the one Sam's office was located in, albeit a little cleaner and brighter.

Sam stopped before yet another locked door. This one was metal, however, and there was no window or visual access of any kind into the room beyond. The security sensor was in the same place as on the other doors—right side about chest height. This time, instead of waving his phone at the sensor, he entered a string of numbers on a keypad. Right above it was a hand-lettered sign that read "Cat Box."

I looked at the sign and raised an eyebrow.

"I'll tell you inside."

I hadn't been in one of Sam's labs since undergrad days, so I didn't have a clear mental image of what a modern lab should look like, but nonetheless, I was totally unprepared for the sight of this lab, because it was filled with...

Nothing.

The large room we had entered was almost completely empty. Sam's office was smaller than my girlfriend's...my *ex*-girlfriend's closet. This room was the size of a large college classroom and utterly vacant except for two areas. One was a computer workstation on a standup desk in a near corner. Two high stools rested near the desk. The other was a third stool, identical to the other two, which sat in the center of the space, well away from anything else, and looking a little forlorn.

On top of the stool sat a plastic box, about eight inches high, with a T-shaped handle on the top. The box was white, except for the horizontal cross of the T, which was black. As I examined it, I decided it didn't look so much like a handle after all, but more like the handheld barcode reader the Target clerk whipped out when the item you were buying was too big to pass over the scanner on the conveyor.

"Impressive," I finally said.

Sam grinned, picking up on my sarcasm. "Yeah, the days of big machines with cool lights and spinning tape decks are pretty much gone. Especially when you're scanning for what we measure in here."

"Which is?"

"Well..." Sam hesitated. "I've been living with this for so long, I don't really even know where to start. Okay, you know that my area is particle physics, right?"

"Yeah."

"And that when you get to the size of the particles we study, that they don't act much like matter at all?"

"Sure. I roomed with you, didn't I? Tiny particles like quanta...note my correct use of the plural, by the way...basic building blocks of everything...you can measure their location OR their momentum, but not both at the same time. That's your Uncertainty Principle. Which leads to the idea that the act of observing a particle can actually have an impact on its behavior, and that's when Schrödinger puts his cat in a box and fills it up with poison gas, and you have the famous cat who is somehow both dead and alive."

Sam looked impressed. "I can't believe you were actually listening all those times."

"Even a semi-literate criminal justice major can't help but pick up a little bit after a couple of hundred beers and bong hits with you guys."

I paused.

"Cat Box. I just got that."

"Yeah, it's the most over-used scientific illustration ever. But in this case, it fits."

"How?"

"Well...actually, you've started down the same path that we did. If observing a particle causes an impact on its behavior, how can you eliminate that effect? In essence, how can you observe without having the effect of observing?"

"You can't," I objected. "That's what all this is about, right?"

"Right," Sam continued. "And if you can't separate the observer from the observed, then it's the observation that *creates* the reality."

"What? Now you've completely lost me."

"Well, if you accept the idea that the observer affects the outcome, and experiments have demonstrated that very thing since Einstein's time, it's a short jump to the idea that nothing really exists until it's perceived by a consciousness. Like the tree falling in the woods with no one to hear it, also from the Land of Over-Used Analogies. If there is no auditory mechanism to receive the sound, is there sound at all? It takes both pieces. The transmitter and the receiver. Matter isn't so much a discrete, unchanging, physical thing. It's a collection of a range of probabilities that don't coalesce until our minds put them together."

"Okay. Still lost."

Sam sighed. "Try this. Have you ever lost your keys, and looked all over the house for them?"

I nodded. "Of course."

"And then, when you're about to give up, you go back through every place you looked one more time. And sure enough, even though you KNEW you already looked under the sofa cushion, when you look there again, you find the keys."

"Right. Because I missed them the first time. Or thought I had already looked there."

"Maybe. Or maybe the range of possibilities that form the location of your keys came into focus a little differently each time you looked at that spot. Or…think of the first time you looked for your keys as happening in one universe, and then you finding them in another, parallel universe."

"I wondered if we were going to get to parallel universes. So, my keys went to a parallel universe?"

"No, that's the point. The observer affects the observation. Your perception effects the outcome of you looking at a probable location of your keys. And something happened to cause the probability wave form to collapse a little differently the second time. Or, if we want to stick with the many universes concept, you moved from a universe where the keys weren't under the sofa cushion to one where they were."

"I went to another parallel universe? That's insane."

Sam shrugged. "That's what the data seems to indicate."

"So how do I get back?"

"That's just it. You don't. No backsies. THIS is now your reality. One where the keys were under the sofa cushion all along. Now, here's where it gets interesting. Multiply you losing your keys by the number of little decisions you, and everyone else in the world, make every day.

Hundreds of millions of chances for the waves of probability to not always collapse in a way that is consistent with previously observed phenomena. Kind of a stutter in reality."

"A stutter."

"Or like a jump cut in a movie. Your keys weren't there, now they are."

"So what happens next? My keys just magically appeared. Why don't I notice?"

"Maybe you do. But keys can't just appear, so you shrug and say to yourself, 'I must not have looked there after all' and forget about it. Our minds 'smooth over' hundreds of inconsistencies in probability and causality every day."

"Okay..."

I was still trying to figure out where all this was going. "So, even if this is true, our brains edit it out. You can't measure it."

"Ahh, but you can."

Sam, clearly enjoying himself, held up a finger. "If this theory is true, new quanta from adjacent realities, we call them streams, are arriving here in *our* stream all the time."

"Wait." I held up my own hand. "Don't I remember that matter can't be created or destroyed? What about that?"

"Wow. You really did pay attention. Blue ribbon to the semi-literate criminal justice major. The quanta that come into our stream are always exactly balanced by the quanta going out. In the stream you moved into, your keys are under the sofa cushion. Meanwhile, over in the next stream, another Trav is just as puzzled because he could have sworn he looked in his coat pocket, but there they are."

"But it's still a dead end. The keys exist in both realities. There is nothing you can measure."

"But...what we found out is that we CAN measure those little discontinuities, those stutters in reality that are the quanta arriving or leaving our universe from another stream."

"Which does...?"

"Right now, we're trying identify and map particles as they come and go. Long-term, the idea is to use that map to identify probability wave forms *before* they actually collapse."

"Wait. You're telling me your goal is to predict the future?"

"Well..." Sam hesitated. "When you get into this territory, words like 'future' get kind of fluid. Could we someday watch an event in real time and try to somehow nudge the wave form to collapse in one direction as opposed to another? Maybe. But it would take a level of processing power and refinement of the code that we won't see for years, if ever. And that is, as we like to say on final grant reports, 'beyond the scope of this project.'"

"Good," I said firmly. "I'm not sure I'm ready to let you drive us into some alternate reality with no way to get back."

"Not much chance of that," chuckled Sam. "Unless I could be sure it was one where the mini-skirt was always in style. Anyway, that..." He gestured with a flourish to the box sitting on the stool, "...is what the Cat Box does."

"Brings the mini-skirt back into style?"

"Funny."

"So, how does it work?" But before Sam could start another monologue, I quickly added, "Shorthand version."

"Well, we've removed as much external stimuli from this room as we can, to keep to the smallest possible number of arriving particles. Right now, we can only measure very small amounts. Any area with normal physical activity can have hundreds, even thousands of 'stream jumping' events every second. It completely overwhelms the device."

Something attracted Sam's attention to the computer.

"Hmm. That's weird."

"What?"

"Oh, the screen is really jumbled." Sam had wiggled the mouse, and when the screen woke up, the display was solid blue.

"It's not supposed to look like that?" I asked.

"No," replied Sam. "Lemme re-boot."

He reached down and pressed the reset button on the CPU case. The screen immediately went black and the computer began the familiar whirring and clicking of a restart.

"This is one of the new 3-D monitors," Sam said as the machine chugged through its startup routine. "What we should be seeing is a representation of this room. When the device measures quanta entering the stream, we'll see some blue specks or streaks. Particles leaving our stream will show red. Of course, we're not seeing the actual particle activity, just a graphical representation of what's going on at the quantum level. The actual data is written to a database. The picture we see gives us an idea of where within the room the activity is taking place."

What looked to me like a fairly normal Windows desktop had finally appeared on the screen. Sam launched an icon—a cartoon cat, of course.

We watched as the program loaded. As Sam had promised, a very lifelike 3-D image of the room seemed to spill out of the monitor, followed almost immediately by a silent explosion of blue that erupted from a corner of the monitor, covering the entire screen. Because of the 3-D effects, the blue wave seemed to leap out of the screen at us. I had to resist the urge to rear back as if I expected to be showered by paint.

"What the hell?" muttered Sam.

He restarted the computer again.

"That's funny. It's kind of like the first few tests we did, the ones I mentioned that overwhelmed the application because there was too much stimuli. But, nothing like this has happened since we moved everything into this room."

This time, when he launched the Cat Box application, he typed several commands as the program was loading.

"There, I've slowed down the display several thousand times. Should give us at least a glimpse of what the Cat Box is reacting to before it spits up the blue again."

We both leaned toward the screen and watched as this time, the blue filled the screen much more slowly. It began as a small point in the corner of the display that seemed to correspond to the spot where we stood. I watched as the spot of blue began as a pinprick, but even with Sam putting the software into slow motion, the small circle flared out into five elongated ellipses before overwhelming the screen like before.

"Let me slow it down even more," Sam said.

He did so. This time, for a second, it was very clear that the shape the blue pinprick grew into before exploding was the silhouette of a human form.

Sam looked at me, his eyes wide.

"Did you see that?"

"Yeah...what does it mean?"

Sam stared incredulously at the screen. "It means that what's driving the application crazy is that there is a huge amount of matter recently transferred to this stream. Too much for the detector too measure, so it locks up. And the only thing that's new to this room is you."

"You're not from this stream."

4

"*I'M NOT WHAT?*"

"You're not from this stream," repeated Sam, his own excitement moderating a bit as he processed what had just happened.

"I know, sounds really weird, doesn't it?" He gave me a reassuring smile. "But don't get too worked up. Based on what we're learning here, people and things shift from stream to stream all the time. We've actually seen it in the Box with stuff, and a couple of times we got indications with people, but never to this extent before. We call it the 'blue shift,' because on the screen incoming particles are represented in blue, like a Doppler shift in astronomy. Remember from Van Allen's class? Objects coming toward you have a blue shift, because the light waves coming from them are 'shorter' from the perspective of them approaching you? Things moving away from you have a red shift. Anyway, the law of averages says this was going to happen eventually, but I never imagined it like this. Congrats!"

"Thanks. I think. What happens next? Is this where you bundle me off to Area 51? Take samples of alien tissue? Anal probe?"

Sam chuckled. "Don't flatter yourself."

He leaned back in the stool and folded his arms.

"I'd like to say this was a huge breakthrough, but the reality is, since this is the first time you've been in the Box, we don't have a baseline or control reading on you. It sure looks like you're a giant quivering mass of particles freshly arrived in this universe, but the only proof I have is this one reading. Unless..."

"What?"

"Well, in our experience, the adaptation to the new stream doesn't take very long at all. Just a few hours, actually, and all traces of the blue shift are gone. Which means that you...well, arrived...pretty recently. It's nothing we could actually use as a part of the research, but think back over the last day or so. Is there anything you remember that seems strange, out of place?"

I thought for a minute, mentally running through the day. "Not really. Wait...did we ride to work together yesterday morning?"

Sam shook his head. "No. Just today. Why? Did you think we did?"

"No, I guess your asking me is what I remember. Weird."

"See, though?" In spite of himself, Sam was getting excited. "It could be the adaptation at work. Your memories become consistent with the new reality, sloughing off anything that doesn't fit. Just like the quanta lose the blue shift after a while. Anything else?"

I opened my mouth, then shut it and shrugged.

"I dunno. I got to work. Got a medal...which was a surprise. Pretty big bust at The Kremlin. Busy day, but nothing too weird. Until now."

"Hmm." Sam chewed on his lower lip. "Which could still be the adaptive process. Well, if you don't mind, I'm going to go ahead and write this up. Even though we don't have the empirical data we need to conclusively state you're from another stream, the apocryphal observations could be useful at some point. And, I'd also like you to come back in a day or two. Another reading might tell us something about the rate of adaptation to the new stream, which we don't have for organic material."

"Wait. What about the Trav who started out here on this stream? Did I replace him, or what?"

Sam shrugged. "No idea. Our models are still pretty theoretical at this point. We're studying quanta, not people. But remember, matter *in* has to equal matter *out*. The fact that you're *here* by definition means that *he* has moved onto another stream."

"Okay. If you say so. And I don't go back?"

Sam smiled tolerantly. "It's only in the movies that parallel realities are places you can pop in and out of. There is no 'back.' Just a set of probabilities. And remember, streams are created constantly by relatively small and benign occurrences. Even if it was possible, you'd have to skip over dozens of streams before you reached a reality substantially different from the one you left. That's why we picked the 'stream' analogy. Time, like water, only flows one way. Plus, after a river forks, the water in one stream can't jump over into another. No backsies. Both streams continue their one-way journeys toward the ultimate destination."

"But streams are tributaries of bigger rivers and stuff. They don't fork off and stay separate forever."

"Well, it's not a perfect analogy," he admitted. "Maybe a better one is a delta, where a river splits off into smaller streams on its way to the ocean. Anyway, the point is that whether you stay in the same stream or get shunted to another, it's a one-way trip. We're all just twigs floating downstream to the future."

Sam smiled, but he knew me well enough to tell that I was still a little freaked out over this revelation. He put a hand on my arm.

"Dude. Seriously, I know this feels weird, but take my word for it. It happens all the time. Don't obsess over it. Go. Explore your new home!"

I gave him a withering look. "But if I show up here tomorrow and you've got a little Van Dyke beard, I reserve the right to totally freak out."

"Well, if the secretaries are wearing mini-skirts with bikini tops, then everybody wins," he responded.

"Again with the mini-skirts. You guys have pretty much hit all the parallel universe jokes, haven't you?"

"You don't know the half of it. It's non-stop. And don't even start with the *Ghostbusters* puns. I've heard them all."

I held up a hand, palm outward. "I promise not to cross the streams."

"That's it, out! Or I swear to God I'll figure out a way to boot you into a stream where the only jazz records that exist are by Kenny G."

"Anything but that." I raised my hands in surrender. "I'll go. See you later."

Sam turned back to his computer, obviously wanting to go over the bizarre readings one more time. He gave me a dismissive wave.

I retraced the route we'd taken to the Cat Box, through the new part of the building back to the original structure, still trying to figure out how I felt about what Sam's machine had told me.

Was it possible? Could I have actually traveled from one reality to another, and not even known it?

And why was it that, whenever my thoughts went in that direction, it seemed like there was something else, something beyond my mental reach, but somehow important?

Okay, that's it. Stop it and move on. Sam's right. Don't obsess.

I pushed the questions out of my head as I got into the car.

Back at the station, I headed up the stairs toward my desk. I was a little early for my shift, but was happy to have some moments of quiet. Monroe wasn't in yet, and a quick check on the computer revealed that Grymzin was still in lockup.

Monroe showed up shortly after. He stopped by my desk, slapping a massive hip on a corner.

"I got here early, took a run at Grymzin. Hope you don't mind."

I shook my head. "Anything?"

He made a farting sound. "Didn't get shit. He wouldn't say a word. Not even to ask for a lawyer."

"Same as when I booked him last night."

Monroe shook his head in disgust. "And the recording techs loved getting all the audio and video set up for thirty minutes of some ugly Ruskie sitting there picking his nose."

"Picking his nose? Really?"

"Oh, yeah. Seemed to enjoy giving us a show."

"This job is so glamorous sometimes."

He heaved himself to his feet and plopped down at his own desk, pulled out a folder and started reading.

On cop shows, your hero is totally focused on one case, working nonstop till he or she catches the perp, forsaking friendship, home, and life outside the job till successful.

In real life, even the biggest case is one of a dozen you're working. So, like a soldier who learns to sleep whenever and wherever he can, a good cop learns to work on a case when there is something to do, set it aside when there isn't.

Police work is like that a lot of the time. Hours, even days of boredom broken up by occasional moments of abject terror.

Today was shaping up to be one of the former. I worked on paperwork for a couple hours, ran to the sub shop next door for a sandwich, and ate it at my desk, munching on the ice from my giant glass of tea with a satisfying crunch.

I had gone back to staring at my computer screen when my phone buzzed with the tone signifying an intercom call.

"Becker."

"Trav." It was Saunders, the desk officer. "Visitor for you."

"Be right down."

I crossed out of the offices and headed downstairs to the reception area. It was typical of most cop shop layouts. Large desk with a half-dozen video monitors displaying jumpy black and white images of various zones of the station. Couple of computers for taking reports, attached to huge CRT monitors. Budget cuts hadn't allowed the force to fully convert to flat screens. Like most areas of the station, the walls were painted in government-issue sea green, with plain but durable seating for the public.

A young woman leaned over the counter in familiar conversation with Saunders as I pushed open the door. She wore a bright green tank top untucked over slim jeans that did little to conceal some very attractive curves. A square bag hung from one hand. Coal-black hair floated down her shoulders. The institutional fluorescents were unflattering at best, but the harsh light couldn't completely blot out the healthy glow of her smooth, lightly-tanned skin and the twinkle of mischievous green eyes.

My breath caught as I came into her field of vision. She gave me a measured glance. Once upon a time, those green eyes had flared with passion when they met mine. Now there was only steel.

"Hi, Trav," Mary said. "Can I talk to you a minute?"

"Uh, yeah, sure." I caught the door with a hand behind my back before it shut and held it for her. She smiled tightly as she passed.

She'd said she was going to leave the album at the desk. I wondered what it was that she wanted. Hadn't we agreed yesterday there was nothing more to say?

I led her down the hall to an empty interview room and opened the door for her. She set the sack down on the table as I pulled the door shut, then spun around.

"C'mere, you."

And suddenly my arms were full of delicious girl. Her lips sought mine as she pulled me close. Acting all on their own, my arms snaked around her waist. I moaned softly as we came together.

The kiss left me breathless.

"Wow."

Mary narrowed her eyes in mock scorn. "That's more than you deserve, making me drag you to an empty room because you don't want any PDA in front of your fellow cops. *I* think *they* would think you were weird to have a hot number like me and not be all over her."

"I, uh…"

I was completely at a loss. Mary pulled back a little more, sticking her thumbs in the waistband of my jeans to keep her balance.

"Trav, what's wrong?"

"Nothing."

Some of the steel came back into Mary's eyes.

"Trav. Are we back to that again? Why can't you *tell* me what's bothering you? Is it so hard to talk to me?"

Sometimes when you're with someone you know well, talking over a familiar subject can be comfortable, like slipping on a leather glove formed to your hand by years of use. But this conversation possessed all of the familiarity of well-covered ground but none of the comfort.

I ran a hand through my hair, suddenly determined to not let this discussion escalate into the usual argument.

"I know. I, uh…okay. If I said I'll tell you all about it later, would you trust me? It's been a strange…morning. I guess I need to process it myself a little more before I can go into it."

Mary's gaze softened.

"Fair enough." She poked me in the chest. "But I'm going to hold you to that."

"I know."

This wasn't really being fair to Mary. Not opening up to her was the main thing that had stressed our relationship. It had been a minor irritant at first, but had grown and grown until it was more like a wall between us. I'm not a big one for talking about my feelings. Add to that the usual cop's reluctance to tell his girl things that would scare her, let alone were confidential, and it was a perfect recipe for feeling left out.

I wanted to tell her what was really bothering me, but where to start?

Sorry I'm a little confused hon, but I just flew in from a parallel universe where we're broken up.

"Mary, I..."

She put a finger on my lips. "We can talk later. I know you don't have a lot of time. And I have to get ready for my concert tonight. But I wanted to give you this."

I noticed now that, in addition to the sack I had seen, she was also carrying her violin case. Mary was concertmaster of our symphony orchestra, a surprisingly high-quality organization considering the size of our town.

She picked up the sack and pulled out a flat cardboard square that was very familiar.

"The seller said it was in near mint condition, but I didn't dare hope it would be this nice."

She handed me the album.

Mary was right. It was in beautiful shape. The blue highlights leapt out of the otherwise monochromatic blacks and grays, just as striking as when it had left the printer nearly sixty years ago. There wasn't a hint of the album-shaped indentation or wear the disc inside sometimes transferred to the cover.

I carefully slid the album free of the protective sleeve inside the jacket. Even that was only a little yellowed, no visible tears or signs of wear.

I never get tired of seeing the rich, inky black of real vinyl. Compact discs are easier to store, MP3s more convenient, but give me midnight grooves any day.

I studied the album label. It was the old-style Columbia stamp from the late Fifties, gray background, red letters.

An original pressing of the finest jazz record ever made, one that had spoken to me ever since Dad had put it on the platter of his vintage Technics.

There were no scratches or blemishes anywhere on the surface. I could hardly wait to put it on my turntable at home and listen to the music the way the artists had intended.

No digital processing or compression, but actual analog sound waves.

When you converted music to a string of 0s and 1s, you also take some of its soul. I like being able to carry my music collection around in my pocket as much as the next guy, but if you want to really *listen* to a piece of music, you should do it on a turntable, powered by an amp with tubes—powering not little earbuds, but actual speakers.

"It's great."

I regretfully slid the disc back into the dust jacket, and the jacket back into the album cover. "Thanks for finding it."

Mary smiled and slid an arm around my waist. "It was the least I could do. After all, it was me who broke the one your dad gave you. The one he'd had since high school."

"It was an accident."

"I'll listen to it with you tonight if you want."

"It'll be late."

Mary smiled and leaned in for a kiss. When she wore heels, we were exactly the same height. That would bother some men, but I liked being able to look straight across into her eyes, without tilting down.

"I'll be up," she promised. "My place?"

It's a measure of the kind of girlfriend Mary was that she had thoughtfully added a turntable to her home stereo so I could bring records over. As a professional musician herself, she had acquired more than a few vinyl LPs, so it wasn't a totally altruistic gesture, but trading off listening to my vintage jazz and progressive rock with her classical discs over multiple martinis formed the framework of most of our favorite nights.

"Casa de Logan. Right."

Mary was almost to the door, but turned back. "Are you sure everything is okay?"

"Yeah, it's been kind of a weird day, and it's early. I'll tell you all about it tonight. I promise."

"I'm looking forward to it."

She came back, gave me another quick, but no less passionate, kiss and swept out the door.

"Bye."

The door didn't even have a chance to latch before I whipped out my phone. I quickly dialed Sam's number.

"Hey."

"Sam, are Mary and I still together?"

"Of course."

"Then, why do I remember us as broken up?"

"Broken up? You guys are the textbook happy couple. It's pretty sickening, actually."

"Spare me the editorial. Why do I remember it differently? You told me that even if I did move between streams, the differences would be little. This is a hell of a lot bigger than my car keys being in a different place."

"You're kidding, right?"

"Do I sound like I'm kidding?"

"And you say you remember being broken up?"

"Yes! That's what I'm telling you."

"Boy, that shouldn't be."

Sam's voice faded, as he obviously was fitting this new data into his understanding of the theory.

"Sam, focus. What do I do?"

"Do? Nothing. There's nothing *to* do. Remember. No backsies."

Now I was the one who stopped listening, as a thought that had been scratching at the back of my hind brain suddenly slid into my consciousness with a chill that flowed down my spine.

"Sam…"

"Hmm?"

"Sam, quit re-writing your equations and listen. Did you do this to me?"

"Me?"

"Don't you think this is a little bit of a coincidence? That you show me your Cat Box and a half hour later I have memories different than everyone around me?"

"Wow. I never thought about that. What do you think I did?"

"How am I supposed to know? You're the damn quantum physicist! Would you get your head out of your computer and think about this for a minute?"

"Yeah, sure, Trav. Just calm down."

"Easy for you to say."

"To answer your question, no, I didn't *do* anything to you. There is nothing *to* do. All we're doing here is measuring discontinuities in probability wave forms as they collapse into our space. The Cat Box is not a magic transporter that moves people from stream to stream."

"Well, this still doesn't make any sense."

"You're right there."

There were several seconds of silence.

"Tell you what," he said finally. "Maybe you should come back over to the lab. Let's put you in the Cat Box again and see if it spits up like it did before."

"The Cat Box spitting up. Funny. I've come unstuck in time and you're making jokes."

"Sorry. Can you come over here?"

"Not right now. Maybe later. I'll let you know."

I snapped the phone shut.

Now what?

I leaned against the table and tried to make sense of the last few minutes. I was actually now in a parallel universe.

Holy shit.

This was beyond crazy. If I hadn't seen my scientist friend show me proof on my computer screen, I would assume I was going insane.

But Sam had been so matter of fact. *We're moving from stream to stream all the time.*

It didn't feel normal from my end.

Despite the fact that this world was so much like mine, differing only in certain details, this was not the world I had grown up in. How was I supposed to deal with that?

I took a deep breath, trying to calm my racing pulse. I couldn't give in to the fight or flight reflex.

There was no place to fly *to*.

After a minute, I took a shot at evaluating my situation. On the one hand, I felt like an imposter. Or the victim of the weirdest case of mistaken identity ever. On the other hand, the differences here seemed to be in my favor.

I was back with Mary. Well, not back exactly, since on this stream we apparently had never broken up. And, according to Sam, there was no returning to my original stream.

I decided I could live with that.

Hoping there weren't any other big surprises in my Brave New World, I headed back upstairs.

I got back into the squad, and Monroe looked up as I came in.

"Cap will be back in an hour. Wants to see us as soon as he does."

I nodded. When I sat down, I checked the arrest status screen on my computer. Grymzin was still in holding, still not talking, hadn't asked for his attorney.

Captain Martin finally returned about two. He caught our eyes and jerked his head toward his office.

Monroe and I followed him in his office. It was stuffy inside, the result of too many closed-door meetings overloading our half century-old HVAC, but I shut the door anyway.

None of us sat. The captain turned and looked from one of us to the other.

"I didn't want to wait, so asked Alex to go over The Kremlin bust with me even though you weren't here yet. Hope you don't mind."

"No problem."

"He told me how you picked the suspect out of the crowd. That was good work, regardless of how the rest of this turns out."

I looked over at Monroe. He returned my glance coolly.

He wasn't going to say anything about my lapse. Alex Monroe would not rat another cop out. I could let this slide, and he wouldn't say a thing. Of course, he'd never trust me again, but he was leaving it up to me.

"Well, don't be so quick to congratulate me, Captain. I may have compromised our CI at The Kremlin."

Martin's eyes widened a fraction of an inch, the equivalent of ashen-faced shock for most people.

"What happened?"

I explained how the bartender and I had exchanged looks, Monroe adding that our conversation might have been overheard.

"And the girl?" Martin asked.

"She's part of the stable that services Kaaro's favorite customers," Monroe said. "We've had her in a half-dozen times. Claims to not have much English beyond 'three hundred for all night,' but I always wondered if she wasn't a lot more aware of what was going on than she was telling."

"Can you get to Lennox and tell him to be careful? Maybe even pull him out of there."

Monroe nodded.

"Do it. Trav, stay for a minute."

Monroe opened the door and slid out.

"Damn," Martin sighed. "Rob's a decent kid, not like most of the scum who take our money and roll over on their friends. And nothing happens in that bar that he doesn't notice. In a way, he's the worst kind of informant. The kind who wants to do the right thing. But I don't have to go into that with you, since you're the one who brought him to us."

Well, so much for no more surprises.

I looked at the captain, trying to think of something to say, which was made even more difficult by the fact that I had no idea what the hell he was talking about. I was saved from openly displaying my cluelessness by the door opening up again. It was Monroe, back too soon to have done what the captain had asked.

"Uh...Leon..."

"I don't need to be announced, Detective," came a resonant voice.

Anton Kaaro and another man I had never seen before squeezed into the office. I would have made some joke about a clown car, but the look on Martin's face stopped me. I backed around the corner of Martin's desk to make room and studied the two men.

This was the first time I had seen the immigrant crime boss up close. Anton Kaaro was dressed head to toe in gray. Gray suit, gray shirt, gray tie—right down to his shoes, which gleamed even in the dim station fluorescent lights. The only color breaking up this tone-on-tone look was his hair, which was midnight black.

The lawyer, because that was who the other guy had to be, could not have looked less like the attorney for a businessman/crime lord.

He was tanned and blond, wearing a European-cut suit worth more than my car. His tie was a riotous splash of color, matched by a pocket square. When he saw Martin, his eyes lit up like he was meeting a long-lost relative for the first time.

"Captain Martin!" He lunged forward and grabbed the captain's hand in two of his. "I can't tell you how much of a pleasure it is to meet you. I've admired your work in the department for years."

"Really?" the captain said skeptically. "And you are?"

"Charles Shaw. Call me Chuck. I'm Mr. Kaaro's attorney."

"Don't you mean Mr. Grymzin's attorney?" Martin asked.

"Of course," the lawyer said with a rueful, *you got me* smile, displaying perfect white teeth.

"Well, Charles-call-me-Chuck," Martin replied, "*Your client...*" He looked pointedly at Kaaro, "is being held *downstairs*. I'm sure Mr. Kaaro can direct you. He's been here before."

Kaaro studied the captain without expression for a moment, then looked at Monroe. I thought I saw one eyebrow twitch slightly as his gaze swept over me, and his eyes narrowed.

Shaw continued speaking.

"Well, Leon...can I call you Leon?" Shaw ran a hand through his hair. "That's what Mr. Kaaro and I came up to see you about. You see, he and I had a chance to do some follow-up with his employees after you all left. Now, I'm not going to say that your officers jumped to conclusions when they arrested Mr. Grymzin, but we can't find anyone who saw him anywhere near the, uh...altercation."

"Shocking," the captain said. "No one would tell their boss one of his chief lackeys committed murder right in front of them. Who could have imagined that?"

"There's no need for sarcasm, Captain."

An edge crept into the attorney's tone. "The bottom line is, you're not going to locate anyone who will be able to place my client near the attack. Why not save the DA some time and release him? That's what is going to happen eventually anyway."

"I think the DA will be perfectly willing to spend some time on this case," Martin said. "And who knows, maybe someone did see something, and they simply didn't tell *you.*"

"No one will be testifying against Bilol."

We all looked at Kaaro. He had been so silent and willing to let his lawyer do all the talking, it was almost as if a statue had started speaking.

His voice was soft, but resonant. And despite his heritage, it held no discernible accent—just the slightly more formal construction you hear from someone who didn't grow up speaking English.

"You don't know that," said the captain.

Kaaro shrugged. "So you say. I know what each of my employees saw."

His gaze drifted to me once again.

"And *said.* Or didn't say."

His eyes held mine a little too long. Then he turned to Shaw.

"This is not a productive use of our time. We will go get Bilol now."

And just like that, he turned and left the office.

It was as if someone had shut off Shaw's spigot. About to speak, his mouth snapped shut and he followed Kaaro out.

We all watched them go. After they disappeared down the stairs, Martin turned to me.

"Sounds to me like Lennox is blown. But if he's as smart as you say, maybe he knew enough to find a hole to hide in. Do you have a secure way to get in touch with him?"

Martin and Monroe both looked at me expectantly. I tried to keep a calm look on my face, but my mind was racing.

The entire total of my relationship with Rob Lennox was one silent exchange across a room. All I really knew about him was what little I'd been able to pick up in the last few minutes from Monroe and the captain.

Sam had said that in order to get to a stream more than marginally different than the one I had come from, I would literally have to jump over hundreds of others in between. Between Mary and this, things were way different.

But I couldn't waste time thinking about that now. I had to think like the Trav of *this* stream.

He had been working with Lennox for weeks, maybe months. There would be some documentation. It was required even of a confidential informant. Lennox would have signed a document that could be produced later in court to prove his relationship with the department.

However, that document would be in the captain's possession. And asking to see it would reveal I had no clue what was going on.

But...there was one more chance that might save me. And Lennox.

I had never worked a CI before. But I had worked on plenty of sensitive cases. And I was religious in keeping copious notes on details of cases and meetings.

I just had to hope I could find the information I was looking for.

All of this flashed through my mind in the few seconds Martin and Monroe were looking at me expectantly. Hopefully, the pause hadn't been too long.

I did the only thing I could do.

Nodded and said, "Yeah, I do. It's on my computer."

And hoped it was true.

Martin nodded back.

"Then get to it."

I turned to leave, Monroe in my wake. As we rounded the corner toward my desk, he was saying, "Pull up what you need and then let's get out of here. It should take a couple of hours to process Grymzin out, but you never know. With a guy like Kaaro, the usual rules don't always apply. How long will it take you to reach him?"

"Trav?"

I had stopped in my tracks, totally oblivious to his words, and even him calling my name didn't really register as I took in the sight around my desk.

And the other reason might have been I couldn't be sure if he was talking to me or one of the other six Trav Beckers bustling about the squad room.

INTERLUDE

*B*URTON TUPPER WATCHED *with approval as they executed the witch.*

The trial had been swift, Tupper made sure of that. None of this emotional twaddle, pleas from her children or husband. The only witnesses he directed the magistrate to allow were the young women who had heard Humility Carver predict the future.

And who could also testify how Mistress Carver took over their bodies, forcing them to remove their clothing, fondle and touch themselves and do unimaginable things to each other with their young lips and tongues.

It had, of course, been the moaning and screams that had attracted one of the girls' fathers to a clearing in the woods near his home, where he witnessed the debauchery.

Fortunately, even through his shock, the man had the presence of mind to realize some demonic power was at work, and had gone immediately to the worship house where Tupper was working on the week's message.

When the pastor came on the scene, the spell had immediately been broken, and it wasn't long before he got the truth from the sobbing and now-contrite girls.

Mistress Carver, not surprisingly, had denied everything when a group of elders pulled her from her bed. She had even bewitched her husband and family to believe she had been in the house the whole time.

But Tupper knew better.

He had been watching the young mother for some time. She was exactly the kind of woman the devil used to tempt men. She did nothing to hide the womanly curves that he knew lurked beneath her plain clothing, even after birthing three children. When she spoke to a man, she looked directly into his eyes, not casting her vision downward as proper comportment dictated.

Tupper had encouraged, nay, begged her husband to allow him to counsel her. He favored private sessions with women who his spiritual intuition told him would behave wantonly without his guidance.

But Goodman Carver had refused his generosity, even hinting that he should not be alone with a young woman.

Ever the godly leader, Tupper had turned the other cheek to this affront. But now he had no choice.

At the conclusion of the trial, a trio of bailiffs dragged the woman from the courtroom to the town square, while a group of church elders held tight to her children, and three more kept the husband from interfering.

Humility Carver was made to lie supine on the ground, her legs spread obscenely. But this would be the last time she tempted men in such a way, Tupper thought with satisfaction.

A large square plank was brought and placed over the woman, covering her from neck to knees.

Tupper held up his hand, and addressed the crowd.

"This woman has been duly tried and convicted. Now, Goodwife, I give you one last chance to confess your sins and repent." He looked down at her.

She had remained silent through the trial, and even kept her mouth closed tightly all the while she was brought to the scene of her punishment. Now, her eyes darted wildly among the crowd, searching in vain for a sympathetic glance. Her eyes finally met her husband's, struggling to free himself from the grip of those who kept him from coming to her.

A tear rolled down her cheek, dotting the ground.

"I confess," she said softly.

"What, my dear?" Tupper asked.

"I confess," she repeated. "I did all those things. Just...please, don't take me from my babies!"

"And do you repent of your sins, rebuke the devil whose influence led you to sin?"

"Yes," she sobbed.

Tupper held up a hand, addressing the assembled throng. "The Lord your Father has heard your confession, and will take it into account at your judgment." He gestured to a group of young men standing near a pile of large stones.

"Proceed with the sentence."

"You bastard!" Carver spat, struggling against those who held his arms.

One by one, the stones were brought, and placed on the plank. Young men brought large stones, youngsters were encouraged to place pebbles. All took part in the purifying, even Humility Carver's own children.

Tupper looked on in approval as one child stumbled forward, a generous-sized stone in one hand, the other holding one end of a dog's leash.

The dog, a mastiff practically as tall as his master, pulled the youngster up to the pile of stones, dancing and barking as the boy placed his rock atop the others.

"Down, Toby!"

The child pulled the dog away, and tried to make him heel near where Tupper stood.

Humility's husband should have helped as well, but he stood his ground and was beaten unconscious rather than participate. Tupper would have to spend some time in prayer tonight, to ascertain what should be done with the man. Some might regard his obstinance as a challenge to the Tupper's pastoral authority.

And the man should be grateful, Tupper thought. Some villages burned their witches. Tupper had always thought that punishment somewhat wasteful. A faggot of wood, once consumed, was gone forever, and the pitch used to ignite the flame was not cheap.

Pressing was just as effective, and stones were free and plentiful, not to mention reusable.

Sooner than you might imagine, an impressive collection of stone balanced somewhat precariously atop the plank. Humility's breathing had become quite labored. He was surprised when she opened her mouth to speak.

"Father Tupper…"

Tupper leaned down toward her face, pleased that she had chosen to make a final confession to him.

"Yes, my daughter?" he said gently.

She looked directly at him once again. Then, oddly, her gaze became unfocused and seemed to look past him at something to the side. He tried to follow her gaze, but saw nothing. He turned back to her, and was surprised to see her lips curving up into a strained smile.

She looked back at him.

"Enjoy these last few minutes," she whispered.

"What, my dear?"

"You'll…" a small gasp, "…see."

Thunk!

A large stone was added to the pile. Only because he was so close could Tupper hear a soft crack underneath the plank. A bloody foam burbled up between Humility's lips and her glance once again became a blank stare.

But this time it was the stare of a departed soul.

Tupper once again held up a hand.

"I declare your sins forgiven, daughter," he intoned. He raised his voice, so his entire flock could hear.

"And by your participation in this just act, the stain of sin which dirtied our entire community has been washed clean. Go now, knowing that we have all been purified."

A loud cheer went up from the assemblage.

"Toby!"

The dog, startled by the noise, took off like it had been stung by a bee. The boy's hand was caught in the leash, and he tried to keep his feet as the dog sprinted toward Tupper.

"Easy, easy!" Tupper cried as the dog approached.

He tried to reach down to catch it by the collar, but the dog pivoted quickly, staying out of his reach. As the animal turned, the leash became wrapped around Tupper's legs.

He straightened as the dog circled fully around him, the leash drawing his legs together.

His prayer book flew out of this hand as he tried to keep his balance.

Tupper teetered for a moment, and began to topple toward the pile of stones.

He never saw the jagged rock edge that pierced his temple, but as he tumbled in what seemed like slow motion, his head was turned toward Humility Carver, a bloody smile still adorning her face.

As the blackness descended, Burton Tupper's eyes met those of the woman who had seen his fate.

5

I LOOKED OVER at Monroe, then back at the roomful of Travs.

One was holding a cup of coffee and appeared to be talking to someone, although the space he was directing his face to was empty. Another was sitting on the corner of the desk but appeared to be completely oblivious to the one who was actually sitting at the desk, doing something at the computer. Still another was standing on the other side of the desk, reading a report. A couple more loitered nearby.

"Uh, Trav?"

Monroe was looking at me expectantly. I looked back at the insane tableau and now noticed that, while each and every one of the crowd surrounding my desk was undeniably me, they also had varying degrees of solidity.

The ones standing around were practically transparent. The ones reading or engaged in a discrete task while standing were not as see-through. And outlining their profiles was a faint, but distinct, *blue* tinge, like someone had taken a glowing blue marker and traced around them.

The one at the computer was the most solid and normal-looking of all. He also had a glowing outline, but his was red.

I looked back at Monroe. He was still waiting for me to say something. He also had glanced out at the squad, but obviously didn't see anything out of the ordinary.

I didn't have time to decide whether or not I found it comforting that this was apparently my own personal hallucination. Monroe was waiting for me to do something.

"Uh, yeah, sorry," I finally said. "I've got what we need right here."

And hoped that was actually the case.

I approached Red Trav, trying to look normal.

What would happen if I tried to sit down in the same space as him?

By now, you have probably figured out that, in addition to helping me with my stats and chemistry in college, Sam had also introduced me to geek culture. Whenever he didn't have his head stuck in a textbook, there was some classic sci-fi movie or TV show turned on.

I had tried to ignore it for a while, but eventually I got sucked in.

Stargate, Battlestar, Lord of the Rings—I could recite them all line for line. Like I said, he totally ruined me to hang out with real people.

And, of course, *Star Trek*.

Next Gen first, Sam had the DVD set. Then, *The Original Series*, on actual VHS, believe it or not. After our last class on Thursday was over, watching TOS was a weekly ritual.

Of course, since it was college, we also made a drinking game where you had to chug a beer every time Spock did that raise-one-eyebrow thing.

Anyway, remember that episode where two doppelgängers from parallel universes dared not come into physical contact, lest the meeting of matter and anti-matter annihilate everything in existence?

That's what I was thinking about as I approached Red Trav and prepared to sit, um...*in* him.

Although, blowing up the universe would certainly take care of the issue of my not knowing how to find Rob Lennox.

"Tick tock, Trav."

I took a deep breath, hoping that Monroe would think my nerves were related to the time pressure of our task, and gingerly sat down.

No explosion or fatal tearing of the fabric of reality.

In fact, I didn't feel a thing, but I could still see a little of the blurry red outline where Red Trav and I weren't occupying the exact same space.

Like our hands.

Mine were in my lap, his were slowly and deliberately depressing keys.

What the hell, I don't have any better ideas. I'll just follow along.

I quickly figured out that Red Trav was going through the login sequence to my...er, *our* computer, so I followed suit.

I quickly typed in my password, *MdJcCaWkBePcJc*.

Now, just because I'm not a technophile, you shouldn't get the idea that I'm lax in cyber security. But, it was easy to remember a twelve letter password when it was the initials of the Miles Davis Sextet. Song lyrics work just as well. One was the lyrics of the Poco song I mentioned earlier—in Spanish for an added level of complexity.

I could thank Sam for making me a sci-fi geek. I had my dad to thank for the musical education.

As a kid, I hadn't realized how much I had absorbed during those road trips and long winter nights spent by the stereo. It wasn't until years later I realized how thoroughly those nights playing board games and hanging out while his music played in the background made most music recorded after 1985 sound derivative and simplistic.

And Dad definitely provided a varied musical menu. I've already mentioned Poco, who would be a country band if they came on the scene today. But his collection also included Yes, Dave Mason, J.J. Cayle and Traffic, as well as Miles, Coltrane, Cannonball.

Not surprisingly, I'd rebelled in my teens by insisting on a deep love for a particularly atonal brand of house music.

But now that Dad was gone, coins worn nearly smooth from his magic tricks and an iPod-full of old jazz and progressive rock tunes were the main things I had to remember him by.

As I typed the final *c*, I had almost caught up with Red Trav's fingers, and we hit the return key at virtually the same time.

The login screen gave way to my familiar desktop.

Conscious that Monroe was watching me, I quickly navigated to my Reports module, a secure software suite that had replaced most of our manual reports.

That called for another password (the first two lines of "In the Court of the Crimson King"), and pretty soon I was digging through my secure reports.

I wasn't sure what I would find. I didn't like storing sensitive information electronically, no matter how safe we were told it was. I had to assume the Trav from this stream was the same way. But the reports program we were now required to use also allowed the user to set a security level on data that would result in only that user and Captain Martin being able to view it.

If this Trav hadn't followed the rules and kept his records here, I would be out of luck.

I entered Rob Lennox's name into the search field, held my breath and pressed the return key.

I was rewarded with a lengthy list of date-stamped reports that scrolled for two or three screens-worth before stopping.

Trying not to sigh audibly in relief, I clicked on a box labeled *info*. A page of detailed information sprang onto the screen. Lennox's phone number and address were the first things listed.

I flipped open my phone and started pressing keys to send him a text.

Need to meet. R U home?

Monroe looked at the phone, then at me.

"New phone?"

"Uh, no."

I gave him a confused look, but he shrugged. "What now?"

"I don't want to wait to see if he answers. Let's head that way."

Monroe nodded.

We were headed toward my car when the phone rang. I glanced at the screen.

Mom.

I suddenly realized what today was. Even in the midst of all this chaos, I couldn't miss talking to her.

I looked at Monroe and shook my head.

"Not him. But I should answer this."

"Do you want me to drive?" asked Monroe.

"Yeah, that's fine."

We changed directions toward his car as I flipped open the phone.

"Hi, Mom."

"Hi, Travis."

Mom was the only person who called me Travis.

"I wanted to check in with you," she continued.

"I know. You beat me to it."

We approached Monroe's car as I talked. He fished for his keys, and the door locks disengaged with a *thunk*.

"How are you doing?" I continued.

By now, we were in the car, and we took off.

A sigh.

"Fine."

"Are you getting out some?"

"Oh, of course. The reunion committee is meeting again."

"You just had your reunion three months ago."

"We like to start early. The fifty-fifth is a big one." I could hear a little smile creep into her voice. "All right, it's really an excuse to get together for lunch every month."

"Still doing the tai chi?"

"Yes, yes. And eating right, and taking my medicines. You don't have to worry about me, sweetheart."

"I want to make sure you're taking care of yourself."

"As much as anyone my age can, dear. But as we both know, there are no guarantees, no matter how much exercise or good diet you get."

"I know, Mom."

"How are *you* doing?"

"Fine, Mom. It's just…"

Monroe wasn't looking in my direction, focused almost too much on the road. He wouldn't eavesdrop on purpose, but I still couldn't go into this right now.

"You're not alone, are you?"

Mom ESP. If I had it, I'd strike fear into the heart of every criminal who crossed my path.

"No."

"Well, we can talk later. I wanted to let you know I was thinking about you. And your dad."

"Me, too. Every day."

"Love you, Travis."

"Me, too."

I snapped the phone shut. Monroe was still staring straight ahead.

"My mom. Dad died a year ago today."

"That sucks."

"Yeah."

He didn't say anything else, and I didn't offer more details.

Fact was, even after an entire year, even the briefest thought of my dad created a throat-tightening wave of despair that I still hadn't been able to shake.

I had finally gotten to the point that I could go a few days without thinking of the Mike Becker-sized hole in my soul.

Look up "jack-of-all-trades" in the dictionary, and my dad's picture should have been there. I have already mentioned the music and the magic tricks. But that just scratched the surface. He was the department's best sharpshooter until his retirement, and spent hours in a tree stand during deer season. The Internet fascinated him, and for a while he kept a very entertaining blog. His agile mind was always looking for something new to try, especially with the free time he had after retiring.

He didn't slow down at all, training as a museum docent, and doing magic gigs, both paid and free, right up till the icy night he'd been driving home from doing a show for disabled kids and lost control of his pickup.

That was the real reason I wouldn't do card tricks anymore, no matter how much Holli begged. I couldn't even look at a deck of cards.

"So, what's the plan?" Monroe asked, interrupting my reverie.

I snapped back to reality, processing how far we'd driven. We'd be at Lennox's place in a few minutes. Time to get my head back in the game.

Monroe parked about a block and a half away. We approached the building casually, but swept the street for anything that looked out of place.

"He's on the third floor," I said as we got to the building.

"Figures," Monroe harrumphed. It was more for show than anything else. He was very light on his feet for a big guy. I'd watched him chase down more than one fleeing suspect, shocked when the portly cop grabbed them from behind.

There was no security on the building, so we quickly, but quietly started up the stairs.

I led the way, since I was the one who allegedly had been here before. The building was eerily quiet. Usually a place like this was never silent. The floor generally pumped with the bass beat of rap music, the fake life of some reality TV show. Or, the real life of some couple having a knock-down drag out.

Except for the distinct smell of Chinese food wafting along on top of the old building smell, you'd have sworn no one lived here.

We got to the top of the stairs. I looked down the hall and spied Lennox's apartment number, *9*.

We trod quietly down the corridor. As we approached Lennox's door, we saw it was ajar. I silently drew my weapon, knowing without looking that Monroe was doing the same.

The door was cracked open maybe two inches, black behind, meaning the lights were turned off inside.

Great.

Still in the lead, I stopped at the door and listened.

Nothing.

I quickly crossed to the opposite side of the door, where the knob gapped away from the frame. Monroe stood back behind the door frame. Not many targets easier to hit than a silhouette in a doorway.

I pushed the door open with my gun hand.

"Rob?" I called.

Still nothing. I sensed there was no one breathing in the apartment, but played it safe even so.

I glanced at Monroe, and raised one eyebrow. *Ready?*

He gave an almost imperceptible nod.

I snaked a hand inside the door frame and felt for the light switch. I switched it on, and my suspicions were confirmed. Empty.

Carefully, we peeked around the door.

A one-room studio apartment lay before us. The space was small by any measure, but the litter of trash and overturned furniture covering most of the floor space made it seem even more confining.

The little place had been trashed.

Two chairs in the tiny kitchen area were upended, and the shards of some broken plates littered the floor.

There was one overstuffed chair in the sitting area. It was on its side as well.

The bed was unmade, and there were a couple of stained towels on it.

We cautiously entered the room, even though there was nowhere someone could hide in the small space.

I approached the bed, examining the towels. They were stained with dried blood.

Monroe moved past me, to an open door that had to be the bathroom.

"It's clear," he called a moment later.

He emerged, carrying a damp washcloth, which seeped more blood. He started to say something, then his eyes darted toward the doorway.

"What the hell did you do to Rob?" cried a voice behind me.

I whirled, gun coming up. A young woman stood in the doorway.

I opened my mouth to tell her to put her hands where I could see them, but before I could, Monroe gave a relaxed grunt.

"Geez—Harper, that's a good way to get shot."

I frowned and studied the woman. She wore a faded t-shirt, cut off to expose a trim, pale belly, and worn jeans that hugged her hips and thighs without a crease, tucked into a pair of black motorcycle boots. Her blonde hair was straight, but teased out to create about twice the volume it should have had.

I mentally pulled the hair back in, tied it in a bun and subtracted the striking black and purple eye makeup she wore.

Then I put a uniform cap on her and realized I was looking at Officer Amy Harper.

"Changed your clothes," I said, putting my weapon away. Monroe did the same.

She shrugged. "Can't visit this neighborhood in my uniform."

"What are you doing here?" I asked.

"Same thing as you," she replied with a small frown. "Looking for Rob. Did he call you?"

"No, I sent him a text but he didn't answer."

She nodded. "He left the club not long after you all did. No one has heard from him since. I figured it would be okay for his 'girlfriend...'"

She hooked her fingers in air quotes.

"...to show up to check on him."

I nodded. This was starting to make a little more sense. And it also explained why she hadn't wanted to go inside the bar when Monroe and I had encountered her outside.

Having a woman serve as Lennox's contact wasn't a bad idea.

It might look odd for me to show up at Lennox's apartment. Even if no one made me as a cop, they might ask Lennox who this guy was who kept hanging around.

But a pretty girl could chat him up in the bar or slip into his building and he wouldn't have to explain anything.

And, as Harper had just proved, her girlfriend persona bore little resemblance to her in uniform. She'd been right to be cautious last night and not go into the bar. But hell, she probably could have waltzed right in and questioned guys who'd been checking her out the night before and they wouldn't have been the wiser. She was a little green to be doing undercover work, but looked to be handling it okay.

"So, they said at the bar he'd gone home?" Monroe asked.

She nodded. "Left probably an hour ago."

She looked around, taking in the disarray of the room for the first time, the blood on the sheets and on the cloth Monroe still held. She bit her lip and inclined her head toward the bathroom.

"Wh...what was in there?"

"Just this," Monroe replied, holding up the washcloth.

"I'd say someone showed up here and roughed him up some," Monroe continued as we all looked around the room once again. "But gave him a chance to clean up a little before they took him out."

"Even in this neighborhood, hauling a bleeding man out of his apartment would attract some attention," I offered, wanting to contribute something to the conversation.

Harper turned to a small table that sat to the left of the entry door. She held up a phone.

"He wouldn't have left willingly without this."

Monroe and I nodded. He turned to me.

"Any ideas where they might have taken him?"

"Not a clue."

Monroe sighed. "Shit. Well, there's not much we can do here. Might as well head back to the station and break the bad news."

"I'll stay here for a few minutes," Harper said. "Best for me not to be seen leaving with two cops, just in case."

"Lock up before you go," I said.

She nodded. "I have a key."

Monroe and I headed back to the station, where predictably, Capt. Martin did not congratulate us on our fine work. In fact, he only favored us with two words.

"Find him."

We hustled out to our desks. Just as I was sitting down, my phone vibrated with the arrival of a text. It was from Sam.

Need to talk to you.

Ok. When?

Now. Am downstairs.

"I'll be back in a couple," I said to Monroe. He grunted, not taking his eyes from his computer.

I grabbed my jacket and headed downstairs.

As I stepped out onto the sidewalk, a Toyota hybrid, running silent on its electric, glided toward me. The passenger window rolled down.

Sam leaned over, squinting up at me through the opening.

"Get in."

"What's going on, Sam?"

He shook his head, lips pressed tightly together.

"Wait. I thought your car was in the shop."

"Never mind that. Get in."

I slid in. Sam gunned the tiny engine before I even got the door shut.

"Where's the fire?"

Sam shook his head. He quickly swung the little car into a three-point turn and pulled out into the street, one hand on the wheel, the other fiddling with his phone.

"Wanna watch where you're driving?"

"We have more to worry about right now than a fender bender," he replied grimly.

He fell silent, dividing his attention between the road and his phone. Something was bothering me about his appearance, and after a few seconds I figured out what it was.

When I had left his lab a couple of hours ago, he'd been wearing a navy blue t-shirt that said, "Trust me, I'm the Doctor" on the front. Now his shirt was green, bearing the Green Lantern symbol.

He also had managed somehow, in the last two hours, to acquire a two-day's growth of scraggly, ginger beard.

"Spill something on your shirt?"

He didn't answer, and refused to speak for the rest of the trip, until finally we pulled up at a familiar door.

"This is my place."

"No shit. C'mon."

Sam took the steps up to the apartment building two at a time, no small feat considering his stature. I hurried to follow, pulling keys out of my pocket. When we got to my door, Sam pushed past me. Then he half turned to me and held a finger to his lips. He brought his phone up and swiped the touch screen a few times, frowning. Finally, he relaxed.

"Okay, it's clear." He reached past me and turned on the light.

"What's clear? What the hell is this all about?"

"C'mere."

Sam led me across the room to the closet. He put his hand on the knob and began to turn it, but stopped.

"Uh…this is probably going to be a little weird."

"Like it's not weird now? Just tell me what is going on."

"Let me show you this first."

He swung open the door.

Maybe Sam's warning should have prepared me for what I saw. Or maybe I should have been warned simply by the chain of all the other impossible events I'd been through in the last few hours. Although at this point, I'd kind of forgotten a lot of them.

Regardless, nothing really could have prepared me for this.

Propped in a semi-sitting position against the boxes of out-of-season clothes, books, and old stereo components that filled my living room closet was a corpse. It was dressed identically to me, right down to the Cardinals baseball jacket. Which made sense in a way, because it also wore a face identical to mine.

Identical in every way except for the quarter-sized, bloody hole in the side of its head.

6

"U^{H, TRAV?"}

"U H, TRAV?"
I tore my gaze away from my own dead body and looked at Sam.

"Do you...wanna sit down or something?" He said uncertainly. The iron purpose driving him since picking me up seemed to have completely drained away.

I slowly swung the door shut just far enough to obscure Trav-in-the-closet.

"Will you please tell me what the fuck is going on?" I said, slowly grinding each word out.

"Can we sit?" asked Sam.

I motioned to the couch.

Sam sat down and ran his hand over the coffee table, wiping an imaginary speck of dust from its shiny surface.

I sat at the other end of the couch. It took every mental muscle I had to not look back over at the closet. I'd like to be able to describe how I was feeling, but until you find yourself staring into your own dead face, I doubt you'd understand.

I folded my arms and turned toward Sam.

"Well...it started in my lab."

"I guess I figured that."

"No, not the lab you were in."

"There's another one?"

"Yes. No."

Sam stopped, and ran a hand through his thick bush of hair. "Okay. Let me start at the beginning. The lab I'm talking about is *my* lab. In my stream."

"You're from another stream?"

"Sure. And so are you."

"I know. You told me earlier."

"That wasn't me. It was the Sam from this stream."

"There's two of you?"

"Sure. There's two of *you*." He gestured toward the closet. "Well, there was, at least."

I suppressed a shudder.

"This is not getting us anywhere, Sam. How about you back up a little? Can you start at the beginning? Is there a beginning?"

Sam thought for a minute. "It would probably be easier if we started with what *you* know. Or think you know."

"I went to your lab today. You showed me the Cat Box. Which went crazy when you, although now you say it wasn't you, turned it on. The... other Sam said it was because I had just arrived from another stream. Later, I saw Mary..."

I paused.

"And?"

I frowned, trying to recall what had bothered me about my conversation with Mary. I remembered being confused, but couldn't quite put my finger on why.

"Things were, different. But I don't exactly remember how they were different."

Sam nodded as if this was no surprise to him. "Did he, the Sam you were with, talk at all about how streams work?"

I shrugged. "We move between streams all the time...the Cat Box was designed to measure the stutters in reality created by movement between streams. And that the motion is only one way."

"No backsies."

"Yeah."

"Well, sounds like he gave you a pretty complete picture. It's all wrong, of course."

"Wrong?"

"Well, incomplete."

"Are you going to enlighten me? I've had kind of a long day. Apparently, I can't trust what I thought I knew, and there's a body, *my own* body—in the closet."

"I'm sorry, Trav. None of this is your fault. I'm sorry you got caught in the middle, but..."

"But what?"

Sam sighed. "Let me start at the beginning."

"That would be nice."

"Well, first off, like I said, I'm not from this stream. In the grand scheme of things, where I'm from is not that different than here. But in my stream, we've gotten a lot farther in figuring out what the full capabilities of the Cat Box are."

He paused, looking at me intently.

"You with me so far?"

I nodded. "Go on."

"Well, the Sam here told you the Cat Box was designed to measure the incoming and outgoing quanta, right?"

I nodded again.

"Okay. Well, in my stream, we've gone a little further than just measuring. I figured out how to actually *choose* which quanta move from stream to stream."

I sighed. "Now you've lost me."

He nodded patiently. "With enough computer horsepower to decode the wave forms, I can not only track when people and things move from stream to stream, I can direct those movements."

"So, this is all *your* doing?" I waved a hand at the closet. "What the hell were you thinking?"

Sam held up a hand. "Wait. Hear me out. I'm so sorry if you feel like you've been bounced around. Believe me, it wasn't the plan to jerk you in and out of streams like you have been. But circumstances kind of forced my hand."

"What circumstances?"

Sam turned his attention again to his phone and again stroked and swiped on the screen.

"Just a second. To understand why you're here, first you need to fully understand where you've *been.*"

He punched the screen one more time with a satisfied grunt.

And my brain exploded.

Memories crashed *into my mind.* That's the only way I can describe it.

Full-blown pictures burst into my consciousness. Things that I suddenly now knew I had experienced, but had slipped out of my recall.

The vodka blackout, Sam getting me up and ready for my hearing. Mary out of my life, Adam *dead.*

The kaleidoscope of new images wedging themselves into my head made me dizzy. My stomach dropped like I was riding a roller coaster.

Sam was silent, giving me some time to adjust.

"Ung...God. You could have given me some warning."

"Sorry. There's no smooth way to manage the integration."

"What did you do to me?"

"When you shift streams, your consciousness adjusts, or smoothes over any discontinuities, remember? I mean, you've had an eventful couple of days, right? But when I picked you up at the station you didn't say anything about the streams, or about your disciplinary hearing, or Mary, let alone Adam. In fact, I could tell you didn't really want to talk to me much at all. You were pre-occupied with whatever you're doing at work. Am I right?"

He was. Whatever he had done to me had brought the memories of everything that had happened to me back to the surface—but before we'd gotten here, I had almost totally forgotten the strange situation I'd been in.

Sam was still talking. "Yesterday morning, I gave you a pill. Well, not a pill exactly. It's nano-technnology. It kind of gives you a... marker that I can use to track your individual quanta as they shift from stream to stream. I can also..."

He screwed up his face, wincing a little.

"Well, I guess the best way to put it, is... I can push *reset*, which gives you back whatever got smoothed out. Those are *your* memories, they were there all the time, but re-integrating them doesn't feel very good."

"I'll say. So, you've done this before?"

"Not to this extent."

"Who were your other guinea pigs?"

"That's not important now. You understand everything I said?"

I nodded, although I was still trying to follow.

"You can go to another stream," I said slowly.

"Yeah."

"And back again?"

"Right."

"And you can move me, too?"

He shrugged. "That's kind of a simplistic explanation, but essentially, yes."

"*Why?* Why am I here, instead of drunk, alone and suicidal back where you found me?"

"You want to go back there? You forget. I was with you. Not much fun."

"Doesn't matter." My head was slowly beginning to clear. "No backsies, remember?"

"Well, that's another thing we figured out in my stream. If you can jump from one reality to another, you can certainly jump back. As long as you can keep track of where you are *vis a vis* the other streams, that is. Which is where this comes in."

He held up his phone. "This is linked to the version of the Cat Box in my home stream, which I call Stream Zero. With it, I can track, monitor and move from stream to stream."

"You still haven't answered my question. Why? And why me?"

"Because I need your help."

"Help? What kind of help?"

"I need you to help me catch the guy who did that." Sam gestured to the closet.

"Do you suspect someone?"

Despite everything I'd been through in the last few minutes, let alone the past two days, the cop took over.

Sam nodded. "I don't just suspect, I *know* who did it."

"Who?"

"You."

"Me."

"Yeah."

We sat for a moment while I digested this. Finally, Sam broke the silence.

"It was an accident."

"What was?"

"Getting you...well, *my* you..."

"MY you?" This was making my head hurt, beyond the dull ache that still throbbed behind my eyes from having a bunch of memories wedged sideways into my consciousness.

"Is there a less confusing way we can talk about this?" I complained. "I can't keep all of us straight. You said you called where you come from Stream Zero, right? That makes you Sam Zero and me...*your* me, Trav Zero."

"Fair enough."

"So, what do you call this stream?"

"Linear measurements don't make much sense in this realm, but you can think of it as being 'close' to Stream Zero. I had to jump you a couple of times to get you where you needed to be. Call it Stream One."

"And the Sam who showed me the Cat Box is the Sam from this stream, not you?"

"Right."

"And where did I come from originally?"

Sam thought for a minute. "Uh...four, I guess."

"Fine."

94

Oddly, I found myself wondering why I couldn't have at least started in the top three. But I forced myself to stay on topic.

"So, it was an accident?"

"Yeah. Well, like I said. In my stream we've moved beyond tracking matter as it enters and leaves our stream, and can actually track it from stream to stream."

"Not just track it but follow it, apparently."

"That came later. Where it started with you was…I called you a few weeks ago for help. You know that both Mary and I were encouraging you to quit the force and go to work with your old partner."

Gene Palmer, whose wife had introduced me to Mary, was my first partner on the force. I was as green as Adam when he got hold of me, and he had trained and mentored me until retiring a few years previously.

He'd since hung out his shingle as a security consultant, just in time to take advantage of the continuing corporate nervousness about terrorism, of both the physical and cyber varieties.

In a couple of years, he'd gone from being a glorified security guard to running a pretty big company providing personal security, background checks, and Internet safety to both individuals and corporations. Gene had been after me to join his company for several months, and had even offered to make me a partner.

I sighed. This had been one of the major friction points in my relationship with Mary, in my home stream at least. She worried about the dangers of work on the force, particularly after the mess that had killed Adam. She had encouraged me to accept Gene's offer, but even in the aftermath of the Adam disaster, I wasn't willing to quit. The resulting row had pretty much ended our relationship. In Stream Four, at least.

"I wasn't working for Gene in your stream, was I?"

Sam looked a little uncomfortable. "No, but we had been having some unauthorized access attempts in the lab and I asked you to look into it. In my stream, Adam wasn't killed, but it was a hell of a close call for both of you. Mary was scared to death. Honestly, we were hoping a taste of that kind of work would show you going to work for Gene wouldn't be so bad after all."

95

I pushed aside the annoyance of my friend and my girl conspiring behind my back. "So, what happened?"

"Well, you came into the lab, and the Cat Box went nuts. But differently than the way you described it. The readings weren't showing Trav Zero had arrived in the stream, but every time he was in the room with the device, it started to spew out gibberish. Huge amounts of traffic both in and out of the stream not substantiated by any other readings, streams coming together, streams moving apart—it didn't make any sense. We figured it was a glitch in the software, until..." Sam paused.

"Until what?"

"Until Trav told me he was seeing into other streams."

"What?"

"He said that he had started seeing...well, he described it as shadows, or like after-images you get when a bright light shines into your eyes. If he was looking at a person, he could also see shadows of them performing different actions. And, he said if he focused hard enough, one of those particular actions or events would then actually happen."

"You mean he was *making* it happen?"

"No. Or at least I don't think so. What we finally decided was that he was seeing the potential new streams that might result from a given behavior, or action. And that if he concentrated on a given outcome, he could, kind of 'steer' toward it, making his potential observation 'come true.' From his own perspective, at least."

I thought about the roomful of Travs bustling around the office. Could that be what he was talking about? But what Sam was describing was way beyond getting pushed into different streams. It was more like...*being able to foretell the future.*

"Yeah," said Sam. It was only then that I realized I had said that last bit out loud.

"Time seems to run at slightly different rates on different streams. Again, like the branches of a river. Headed eventually to the same place, but one might get there faster than another."

Which explained how I could hear about Grymzin's arrest on Stream Four, then take part in it a day later on Stream One.

"What happened then?"

Sam sighed. "And then things totally went to shit. The visions, or shadows or whatever you want to call them started to make him crazy. He couldn't tell the difference between things that actually happened and things that only might happen. And then..." His voice trailed off again.

"What?"

"Well, he made a big bust. And later didn't know if he had actually caught the right guy or if he had moved into a stream where that guy had done it. It drove him nuts. He showed up at the lab, pulled his gun on me. On ME, for Christ's sake. And said we had to destroy the machine. That no one should have this kind of power."

"So did you?"

"No! That's the thing. As near as I can figure, the Cat Box didn't have anything to do with Trav's 'power,' or whatever you want to call it. Whatever 'power' he had wasn't coming from me. It came from something else. I have no idea what. Turning off or dismantling the machine wouldn't do anything."

"Did you tell him that?"

"Of course. Well, that pulled him up short. He said, 'You're right. But this is still too dangerous. And I'm the only one who can fix it.' And then..."

"Then WHAT?" These long pauses between Sam's conversational bombshells were really driving me nuts.

"He disappeared."

"He what?"

"He disappeared. Right in front of my eyes. I didn't even know that was possible. It took me weeks to re-figure all my equations and recalibrate the Box till I figured out how he had done it."

"And that's how you learned how."

"Kind of. I figured out how to modify the Cat Box software to allow me to move to another stream. But I have to use software."

He waved his phone again.

"He did it without any machinery. And I jump blind. I generally have a pretty good idea of what stream I'm heading for, but I can't always be sure. Which is why it took me multiple tries to get you to where we needed to be. Trav... Trav Zero that is, said he could actually see where he's going."

"How?" I asked.

"He couldn't ever explain it to me," Sam replied. "All he ever said was, 'I follow the red shift.'"

Follow the red shift. The Travs in the office had pretty much all had a bluish aura around them. Except for one. And the one tinged in red had been the one whose actions I had decided to follow. But I didn't know why, and the cryptic phrase from Trav Zero didn't help much.

"Follow the red shift? What does that mean?"

"No idea." Sam said.

We sat in silence again, Sam stroking and sliding numbers and icons around on his phone. I stared at the closet door, knowing that sooner or later I would have to open it again and confront what was in there. Which caused me to recall what Sam had said when he'd shown me the body.

"Wait."

Sam looked up from his screen.

"You said *I* did that." I waved my hand at the closet. "You think it was Trav Zero?"

Sam nodded.

"I know it was. I've been following a trail of dead Travs for days, trying to catch up to him. Whatever it is that caused him to develop this ability to jump between streams also has caused him to become completely unhinged. As near as I can figure, he's decided that the only way to keep anyone else from disturbing the natural continuity is to get rid of anyone else who might develop the ability to manipulate it."

"So, he's going from stream to stream killing *himself?*"

Sam shrugged again. "I didn't say it made any sense. Anyway, I've been trying for a week to jump far enough ahead of him to get to a Trav he hadn't found yet. Then I had to bring you back to a stream that was close enough that you could help."

"Help? Help do what?"

Sam looked at me as though the answer should be obvious. "Find Trav Zero, of course. Before he finds you."

"And how do I do that?"

Sam looked at me intently. "You're a detective, Trav. I can't do this. I work in a lab. I'm lucky that he hasn't targeted me, or I'm sure we wouldn't even be having this conversation. I need help. And who better than someone who has a vested interest in the outcome?"

"A vested interest," I repeated numbly. "You mean I'm the bait."

"Don't think of it like that. You're a cop. He's going around killing people. Isn't that the kind of thing you generally try to stop?"

"He's killing *me*. Or mes."

"And the best way to get him to stop is to find him before he gets to you."

"And then what? Arrest him? So I haul *me* into the station and book *me* on the charge of murdering *me*?"

"I think you know we can't do that," Sam said quietly. "But let's find him first. Who knows, maybe you can talk some sense into him."

"You couldn't."

"I'm not you," Sam shot back.

"Yeah, you're about the only one."

I held up a hand, forestalling his rejoinder. "You're right. Find him first."

"Trav, look on the bright side," Sam said.

"There's a *bright* side?"

"Yeah. Think about it, man. In this stream, you're a decorated hero, Adam's still alive. You and Mary are still together. Help me fix this and you get to *stay here*."

I stared at Sam for a minute, speechless.

Stay here?

It was a damn sight better than the place I'd apparently started out from. I shuddered at the memory of being so despondent I had considered eating my gun.

And earlier, when I thought I had arrived in this stream by natural means, I had easily reconciled myself to staying.

Why not?

Sam obviously was following this train of thought.

"And it's not like you'd be taking anything from someone else." He inclined his head toward the closet. "Actually, you'd be doing everyone here a favor. In this stream, Trav doesn't *have* to die."

A thought suddenly occurred to me.

"When did he...you know, get shot?"

Sam scratched his head. "Well, like I said, time doesn't flow at exactly the same rate from stream to stream, but...call it night before last."

"So, he was in that closet when I came home last night."

Sam looked uncomfortable. "Yeah. You see, my original plan was to come get you at the end of your shift yesterday and have this conversation. But when I came to get you, you were out on a call. Then I..."

He paused, opening and closing his mouth a couple of times.

"Then what?"

"Well, then I thought I saw Zero skulking around so I bugged out. This was the soonest I could get back."

Had I gathered Mary's stuff out of the drawers and bagged it last night, as I had thought about doing, I would have put it in this closet.

What a surprise *that* would have been.

"Okay. Well, what do we do now?"

"You're the cop," Sam said again. "I'll handle the inter-dimensional travel, you handle the murder investigation."

"Funny," I snorted.

I thought for a second, then looked reluctantly over at the closet. It was awful, but had to be done. "Okay. Help me get him out of the closet."

Sam's eyes widened. "Are you serious?"

"We start by examining the scene. I could root around searching the apartment, but if there are any clues, they'll probably be with the body."

I stood up. After a moment's hesitation, Sam did too.

I paused for a second at the door, mentally preparing for the sight. I'd worked dozens of accident and murder scenes and had no problems with blood or handling a corpse. But this...

I opened the door, and stared once more into the face that looked back at me in the mirror every morning. Minus the vacant, lifeless stare and bloody mass on the side of his head, of course.

Jesus.

"Take his feet."

"Are you sure?" If it was possible for Sam's pasty, indoors-worker complexion to get even more paler, it definitely had.

"C'mon," I said shortly. "Let's get this over with."

Sam gingerly took hold of the ankles, and I got a grip underneath the corpse's arms. As we pulled, Dead Trav's pants began to bunch up around his calves, revealing the Nike logo on the top band of a pair of low-rise athletic socks.

I was wearing the exact same pair.

Together, we eased the body onto the floor. The joints were only somewhat stiff, meaning rigor mortis was beginning to dissipate. Consistent with what Sam said about the time of death.

What had I been doing thirty-six hours ago? Drinking myself into a stupor and thinking about suicide. It was a good thing Trav Zero hadn't come hunting yesterday in Stream Four, since I would have been an easy target. Hell, I might have saved him the trouble.

Now that we had moved him, we became conscious of the sickly-sweet smell of a decomposing body.

Sam made a sour face.

"Ugh, what's that smell?"

"Good luck."

"What?"

"Good luck that's *all* we're smelling. He either hadn't had anything to eat or drink before he got shot, or he had just been to the bathroom. Otherwise, we'd be smelling whatever had voided from his bowels when he died."

"Oh, God."

Sam jumped up and ran to the bathroom. I tried to ignore the subsequent retching sounds, locking my jaws to keep my own gorge from rising.

With the body now supine on the floor, I squatted down and gave it a closer look.

Trav-that-was wore jeans and a black long-sleeved t-shirt, both of which I recognized easily from my own closet. Socks, shoes and Cardinals jacket were the exact twins to what I was wearing. Which reminded me that I was getting uncomfortably warm. I shrugged out of my jacket and tossed it over to the couch.

"Well?" Sam asked, returning from the bathroom. His eyes were still watering a little and his green complexion did not complement his red hair.

I shrugged. "He's been dead more than twenty-four hours, but less than forty-eight, or he'd really be stinking. No visible exit wound, so the murder weapon was low-caliber, probably a pistol. Maybe a twenty-two." I lifted the head slightly and felt the side opposite the wound, confirming my theory.

Next, I reached inside the jacket, and pulled a pistol out of Dead Trav's shoulder rig. I sniffed the barrel, then ejected the cartridge. The clip was full. "Hasn't been fired," I said, "so he was probably taken by surprise."

I lifted the corpse's left hand. It was cold and pale, but it was easy to make out a crisscross of fine scars on the knuckles, twin to mine—souvenirs from an encounter with a knife-wielding meth addict. "No defensive wounds, so he probably knew his attacker."

"Ya think?"

I chuckled in spite of myself.

Yeah, it was a pretty short suspect list.

"Right."

I leaned back on my haunches. "Well, in that case it was probably more shock at seeing himself on the other side of the gun. He didn't have a chance to take off his jacket, so Zero must have grabbed him either in the hall or after he walked into the apartment."

"Couldn't he have been here waiting?"

"Uh, yeah, I guess. He would have had a key."

I set the gun on the floor and checked all of Dead Trav's pockets, starting with the jacket and then moving to the jeans. Sam helped me roll the body over slightly to get at the back pockets, and I added a wallet and shield to the small pile of articles already on the floor. I stared at the collection, most of which was, of course, duplicated in my own pockets.

Chapstick, a dollar or so in change, little pack of mints, the notebook every cop carries where he jots thoughts about current cases.

"What the hell is this?"

I had just reached into the inside pocket of his jacket and drawn out a lightweight block of glass and aluminum.

"It's a cell phone, Trav."

I dug my flip phone out of my own pocket. "No. *This* is a cell phone. I don't know what the hell he's doing with a smartphone."

Sam rolled his eyes. "I helped him...well, the Trav from my stream, pick out a smartphone a month or so ago. He got tired of looking up phone numbers in a book and having to go to his desk to check email. This Trav obviously did the same thing."

Dimly, I remembered having a similar conversation with the Sam in my own stream, and he had almost convinced me to upgrade. Then the thing with Adam had happened and keeping in touch with the outside world had become a lot less important.

I hefted the device in my hand. Despite not having ever used one before, the phone was a comfortable weight and shape.

"We can find out where this has been, right?"

"What?" Sam frowned, then his expression cleared as he figured out what I meant. "Oh, location data. Yeah, allegedly you are supposed to be able to turn location services off. But hardly anyone ever does, and even if they do, the information is still in there, just harder to get at."

"Can you get it out?"

He shrugged. "Sure. Not something I've tried before, but it wouldn't take long to get the code from a hacker site."

"Can you get to work on it? Knowing where this Trav was in his final hours may help us."

"Sure."

I reached for the wallet next, intending to look in the side pocket where I habitually stashed ATM and debit card slips, which would provide some clues about Dead Trav's movements.

But when I cracked open the billfold, I got a surprise.

"Holy shit."

"What?" Sam, on the opposite side of the body, leaned over to get a closer look. I opened the wallet so he could see.

Dozens of bills crowded the lengthwise pocket in a toothy green grin, many more than were in my own. I thumbed quickly through the stack. A few twenties and fifties, but as I exposed the face of most of the bills, the enigmatic gaze of Ben Franklin met my own. Most of them were hundreds.

"Damn. There's at least two grand in here."

Sam whistled. "That's a little more than you usually carry around."

"It's more than I have in the bank."

"Where do you suppose he got it?"

I shook my head.

I looked through the rest of the wallet quickly, finding nothing else out of the ordinary.

I surveyed the small tableau of belongings again. One of the nice things about knowing the victim, well...intimately, was I could immediately see if anything was missing or out of place, like the phone.

It would also make searching the apartment easy.

Which caused another thought that had been niggling around at the back of my mind for the past few minutes to push its way to the front of my awareness.

"I'll be right back."

I pushed myself to my feet and went down the short hallway that led to the apartment's two bedrooms.

As I mentioned before, the near one was outfitted as an office, pretty normal for any single man. My computer was there, a Dell that was a couple of generations behind the current version of Windows, and a few mementos hung on the walls. A portrait photo of my parents, some vacation pictures with Mary, a sharpshooting award.

I went to the closet.

Most cops—hell, anyone who owned guns and a brain—also owned a gun safe to store them in. Locking your weapon up when at home was a good idea even if you lived alone. The cop who slept with a gun in the nightstand drawer, or God forbid, under his pillow, is an invention for TV. And a good way to shoot your own ear off.

Over the years, heading to the bedroom and locking the gun up in the safe immediately on arriving at home had become second nature.

But the only weapon in the safe right now was Dad's old shotgun, whose barrel was slightly shorter than was legal. He had called it his "homeowner's insurance."

On a shelf in the cabinet sat a box with the few important papers I owned, and the remainder of Dad's legacy: his favorite coins for magic tricks, and a small but ornate cups-and-balls set.

I picked up a couple of the coins and rubbed them together, thinking about Dad. Then shook my head. I didn't have time for woolgathering. I took the box out of the cabinet and set it on the desk nearby.

I then reached around to the back of the shelf.

One nice thing about being the son of a magician was a full education in creating and hiding locks, springs, and safety catches. I pressed a button on the back of the shelf and was rewarded with a soft *click*. The floor of the shelf, which had appeared to be part of a solid block of wood, popped open.

I tilted the piece of wood up so I could see inside. The secret compartment contained, as expected, a pistol. My "insurance" weapon—an unlicensed .22, my other inheritance. Dad never would have used a throwdown weapon to justify use of deadly force, but he'd come into possession of it at some point, and I'd ended up with it.

I sniffed the barrel.

Nothing. But I'd be willing to bet that even though *this* weapon hadn't been fired recently, a ballistics test would match the bullet that had killed my doppelgänger in the other room.

And somehow, I was not at all surprised to find that the compartment was also stuffed with money, several packs of at least fifty one-hundred dollar bills.

I replaced the lid. I hoped Crime Scene Investigations wouldn't end up here searching the place, but no sense in making things easy. I kept the gun, slipping it into my jacket pocket, and returned to the living room.

Sam was back on the couch, putting as much distance between himself and the body as the small living room allowed.

"What were you doing?"

"Just checking something out. There's a lot more money where this came from."

I kneeled down and stared again at Dead Trav for a long time.

"What were you into?" I asked him.

Sam cleared his throat, interrupting my reverie. "What's next?"

I stood up, still deep in thought. "Well, in a normal investigation, we'd get a warrant and search the suspect's home." I waved a hand. "Which strangely, we still need to do. But not *this* home. Even though you say he can do this jumping without any technology, the only place where I can really hope to find a trail is back where he came from. Can you take me back to your home stream so we can search his, er, this place?"

English simply had no pronouns for a situation like this.

Sam frowned. "I think so. It'd be best to go back to the lab. The phone app is good for brute force shifts, but when I need more finesse, I have better luck with the desktop."

"So, we have to go back to your lab to end up back...well, here?"

Sam shrugged. "Sorry. I can't guarantee I'd get you back to the right place."

"That's comforting. Okay, let's go."

Sam looked at his watch. "Yeah, should be okay."

I looked at him curiously. "What do you mean?"

"Well, remember there is already a Sam running around this stream. I can't just show up at the Cat Box any time of the day. I have to wait till Sam One goes home. But we should be fine."

We sat the body up back in the closet. I pushed the question of how I was going to dispose of it out of my mind. Hell, if things went badly with Zero, there might be *two* Dead Travs to get rid of.

106

And since I'd be one of them, neither would be my problem.

I always try to look at the bright side.

After locking up, Sam and I went downstairs and out into the street.

We started walking to Sam's car and were crossing in front of a dumpster in the alley next to the building when I stopped.

"What?" asked Sam, looking at me curiously.

I held up a hand for silence.

I stared out into what would have seemed to Sam to be empty space.

But it wasn't empty to me.

For the second time, another set of images super-imposed themselves on the scene in front me.

Sam was standing next to me, but I was now watching another Sam, and another Trav, moving just ahead of us.

If I concentrated on the sight before me, I could discern a number of other Travs and Sams ahead — or in some cases beside — and even behind us.

But like the last time I had seen this vision, those other figures were fainter and outlined in blue. Whether I was focusing on this particular pair because they were outlined in red, or if they were red because I was looking at them, I had no idea.

Even stranger was the inexplicable set of actions I watch Red Trav and Red Sam act out.

What the hell?

"What are you looking at?" asked the Sam beside me.

And that was when the shot rang out.

I instinctively went down to a crouch, pulling Sam with me, and pushed him backwards into an alley we had just begun to pass. I drew my weapon.

I had a sense the shot had come from across the street and maybe a little above us, but couldn't be sure.

Only a part of my mind was focused on the shooting, however. The rest was still puzzling out the images which continued to overlay the reality in front of me.

Follow the red shift.

"Okay," I sighed.

"Okay what?" demanded Sam.

"Just let me say in advance, I'm really sorry about this, Sam."

"Sorry about what?"

I tucked the gun back into my pocket so I'd have both hands free. Then I grabbed Sam by the belt and neck, quickly lifting him off the ground, and with a thrust from my legs, tipped the little guy headfirst into the open dumpster.

The dumpster lid banged shut from the motion, just as it had when Red Trav had done the same thing to Red Sam.

"What the FUCK?" More swear words emanated from inside the garbage container, but I was already moving, following Red Trav.

This double, thankfully a little more animated than the one back in my closet, didn't seem to be in the least concerned about getting shot. He hurried down the street about a half block, then stopped and turned to face the street.

I followed. As I got close, the image faded away. I turned, now facing the same direction and standing in the same position Red Trav had been.

And as if on cue, a black Volvo pulled up in front of me.

A tinted window rolled down in the back, and an arm stretched out.

The arm was attached to a hand, which held a gun.

"Get in," commanded an accented voice.

7

"**H**ANDS AWAY FROM your gun, please," continued the man. It was Bilol Grymzin, the thug who had done the shooting in the bar.

I obeyed, spreading my arms away from my sides, palms forward in the universal "I'm not holding anything" position.

My mind raced, and not because there was a gun pointed at my chest. If what Sam had said was true, "following the red shift" was the right thing to do.

Although why moving into a stream where I was about to be shot was the right thing seemed a little counter-intuitive.

But if that was the case, Grymzin seemed to be in no hurry to finish the job. He sat unmoving in the car, the gun pointed unwaveringly at my navel.

"Well? Are you going to get in?" he repeated in a bored tone. "Or, can I save Mr. Kaaro much time and bother and shoot you now?"

"Aren't you supposed to be in jail?"

His lips split in a soulless smile. "You will certainly pay for how you treated me. But first, Mr. Kaaro wants to speak with you. He will be angry if I show up with your dead body instead, but I am thinking maybe it will be worth it."

Keeping my hands well away from my body, I slowly opened the door and got in the car. The gunman slid to the other side of the car, barrel never wavering from its focus on my navel. The car accelerated back into traffic as soon as I shut the door.

"Gun," he grunted.

I slowly reached into my shoulder rig and brought out my service weapon, tossing it onto the seat between us. I decided to keep the unregistered .22 and Grymzin didn't seem inclined to search me.

"Phone."

I pulled out my flip phone, again choosing not to advertise I was carrying a second one.

"Turn it off."

I did so, and handed it to him. This was actually a good sign. He could have tossed it out the window. He stuffed both the phone and the gun in his jacket pocket.

So, that pointed to at least a possibility that I would survive this meeting. I decided to be grateful for that.

I was grateful for another thing as well. Thanks to the weird game of Follow the Leader I had just finished playing with Red Trav, it appeared that these guys didn't realize I had been with someone else, or I was sure they would not have missed the chance to grab Sam as a potential hostage.

If I did survive the next hour, I would have some explaining to do to him, but that was the least of my problems right now.

Keeping my face carefully neutral, I studied the man sitting across the seat from me. He hadn't changed much since I had last seen him. In fact, the wrinkled grey pants and cheap faux-leather jacket he wore were very familiar, as he'd been wearing the same ensemble when I'd bundled him into the car. He didn't smell any better now, either.

Grymzin said something in a language that seemed to consist only of consonants. The driver replied with what sounded like a lengthy and phlegmy throat clearing, which caused both men to laugh out loud.

I cocked an eyebrow.

"Gonna let me in on the joke?"

Grymzin shook his head. "I don't think you would find it funny, since we were trying to decide where to dispose of your body."

"Want a little advice? Don't use my apartment. It's kind of crowded in there."

I gave Grymzin a bright smile and turned to look out the window.

Out of the corner of my eye, I could see his predatory smile change to a puzzled frown because his attempt to intimidate me hadn't seemed to work. He chewed on this for a while, but apparently having exhausted his small repertoire of threatening remarks, stayed silent.

Which was fine with me. I needed whatever time I had left during this ride to think.

It looked like I was headed into yet another encounter where the person or persons across the table assumed I knew what the hell was going on.

I needed the time to collate the meager information I had. In the guise of gazing out of the window, I took inventory of what I knew.

One. Three streams ago, while waiting for what I thought was going to be my dismissal from the force, I had overheard Capt. Martin and Alex Monroe discussing a bust involving one of Anton Kaaro's leg breakers.

Two. I then met the aforementioned leg breaker, one Bilol Grymzin, when the same crime was re-enacted in *this* stream. Both shootings (I assumed) were witnessed by Rob Lennox, a confidential informant who *I* had never met, but who the Trav of this stream had a relationship with. And, it was possible that my slipup at the bar had gotten Lennox kidnapped, or more likely, killed.

Then Grymzin and his very large handgun waltzed back into my life. Obviously, he'd just as soon shoot me, but instead was taking me for this ride. Something was keeping him from solving a problem like me the way he normally did.

Which led us to *Three.*

Anton Kaaro.

Whose wishes were certainly about the only thing that could supersede Grymzin's natural instincts to make me disappear.

Before today, I had only ever seen Kaaro at a distance, but now I remembered that funny look he gave me when he and Charles-call-me-Chuck the attorney showed up at the station. He hadn't said anything, but it certainly seemed like he had recognized me.

Could he and Trav One have had some run-ins previously? And what might that have to do with my present situation?

Unfortunately, whatever Trav One had known about Kaaro had died with him. And if I wasn't careful, there might soon be a second dead Trav littering Stream One.

The rest of the trip was made in silence, punctuated only by some occasional wet sniffling and throat-clearing by the driver. Soon we pulled up, not surprisingly, in front of The Kremlin.

Grymzin inclined his head toward my door and grunted. I opened it and got out, Grymzin close behind. Taking my elbow, he steered me to the door under the Red Square sign and pushed it open, nudging me to enter ahead of him.

The Kremlin was crowded, but not nearly as much as last night. And the lighting was back to its normal low level, making it difficult to make out individuals.

But several pairs of eyes followed the two of us as we entered.

The clientele seemed to be a mixed bag, but definitely rougher than the young, upscale group we had questioned last night. Most of the men seemed to have been sent out from the same casting office as Grymzin. Dark, hairy, dressed in blacks and dark grays.

Several unattached women perched on bar stools, some of whom were undoubtedly hookers; all of whom carried the hard, dried look that came from too many cigarettes.

There were also a couple dozen young office types slumming here for happy hour as well. A few of them looked familiar from my last visit.

I hoped the kids all made it home in one piece, but if they were back here tonight one day after a shooting, that was their own fault.

Grymzin led me to a door to the right of the big mirror that lined the back of the bar marked Employees Only.

The door opened onto a short hall, also lit in red, but this time by red light bulbs, probably less expensive than LED for this "backstage" zone. We walked past an open door with janitorial supplies, and another with shelves of liquor on one wall and a line of kegs on the other, before stopping at a door at the end of the hall.

Grymzin knocked. I heard a low sound that could have been something in native Whatjikistanese—or maybe a grunt. Hard to tell.

The office was a striking contrast to the dim atmosphere of the bar. The room was brightly and tastefully lit. The decor was ultra-modern, all rounded corners—metal, glass, and light wood. Scandinavian, but obviously from the original designer, not IKEA knockoffs.

At one end of the room two uncomfortable-looking chairs that reminded me vaguely of sleighs sat in front of a desk. Its large top was made of glass, and four pedestal legs matched the carpet so well it looked like the elbows resting on the desktop were floating.

Anton Kaaro was attached to the elbows.

He was smiling.

In the canine world, baring teeth is a sign of aggression, not of welcome, which is one reason that smiling at a dog who doesn't know you can be risky.

That was the kind of smile on Kaaro's face.

"Travis! Welcome!" Kaaro said in his rich baritone. "Sit."

Okay, so two people call me Travis. My mom and a Russian crime lord.

He waved a hand at one of the chairs in front of his glass desk.

Yep, the chair was just for looks. Uncomfortable as hell.

"Bill," Kaaro said to Grymzin. "Get Mr. Becker something to drink."

"No, thanks," I said.

My back was to "Bill," and I didn't want to crane my neck to look at him, but I wished I could see the man's face from this angle. He certainly must have thought he'd be serving me a can of Whoop-Ass rather than a drink.

"Suit yourself," said Kaaro, "but I will have another."

He slid an empty highball glass across the desk, leaving a trail of condensation on the clear surface. Grymzin took it over to a bar set that occupied a set of shelves near the door.

I inclined my head toward the bar. "He doesn't look like a Bill."

Kaaro shrugged. "His mother was Uzbek."

As if that explained everything.

Grymzin returned with Kaaro's drink.

The silence stretched on for a few moments as Kaaro swirled his glass, regarding the ice as it spun round and round. Finally, he spoke.

"You missed our appointment."

"Our appointment?"

"Why else would I have to send Bilol and Georg after you?" He pronounced it the German way, *Gay-org*.

"I didn't recall we had an appointment."

Which was the truth. From my point of view, at least.

"I thought we had an agreement that you would do me the courtesy of informing me in advance when I or one of mine became involved in one of your investigations." He waved a hand at Grymzin. "I had to hear from the wait staff it was you who took Bill to your headquarters."

I couldn't stop to think through the implications of this statement, particularly what it indicated about Trav One. Kaaro would read any hesitation in my replies as trying to cover.

How to play this, without letting on that I had no memory of our "arrangement?"

I stalled.

"I didn't exactly have the time or the opportunity for a secure conversation. By the time I got there, the place was full of cops, as I'm sure you heard."

Kaaro nodded.

"True. And at least you were able to signal to Madina the identity of the informant."

Aw, shit.

It *had* been me who had given Lennox up.

"She told me it was cleverly done." He was giving me another one of those predatory smiles. "You seemed to be having such trouble finding the source of my troubles with information leaking, I had begun to think my money would be better spent on someone else."

Which seemed to answer the question about where all of Trav One's cash had come from.

"What's going to happen to him?"

I tried for a tone of idle curiosity.

"That is not something with which you need to be concerned."

"It is if people make a connection between Lennox, you, and me."

"I am not worried. You are not the only source I have within your department. I am confident I will get some warning if the investigation takes an uncomfortable turn, even if for some reason, you are again unable to inform me."

Not hard to pick up the subtext there.

"Have you killed him?"

Again the smile of a predator. "Killed him? Travis, I am simply a semi-literate European refugee who scratches out a bit of a living owning this bar. I don't kill people."

"Right."

"Mr. Lennox is safe. Soon, he'll be telling me what he has told your department and who in particular he has been working for. After that, I think he will want to get out of the city, go back to his family in...Iowa, is it?" He looked over at Grymzin, who shrugged.

"You'll just let him go."

Kaaro shrugged. "I can't guarantee he will arrive there breathing, but there will be nothing to connect him to me at that point."

Well, this had been a delightful exchange. I had learned that my analog in this stream was a bent cop, and that I would be responsible for the death of a guy Trav Becker had certainly promised to protect.

It was time to get out of here before I got any more great news.

"Anything else?" I stood up.

Kaaro frowned, disturbed at someone leaving before they were dismissed. But after a minute he shook his head.

"Bill and Georg will take you back to your apartment."

"If it's all the same to you," I interrupted, "I'd just as soon not be seen getting out of one of your cars. Maybe you could call me a cab."

"Good idea." Kaaro turned to Bill and gargled something. Bill reached into his jacket pocket and pulled out a phone. He spoke into it softly for a minute, then snapped it shut.

"Five minutes."

During this little exchange, it occurred to me that I might stir the pot a little. "So, earlier tonight, right before Bill and Gay-org picked me up..."

Kaaro had obviously already checked out from this meeting. He'd picked up his own phone, a Blackberry, and was thumbing the screen.

"Yes?" he said without looking up.

"Someone took a shot at me."

Kaaro looked up sharply. First at me, then at Bill, who grated out a couple of sentences.

"You didn't tell Bill about this."

"Hey, for all I knew, he was the one who fired."

"Why would Bill try to shoot you?"

I shrugged. "I don't know why anyone would try to shoot me. But the guy who showed up two minutes later pointing a gun at me had to be in the candidate pool."

Kaaro rubbed his chin, frowning. "I had nothing to do with this. Maybe something to do with one of your other cases?"

"Maybe. Or maybe my neighborhood is worse than I thought."

Kaaro seemed genuinely surprised and looked at me seriously. "Even in my line of work, I am rarely shot at. I would suggest you look into this."

"I thought you were just a semi-literate refugee scratching out a living in this bar?"

"Remember what I said about staying in touch." Kaaro, choosing not to dignify my flipness with a reply, looked down at his phone again. I had clearly been dismissed.

I turned to Grymzin. "Can I have my gun and phone back?"

He looked over at Kaaro, who waved a hand without looking up. Bill produced my gun and phone.

I followed Bill back out through the club. He opened the front door and motioned for me to precede him, then followed me out. There was no cab waiting.

I turned to ask Grymzin where the cab was just in time to see him reaching inside his jacket.

"Do you think I'm stupid?" Grymzin asked.

"What do you mean?"

"Accusing me of going behind Mr. Kaaro's back. Mr. Kaaro thinks you will be of some use to him. I don't."

Grymzin's hand was still in his jacket pocket, as there were a few people smoking near The Kremlin's door. He inclined his head to an alley between The Kremlin and the next building over.

"I think Mr. Kaaro will be upset if you kill another one of his...uh, employees," I said.

"I will tell him your mysterious shooter had better aim this time." He gave me a wolfish smile. "Thank you for mentioning that. It makes things much easier for me."

He motioned again to the alley. I knew Grymzin didn't want to shoot on a public street, but wouldn't hesitate if I went for my own gun.

But before we could take two steps, a cheerful voice sounded from behind us.

"I didn't expect to see you back here tonight, Detective."

I turned around to see a shape detach itself from the smokers and make its way over to us. Gradually, the figure resolved itself as female and, as she passed under the light of the Red Square sign, I recognized her as one of the women I'd questioned last night.

I searched my mind for her name. "Ms. Foster, right?"

The woman we'd interviewed after the shooting. The psychic.

"Got it in one," she replied with an impish smile. She wore a shimmery, thigh-length tank top with black leggings. The spike heels of boots that hugged her calves almost to her knees click-clacked on the cement as she walked toward us.

She looked from me to Grymzin. "Am I interrupting something?"

"No," I said. The group she had been standing with had turned and were now watching us.

I took the opportunity to back away a little from Grymzin. "Bill here was calling me a cab."

"Oh, my car is right over there. Can I give you a ride?"

She linked arms with me without waiting for an answer.

"Uh, sure," I said belatedly.

I looked at Grymzin, then over at the group of potential witnesses. "We're done here, right?"

Grymzin followed my gaze, totaling which of the smokers were The Kremlin regulars who could be counted on to keep quiet, and which ones would probably cooperate with police in the shooting death of a fellow cop.

Not liking the odds, he pulled his hand back out of his pocket, empty, and used it to smooth his thinning hair.

"Done? No." He glared at me. "But we can finish later."

"I'll look forward to it."

I quickly took Ms. Foster by the elbow and walked her, a little too quickly, in the direction she had pointed. After a few paces, I chanced a quick look over my shoulder. Grymzin was still standing there, watching us go, but wasn't attempting to follow us.

Her car was across the street. She stopped in front of it, digging in her small purse for the keys. I looked up and down the street, trying not to let my nerves show.

She finally found her key fob and beeped open the locks. I opened the driver's door for her, then quickly strode around to the passenger side, sneaking one final glance at Grymzin before I slid in.

She started the car and pulled into traffic. Fortunately, her car was facing away from the bar, so we didn't have to pass in front of Grymzin. The temptation might have been too much for him.

When I felt I could breathe again, I said calmly, "I appreciate the ride, Ms. Foster."

"You can call me Morgan. I think it's okay to use the first name of the person who just *saved your ass*."

"What do you mean?"

"I have eyes, Detective." She glanced away from the road long enough to give me a withering look. "I know that man works for the owner, and he's not a nice person. And judging from the condition of his hair, I don't think he was reaching into his pocket for a comb."

"You can call me Trav. And if you knew things were about to get dangerous, you shouldn't have interfered."

"Oh, please," she snorted. "What was I supposed to do? Let him drag you into that alley and shoot you?"

"That kind of thing only happens on cop shows," I replied with more confidence than I felt. "I'm sure it wouldn't have come to that."

"R-i-i-i-g-h-t," she said, stringing out the word till it had at least seven syllables. "Look, I'm sure you had the situation well under control. But me jumping in quieted things down, didn't it? Or would you rather have had a gun battle right there on the sidewalk?"

She was right about that. Grymzin had been so distracted by her flouncing up and taking my arm, it had defused the situation in a way I never would have been able to do.

"You're probably right."

"I know I'm right." Her impish smile came back. "If it makes you feel any better, I won't repeat the 'saved your ass' part when I tell this to all my friends."

"Fair enough."

We rode in silence for a few minutes. After a bit, she cleared her throat.

"Okay, I have a confession to make."

"You do?"

"Um, yes."

She looked over at me uncertainly. "It's possible that scene weirded me out a little more than I'm admitting."

"That's not surprising, unless you do that kind of thing often."

"God, no. But, now that we're away from there, I just realized..."

"What?"

"I have no idea where I'm taking you."

We looked at each other and burst out laughing.

"Central Station will be fine," I said when the outburst had died down to a chuckle.

I couldn't believe how cathartic that laughter had been. It felt like it had been weeks since I'd had a good belly laugh—and come to think of it, it probably had been.

"Can I ask you a question?" I said.

"If I can ask you one."

I shrugged in assent, then started in. "You know who and what Kaaro is. You look too smart to be hanging out in a place like The Kremlin. Yet, you're there two nights in a row."

"Lucky for you I was."

"You won't get any argument from me, but it wasn't like you showed up there because you knew someone would need to be rescued."

She looked over at me quickly, with an expression I couldn't read, then returned her focus to the road.

"How do you know?" she said quietly.

"What do you mean?"

"How do you know?" she repeated.

"Know what?"

"That I didn't show up because I knew someone would need to be rescued?"

"You've lost me."

"I don't think so."

We caught a red light. She eased the car to a stop and turned to face me. "Sometimes I get a feeling…that there is someplace I need to be. Sometimes it's that bar. And every time I listen to that feeling, something happens later that proves it right. It might be something as simple as finding someone's car keys and returning them. Other times…" She trailed off.

"You mean besides tonight?"

She nodded. "A couple of weeks ago, I was standing next to this couple. I don't know if it was an online dating thing or what, but she kept telling him she needed to leave and he kept hold of her arm. I could tell she didn't like it, but she obviously didn't want to make a scene."

"So, what did you do?"

A mischievous look came into her eyes. "I, uh, kind of spilled my margarita all over him. He was wearing this expensive cashmere sports coat. He dashed into the bathroom to clean it up and while he was gone, she ducked out."

Her look turned serious.

"I had this feeling that if I hadn't been there, things would have turned out very badly for her."

"I remember that you said you were a psychic."

She nodded.

"But that doesn't mean I believe that you're magically drawn to that bar to save people."

"Oh, yes you do."

Honk, honk. The light had turned green.

"I do?"

"Of course," she said, ignoring the car behind us.

"Why?"

"Because you're a traveler, that's why."

8

BEFORE I COULD reply, there was another, *H-O-N-K!* Louder and longer.

Morgan let out a snort of frustration. "Hold your damn horses!" She jumped on the gas pedal and we lunged through the intersection. She squinted ahead and gave a little sigh of satisfaction when she saw a parking spot in the next block. She pulled into it and put the car into park, but left the engine idling.

Freed from having to focus on driving, she turned and looked at me expectantly.

"A traveler," I said.

"Ye-ehs," she replied with that head shake you use when something is so obvious it shouldn't even have to be said.

"What do you mean?"

"Oh, for God's sake!" she erupted. "It's as plain as day, anyone could see it. You're from a different plane! I knew it as soon as I saw you last night."

"Plane?"

"Plane of *reality*." She rolled her eyes. "Dimension, parallel universe, whatever you want to call it. You started in one reality and then you... *traveled*... here."

She enunciated the word very carefully, like she was talking to a two-year-old.

"I've been calling them streams."

"Whatever."

"Wait. And you can see that by looking at me?"

She pointed to her head. "Psychic, remember? Your aura is a totally different color than anyone I've ever seen."

Holy crap. I sat there for a long moment, trying and failing to digest what she had just told me.

"Um, out of curiosity, what color is my…aura?"

She squinted at me. "Red."

"It figures."

"What?"

"Never mind."

Suddenly, she giggled.

"What?"

"Trav. You call yourself Trav."

"So?"

"You're a traveler. Trav is the traveler."

"Funny," I grumbled.

She smiled that impish smile again, then got serious.

"So, what's it like?" she asked softly.

"What is what like?"

"Being a traveler."

"Honestly?"

She nodded.

"Confusing," I replied.

"I'll bet. Is it different where you came from?"

I sighed. "Only for me. I mean, same president, North won the Civil War, Allies won World War II, 9/11, all of the stuff the sci-fi guys like to change is the same. But for me…well, let's just say things pretty much sucked for me there."

"How so?"

"I was ready to get fired. Girlfriend had broken up with me. My partner was *dead*."

"Oh, my God."

I wasn't sure why I was telling her all this. Sure, I had been over all this with Sam, but whenever you talked to him, you could almost see the processors in his brain chewing away at the information, analyzing, and preparing his comeback. Maybe it was the psychic thing, but there was something about Morgan Foster that made it feel safe to be honest with her.

"And here?"

"Here? Yeah, here, everything is great. Adam's alive. I got a commendation."

"The girlfriend?"

"Uh, things are scary good."

"Hmm."

"The only thing…" My voice trailed off.

"What?"

I shook my head. "It's not something you need to be concerned about. I shouldn't even have told you this much."

"Nonsense. Who are you going to tell if not your psychic?"

My psychic. Now I have a psychic. To go along with my resurrected partner and mad scientist friend. If my life was a TV show, it would have been cancelled after the first season cliffhanger and there would have been a fanboy campaign to send candy bars or sandwiches to the network.

"It's the, um, *me* from this stream…plane. He may have been into some bad stuff."

Morgan's eyebrows went up. "Wow. Are you sure?"

"No. I'm not sure of anything at this point."

She was silent for a moment.

"When did you figure it out?"

"You mean, that I…Traveled?"

She nodded.

"It took longer than you'd think. Things are really weird at first, but then you sort of adjust. My friend Sam says the human brain is designed to meld back into whatever reality it ends up in."

"Sam?"

"Yeah. He's a scientist. He's been studying the physics behind this."

"That's kind of a coincidence, isn't it? He's studying it, you're living it?"

"That's what I thought. But he swears he doesn't have anything to do with my...situation."

Morgan pondered that for a moment.

"You said the *you* on this plane was into some bad stuff."

"Yeah, that was what the scene at the bar was all about. Good old Bill doesn't think I'm playing straight with his boss."

"And were you?"

"Of course not. I don't even know what's going on, and the Trav from here isn't going to be any help."

"What do you mean?"

"He's dead."

"WHAT?"

"The Trav from this plane, we call it Stream One, is dead. Somebody shot him."

"Oh, my God."

Morgan reached over and grabbed my arm. Her fingers were cold. "Trav, this is not good."

"I know that. You didn't have to look at him."

"No! You shouldn't ever have seen...yourself. That is not the way it's supposed to be. Something is really wrong."

"You're not going to get any argument from me."

"I'm serious, Trav. Your friend is right. People are designed to adjust when they move to another reality. But things *always* stay in balance. You move into this plane, the...*you* from this plane moves out. You can't ever meet yourself."

"Well, I didn't. Or at least he didn't meet me."

She tightened her grip on my arm, eyes wide.

"You have to take this seriously. It's not the way things are supposed to be."

"You seem to know a lot about this."

Morgan leaned back in her seat, taking her hand back.

"It's something I've always found interesting."

"You've *always* been interested? And how did you first hear about it? I had no idea until my friend showed me his machine."

"Then he's doing his research in the wrong place. History is full of evidence of people sensing, and sometimes reaching, other planes of reality."

"You're kidding, right?"

"Of course not. There are dozens of cases of people disappearing without a trace, and others who suddenly one day started insisting they remembered things differently than everyone else did. There are a bunch of old texts I read. The Church had suppressed them for hundreds of years, but they finally got out on the Internet. The writings suggest that prophets and seers throughout history never predicted the future as much as they somehow could discern a possible course of action from a group of variables and then...well, *steer* toward a particular outcome."

"And you learned about these old texts how?"

She looked uncomfortable. "Some friends of mine in college spent a lot of time researching stuff like that. When you have a talent like mine, you can't talk about it with just anybody. And when you find a group that accepts you, you don't care so much what other stuff they may be into."

"What do you mean by other stuff?"

She bit her lip, weighing whether she was going to explain to me or not. It was cute as hell.

"All right," she sighed, "I can't believe I'm going into this with someone I just met, but it was a group of Wiccans."

"Wiccans."

"Yes, Wiccans," she shot back. "It's not what you think. Wicca is about finding balance with the natural world. No cauldrons, no pointy hats. Most don't even much care for Harry Potter."

"So, you're out communing in the forest, and got talking about parallel realities?"

"Shut up. You can make fun of me if you want, but doesn't this sound like the very thing you've been talking about?"

"Sorry," I said, holding up a hand. "I didn't mean to be flip. You've sat here and listened to my crazy story. You should be driving me to the psych ward."

"You're not crazy, Trav," she said quietly. "It's a gift. Like mine. And one that people have had throughout history."

I thought about that. It was bizarre enough for me to attempt to understand what I was going through. If what Sam said was correct, then my "traveling" and his research into a similar area was coincidental. And if this was happening to me, it stood to reason I wasn't the first.

If a Stone Age tribe had a member who could see into other realities, what would they do with him? Probably make him their shaman. And Morgan had been understandably reluctant to tell me about her Wiccan friends because she thought I'd laugh at her. But there had been a time when she would have kept quiet or risked getting burned as a witch.

Was this the explanation behind prophets and seers throughout history? They just had a window into a stream where time was running a little differently?

It was mind-boggling.

"Follow the red shift," I muttered.

"What?"

"That's what it looks like to me. The outcome I 'steer' toward is outlined in red."

"Wow. You actually have experienced it?"

"Oh, yeah."

"That is so cool!"

"Not so much for Sam."

"What?"

"Never mind."

She put her hand on my arm again.

"Trav, do you know what this means?" she said urgently. "It turns everything that science teaches on its head. Science says that the physical world is the only thing that's real, and humans are merely a bundle of biological processes and conditioned responses. That anything we create, that what we *feel* doesn't have any significance beyond a pattern of behaviors defined by evolution.

"But that's not it at all. *This*," she waved her hand around to encompass the world, "is what's ephemeral and changeable. *This*," now pointing to her head, "is reality. We create and redefine what is real on a continual and constant basis."

She took a deep breath.

"On the one hand, it's so exciting. But…"

"But what?"

"I'm still worried about you."

"About me?"

"Yes." She frowned prettily. "This… bumping into yourself. It's really dangerous."

"Well, like I said, the other me was dead. That may have had something to do with it."

"I don't think so. Those old books are full of stories about people disappearing or showing up talking nonsense. But I've *never* heard of someone bumping into *themselves*. If a twin of someone popped into existence, it wouldn't have been forgotten on some old scroll. It would have been the biggest news ever."

I had been so busy trying to master my own situation, it hadn't occurred to me there was something bigger going on.

I covered her hand with mine and gave it a squeeze.

"If it makes you feel any better, I think I'm in a lot more danger from Uzbek thugs than reality collapsing around me or something."

"Oh, yeah, much more comforting," she replied, still frowning.

She put the car into gear and pulled back into traffic.

"So, what are you going to do now?" she asked as she drove us the final few blocks to the station.

I rubbed the back of my neck.

"Well, Sam and I were going to use some of his technology to try to get a lead on who killed Trav One. Although, now that I know about him and Kaaro, that may not have anything to do with the stream jumping at all."

I decided not to mention Trav Zero. If Morgan hated the idea of me meeting a dead version of myself, I couldn't imagine she would approve of me actively hunting one who was very much alive.

"How are you going to go about it?"

"I'm a detective," I shrugged. "I'll detect."

We had reached the station.

I unbuckled my seat belt. "Thanks for the ride. And the talk."

"I...well, I hope it helped."

"It did. Up to now, I only had Sam's take on all this, the science side. Knowing that it's not all new, that maybe I'm not the only one who has experienced stuff like this, is...comforting."

"What's next?"

"I guess it's like any investigation. You get some questions answered, a bunch more come up. Eventually, you answer more than you create new, and things start to fall into place."

"Will you stay?"

"Stay?"

"Here. On this plane...stream, whatever."

"I'm not sure it's up to me. I've kind of been pushed from stream to stream. I have no idea, other than the red shift thing, how to manage the...traveling...myself."

"I think you have more ability than you might think. Remember that, okay?"

I nodded.

She looked at me intensely. For a minute, I almost believed that she could in fact, read my mind.

Finally she said, "Well, if you do end up here, let me know how it turns out. Okay?" She fished a business card out of her purse and handed it to me.

"Count on it."

She leaned over and gave me a quick kiss on the cheek.

"Take care of yourself, Trav Becker."

I nodded, and got out of the car.

I stood on the curb as she drove off, watching her tail lights fade into the twinkling lights of the city.

"That was some tender scene," said a voice behind me.

I turned around and regarded Adam Yount, who was watching me with a sardonic smile. "You *dog*. Does Mary know?"

"It's not like that."

"I don't know, looked pretty intense to me."

"She's a witness in The Kremlin shooting."

"Do you let all your witnesses drive you around town?"

"Enough."

"Whatever, man. I'm sure you know what you're doing. Anyway, I'm glad I ran into you. Sam has been calling about every five minutes. He's crazy to get ahold of you and he says your cell is switched off."

Sam. Shit. Gun-wielding Uzbeks and psychic Wiccans had kept me from thinking about how I had left him upside-down in a dumpster.

I looked at my watch. Sam should have had plenty of time to extricate himself, though, and get to his lab to prepare for the jump to Stream Zero. I couldn't blame him for wondering what had happened to me. I dug my phone out now to check missed calls.

My flip phone was dead. Which was funny, as I seemed to remember it had plenty of juice the last time I had checked. Then I realized I had another option. I pulled Trav One's smartphone out of my other pocket.

And could do nothing but stare at my own dark reflection in the screen. Trav One's phone was one of those button-less touch screen devices, and I had no idea how to turn it on.

I rubbed the blank screen a couple of times, sneaking a look at Adam, hoping he wouldn't notice my confusion. Fortunately, he had continued with what had obviously been his original purpose in coming outside, a smoke break. He had turned away to light up.

I ran my fingers along the top edge of the phone, finally rewarded by a flash of light as the screen illuminated with a picture of me with Mary, in that silly joined-at-the-head pose that are standard in cell phone self-portraits. After pawing at the screen more or less at random several times, a widget finally dropped down from the top that said, *Three missed calls. Four new messages.* I touched the screen.

All were from Sam. No surprise there.

I decided to look at the texts first, not having any idea how to access the voice mails.

WTF????? Where'd you go?

Okay. Heading for the lab as planned. Looking forward to your explanation.

Everything's ready. Holding up my end. Can transfer you from here after all, just say the word. Where are you?????

I typed. *Sorry. Long story. Am at the station. Do I have to be with you to go?* and sent the message.

"Everything all right?" Adam asked.

"Yeah," I replied. "I, uh, was supposed to give Sam a ride. He's been wondering where I am."

"Apparently."

The phone beeped. It was Sam's reply.

No, can do it from anywhere. Best for you to be alone. Call when ready.

OK.

"See you upstairs," I called to Adam.

He nodded, blowing smoke out through his nose.

I went upstairs to my desk and had just sat down when a shadow blocked the light from the buzzy fluorescents overhead.

I looked up to see Amy Harper leaning on my desk. She was still dressed in civvies, but now wore a leather jacket, and she'd pulled her blonde mane back into a bushy pony tail.

"Any news?" she asked quietly.

I shook my head.

"I went back to the bar," she continued, "but no one knew anything. Or was willing to talk."

I nodded.

"Trav," she leaned close. "Promise me. If you hear anything... *anything,* you'll let me know."

She bit her lip. "I know we're not supposed to get close to our CIs, but Rob is different, you know? I don't know how I'll live with myself if he gets hurt."

I nodded again. "I'll keep you posted."

"Thanks."

"Trav?"

We both turned. Captain Martin had poked his head out of his office.

"Gotta minute?"

"Sure."

I nodded to Amy, pushed myself up from my desk and went into his office.

"Shut the door."

"I just got off the phone with the DA. We couldn't hold Grymzin."

I nodded, not wanting to tell him why this was not news to me.

He sighed, his face was heavy with fatigue. The vibrant and youthful Leon Martin was gone, leaving a tired, middle-aged man behind.

"And, since our CI has disappeared, our friend Charles-call-me-Chuck," Martin's voice turned thick with sarcasm, "convinced the judge that with only the circumstantial evidence of blood spatters, which he could have gotten simply by being in the vicinity, there wasn't enough to make the charges stick. I had hoped for some gunshot residue, but forensics didn't turn anything up. He must have had gloves that he ditched before you found him. Lennox is our only hope at this point. Any more luck on him?"

Rob Lennox was, unfortunately for him, the least of my problems right now. I *had* made that small, if unsuccessful, effort to get Kaaro to tell me where he was, but hadn't given him any thought since. At least the Kaaro encounter had given me one small piece of good news.

"No, but I think he's still alive."

It was a measure of the stress the captain was under that he didn't question how I knew this. He nodded. And I could see a small glint of hope add some life back into his eyes.

"That's something, at least. But Kaaro won't keep him around long. You *have* to find him. Use whatever methods you need to. And, Trav?"

"Yeah?"

"I know I really don't have to remind you of this, but I think we need to keep this extra quiet. Just you, Monroe, and me. I keep thinking about how fast Kaaro and his lawyer got here this afternoon. It was like they knew you'd busted Grymzin before *I* did."

"What are you saying?"

I asked the question because it was expected, but I knew what he was going to say next.

"Kaaro may have a source within the department. It's the only thing I can think of that explains how he stays ten steps ahead of us all the time. But that's my problem. You have enough on your plate. You're not the talkative type, I know. Be extra careful on this one."

"I will."

Actually, that would be easier than he imagined, as the probable cause of the leaks was dead.

I stood up. Time to get out of here before I let the wrong thing slip.

"Oh, one more thing," Martin said as I turned to leave. "Be careful out there, Trav. They said down in Holding that Grymzin was asking questions about you when he was there. He might be thinking of coming after you."

Oh, he's doing more than thinking about it.

"I'll keep my eyes open," I assured him.

I left his office and sat back down at my desk. Absently, I looked through the notepad next to my phone where I jotted random notes down and pulled open a couple of my file drawers. I wasn't exactly sure what I was looking for, but if there was a file labeled *Why I decided to take bribes from a Central Asian crime boss,* I didn't find it.

I also did not find anything that would help me locate Rob Lennox.

Finally, I realized I was putting off what I knew had to be done. While I was still curious about what had made Trav One go on the take, and wanted to set that right somehow, it wasn't my primary concern.

And as much as I hated to leave him in the lurch, neither was Rob Lennox.

Job number one was still to keep Trav Zero from rampaging from stream to stream, killing Trav Beckers. And I remained hopeful that by backtracking to his home stream, I could pick up his trail.

Of course, after my conversation with Morgan, I probably had to add *fix whatever had screwed up the Multiverse* to my to-do list as well.

Simple, huh?

So, as attractive as the idea was of staying here and tackling the more mundane problem of Kaaro and Lennox, what I needed to do was go stream-jumping again.

Well, there was no sense in putting things off any longer. I pushed myself to my feet and headed for the men's room. It was empty, but I locked myself into a stall just in case, and called Sam.

"Took you long enough."

"Sorry. I got called in to meet with the captain."

"Everything all right?"

"First Stream problems."

He chuckled. "Funny."

I needed to get this over with before I lost my nerve.

"Tick tock," I said. "Are you ready?"

"Yeah. But don't think I've forgotten that you threw me into a garbage can."

"Sorry again. But believe me, it would have been better than the alternative."

"Easy for you to say. You're not still picking coffee grounds out of your hair. I assume you're alone?"

"Yeah."

"Good. If we were doing a more gradual shift, I wouldn't worry about it, but since you're jumping from one fairly significant line of causality to another, it is possible that some things or people could be in different locales. And we don't want you appearing out of nowhere right in front of someone."

I could hear the clicking of a computer keyboard in the background while he spoke.

"Now, I'm also sending you an app for your phone. Obviously, we won't be able to communicate across the streams. But I can follow you to some extent, using the tagging system I told you about earlier. When you're ready to come back, launch the app. It will send…well, call it a pulse, that will show up as a tag in my system. That's how I'll know to bring you back across."

Sam walked me through installing the program on the phone. When we were done, he said, "Ready?"

"I guess."

"Here we go. Good hunting."

The pulling sensation that I now knew heralded the beginning of a jump to another plane of reality started again in my stomach, and I took a deep breath. It was an effort not to close my eyes.

The walls of the stall seemed to ripple, changing colors, to yellow, then gray, before snapping back to rigidity and the familiar puke green. I blinked, waited another minute to make sure all the dizziness had passed. I got up from the toilet and pulled open the door.

And nearly collided with Leon Martin.

"What the fuck?" Martin's face clouded over in anger.

"Pardon me?"

"What. The. Fuck. Are. You. Doing. Here."

Martin grated out each word, his voice controlled, but taut with fury.

"I'm, uh, just about to head back out."

"What the hell are you talking about?"

"You told me to find my…uh, CI." No one was around, but despite the way he was acting now, I remembered Martin's warning to keep quiet about Rob Lennox.

"What are you talking about? I *told* you to get the hell out of the station this morning. Bad enough you miss your hearing yesterday, then you show up the next day acting like nothing is wrong."

He sighed. "Trav, I know it's been hard on you. First your dad, then Adam, and I gave you as much rope as I could. I really hoped you'd pull it together. But if you aren't going to help yourself, there isn't a lot I can do. If the brass catches you wandering around in here, it'll be *my* ass. C'mon."

Martin grabbed me by the arm and hustled me back down the hall. As we turned the corner into the office, I automatically looked over at my desk.

It was cleared off and empty. Across from it, Adam's desk was similarly empty, but with a small box of personal effects on top. There was a fine layer of dust coating both desks, as if neither had been touched in some weeks.

As the eyes of the other officers followed us across the room with a mixture of surprise and disgust, I realized that something had gone wrong. Sam had not sent me to Stream Zero to learn more about how this whole mess had gotten started.

Somehow, I'd jumped to Stream Four, where I had woken up yesterday morning in a post-vodka stupor, thinking about eating my gun.

I was home.

INTERLUDE

"*M*R. *LOCKE, THANK you for coming. I'm Dr. Poole.*"

The doctor was a washed-out looking man of late middle age. He wore a dark frock coat, frayed at the sleeves, in the way of a man who spent many hours writing. A cravat that had once been white was knotted loosely around his grimy, starched collar.

The doctor pushed a thatch of gray hair the consistency of straw from his eyes, and peered tiredly up at Robert Locke. He extended a hand, which Locke took.

"I still don't understand why I am here, Doctor," Locke began.

Dr. Poole silenced him, holding up the hand Locke had just released.

"I know. That is why I am so grateful you agreed to come. Please, sit."

Locke took the lone seat in the cluttered office.

"What do you know about our facility, Mr. Locke?" Poole asked.

Locke shifted in his seat. "Er, Bethlehem Royal Hospital is the most famous of its kind," he said uncertainly.

"It's all right, sir," Poole interrupted. "We use the name just like everyone else does."

"Bedlam."

Poole smiled. "We no longer charge the public a penny to come in and poke sticks at the lunatics, but the name is still with us. However, I didn't ask you to come here to discuss the history of Bedlam."

"Why am I here, then?"

Poole paused, a pensive look on his face.

"One of our patients has asked to see you."

"One of your patients? I know no one who…lives here." "Actually, that doesn't surprise me," Poole replied. "But since you did come, would you indulge me for a few minutes?"

Locke pulled his watch from the pocket of his waistcoat. "I have an hour."

"That should give us more than enough time." Poole stood. "Please come with me."

Locke followed the doctor out of the office and through a set of swinging doors past an open lounge where a number of Bedlam patients sat in silence, staring blankly at the two men as they walked past. On the other side of the lounge, a beefy young man at a desk sat reading a copy of the Daily Telegraph. *He looked up at the two as they approached.*

"Jeremy." Poole nodded at the young man. "Just going to see Miss Price."

Jeremy went back to his paper. Locke followed Poole through another set of swinging doors, and down a narrow corridor. The hallway was dim, lit only by a handful of gas lamps in sconces. A row of iron-barred doors lined each side of the hall.

"Please don't think poorly of us, Mr. Locke," Poole said. "As our funds allow, we are remodeling our rooms to make them more pleasant for those being treated here. But this is one of the wings that have yet to be refurbished. It's where we keep our patients who are the most..."

"Dangerous?" Locke asked.

"Deluded," finished Poole. He stopped in front of one of the cells. "Here we are."

The cell was bare, except for a cot with a sheet and thin blanket. A woman sat on the bed. Her knees were pulled up to her chest, and she rested her chin on them, arms encircling her pale legs. She was barefoot, and dressed only in a gray woolen shift.

She was young, Locke noticed. And with a bath, decent clothes, and some attention to the rat's nest of hair that billowed out from her head, she might actually be pretty. She stared blankly at the wall of her cell.

"Grace?" Poole called softly. "How are you today?"

The woman turned and looked at Poole, her face remaining blank.

Until her gaze fell on Locke.

"*Robert!*" *She jumped to her feet and ran across the cell, arms outstretched. She threw her arms through the bars, straining to reach Locke. He drew back.*

The woman's face fell. What little color there was drained from her countenance, and her shoulders slumped.

"*Grace,*" *Poole said in a gentle tone,* "*Remember, we talked about this. I warned you that this might happen. In fact, I told you it was very likely. No one in your family has ever heard of this man. There's no record of your...relationship.*"

"*Our relationship?*" *Locke interrupted.*

"*I'm sorry, Mr. Locke,*" *Poole replied.* "*Perhaps I should have warned you, but I wanted to get your honest reaction to seeing Miss Price. I needed to be sure.*"

"*Sure of what?*"

"*Miss Price is under the...excuse me, my dear...delusion that you and she are married.*"

"*Married?*" *Locke took another step back, feeling as if he'd been slapped.*

"*Yes! Oh Robert, don't you remember?*" *Grace pleaded.* "*We met your senior year at Shrewsbury, married right after you got your appointment at the bank. Our adorable little house in Camden...you look just the same, except...*"

She cocked her head to one side, as if she was trying to figure out what about him was different.

"*You shaved your beard.*"

Locke's fingers flew to his chin. "*Beard?*"

He turned to Poole, now thoroughly confused. "*I am a banker, Dr. Poole. But I live in Brent, and have never married. And I have never worn a beard.*" *Then, to the woman.* "*I'm sorry, Miss.*"

"*Then that means...*" *The animation that had taken over her face caused Locke to see, just for a moment, the happy girl that still lived somewhere inside the asylum inmate.*

But the light in her eyes died and her voice caught in her throat as she said softly, "*Isabel? And Oliver?*"

Locke shook his head. "*I don't know what you're talking about.*"

"You don't know your own children?" Her voice rose. *"What kind of man doesn't know the names of his own children, and denies his wife? Robert, please...if it is something I have done wrong, some way I've offended you, please give me a chance to repent. I can't stand this torture a day longer!"*

Her eyes filled with tears and with a cry she collapsed onto her cot, shoulders heaving as she sobbed into her blanket.

A nurse had slipped quietly up behind them while this was going on. Poole now turned to her.

"Sedate her. But be gentle."

"Yes, Doctor," the nurse replied.

Poole motioned to Locke and they started walking back the way they had come.

"Again, Mr. Locke, please accept my apologies for putting you in this strange situation. Miss Price's delusion is strong, she is able to describe the different aspects of this other life in the greatest detail. These two young children, and..."

"And?" Locke asked.

"Well, you, *sir. She described you to a T, right down to that watch. Did your father give it to you?"*

Locke's hand went to the fob in his pocket. *"Yes. My father was a railway engineer. This watch is railroad approved for accuracy. Not many of them around outside the profession."*

Poole nodded. *"She told me that story."*

"How could she know that?" Locke demanded. *"How could this insane woman I've never seen before know so much about me?"*

"I have no idea," Poole confessed. *"You're sure you have never seen her before today?"*

"Positive. Where did you say she was from?"

"I didn't. But she grew up in Kent."

"Kent," Locke murmured. *"Hmmm. But, no, it couldn't be."*

"What, Mr. Locke?"

"Um, nothing. It couldn't possibly have anything to do with this."

"Please, sir," Poole insisted, *"At this point, I am interested in anything, no matter how far-fetched."*

140

"I'm sure it's nothing, really. It's..."

"Yes?"

"Well, I had a school mate named Price. He grew up in Kent. We were thick as thieves all through public school. I was to spend the holidays with him during our senior year, but he broke his collarbone in a riding accident and ended up having to withdraw. My visit was cancelled, and I never saw him again. It was so long ago, but it seems to me he mentioned having a sister."

"Well, that is interesting," Poole said, "You're right. It is unlikely to have anything to do with Miss Price. Might be worth looking into, though." He pursed his lips in concentration. "There might be a connection."

"How so?"

Despite himself, Locke found himself drawn in to the young woman's plight.

"Well, you say you've never seen her, but it's possible she has seen you. Perhaps on a visit to her brother when you were both in school. And when her condition caused her to have this.. fixation, she picked a face she recalled from her youth as the basis of her delusion."

"Is that possible?"

Poole shrugged. "I have seen many delusions in my career, but never anything like this. In similar cases, the subject usually believes they are the queen, or Napoleon, or the reincarnation of some famous ruler. I've never had a patient who fantasized she was a housewife in Camden, raising two children she had by a banker. No offense."

"None taken."

They walked in silence for a while. Finally, Locke said, "What will happen to her?"

Poole sighed. "I wish I could give you a positive prognosis. But the reality is that, while some in my profession think insanity is a disease like any other, with causes and cures, many of my colleagues still adhere to the belief that mental illness comes from lack of moral character, or inherited feeble mindedness." He snorted. "We might as well blame demons."

They had reached the main entrance to the hospital. Poole reached out his hand.

"Thank you again for coming. I'm sorry to put you in such a strange and uncomfortable situation."

"Think nothing of it."

They shook hands.

Impulsively, Locke reached into his pocket and handed Poole a card.

"Please take this. If Miss Price improves to the point where you think a visitor would not upset her, please contact me."

"You want to see her again?"

"Unless you think it would be problematic for her recovery."

"No, quite the contrary. One way to dismiss a fantasy relationship might be to create a new one based in reality. But, if you don't mind my asking, why are you interested in this woman you don't even know?"

Locke shook his head. "I'm not sure. I don't know her. But I have this feeling that somehow, perhaps I should."

9

KEEPING A FIRM grip on my arm, Martin started to hustle me down the stairs. But as we got there, the upstairs landing was filled with the profile of Alex Monroe, huffing and red-faced as he topped the final step.

"Cap, can I talk to you?"

"Is it important?"

"Yeah."

Martin let go of my arm, putting a hand on the center of my chest and backing me up to the wall.

"Stay."

Martin inclined his head to Monroe, and the sweating detective joined him a few feet away. I didn't have to eavesdrop to follow the conversation.

"Finally got an ID on the John Doe over in the Siemans building."

Siemans Furniture had been closed for over a decade, but its name still adorned a building in the non-rehabbed area of the warehouse district.

"The guy who'd been double-tapped?"

"Yeah. Just like we thought. It was Rob Lennox."

"Damn. And no one knows anything, of course."

Monroe nodded. "Coworkers say he quit a couple of days ago."

"Sure he did," Martin snorted. "Quit breathing. We cannot catch a break with that son of a bitch. Did Lennox give you anything of value before they disappeared him?"

Monroe shook his head.

"Great, just great. Well, have the SI team go over the scene with a goddamned microscope. If there is even a carpet fiber that might link it to Kaaro, I want it found."

"You got it."

Monroe lumbered away and Martin turned back to me, pointing to the stairs.

When we emerged into the lobby, Martin propelled me past the genetic bouillabaisse that tended to stew up around the beat-up chairs in our holding area. A couple of hookers looked up disinterestedly in our wake.

As we approached the door, though, a small body hopped down from a chair right next to the desk sergeant and blocked our way.

"Now?" asked Holli Benjamin.

"What?" asked Martin.

"He promised to do a magic trick for me *yesterday*. My mom will be down any minute. I want to see the trick now."

"Listen, Holli," began the captain. "Trav and I are talking right now..."

"I want to see the trick," Holli repeated, folding her arms and jutting out her lower lip. Any other time, this show of obstinance would have been funny.

I knew I should have let the captain guide me out, but despite the fact that I hadn't picked up a coin or card in months, I suddenly knew what I needed to do.

I disengaged myself from Martin.

"It'll just take a minute."

I put a hand in my pocket. I did not remember taking one of dad's coins from dead Trav's storage box, but I knew just as certainly as I could feel the weight of my gun in its shoulder rig, that when I dug deep down into my jeans I would find an old-style silver dollar there.

I looked at the coin, then looked at Holli, holding her eyes with mine. I showed her the coin, then looked past her face. I was only mildly surprised to see a row of shadowy Hollis spring into view behind the one directly in front of me.

"See this coin?"

She nodded.

"Hold out your hand." She did so, and I put the coin in her palm, folding her fist closed over it.

And, as I stood there, getting ready to do the first magic trick I'd done since Dad had died, a memory leapt into my mind.

BLAM!

I pulled off my ear protection and waited patiently while Dad pulled the string end over end, bringing the paper target from the end of the shooting gallery up close.

We examined the upper-body silhouette critically.

"Nice grouping," Mike Becker said.

"Thanks, but a couple of them went really wide." I pointed to two bullet holes that were well off to the side of the figure.

"True, but if he was coming at you, these would have stopped him. Of course, if you want to be sure…"

"…I know, bring a shotgun," I finished. I was only twelve, but had heard this before. "Pistols are for cop shows."

Dad smiled and ruffled my hair.

"I've been lucky. Twenty years on the force and I have never had to discharge my weapon on duty. Not many cops can say that. Well, had enough for today?"

I nodded and we wiped our weapons down and put them away.

"So, Dad…" I began as we finished.

"Yeah?"

"You didn't answer me earlier about the card trick you did for the lady at the counter."

"Didn't I?"

"No. I thought you were doing the Hindu Shuffle, but you didn't. But you were still able to force the card on her. How'd you do it?"

Dad started to shrug the question off, then sighed.

"I'll be honest with you, Travis. I have no idea."

"WHAT?"

Dad shrugged. "Good eye, by the way. I was doing the Hindu Shuffle. I intended to make sure she had the ten of hearts. But I screwed it up. I wasn't sure what card she had."

"But her card was the five of clubs. And you still made it appear!"

"Yeah..." He paused, unsure about whether to continue. Finally, he seemed to reach some sort of internal decision and leaned closer to me.

"I've never told anyone this before, and it would be nice if you didn't mention it, either. I'm five years from retirement and don't need someone thinking I've lost it. You see, usually when I mess up, I find an excuse to re-start the trick. You've seen me do that, right?"

"Sure, hundreds of times."

He gave me a withering look. "I don't think it's quite that *many. But anyway...I know this is going to sound a little crazy. But sometimes, if I stay calm, trust myself and visualize the trick working correctly..."*

"Yeah?"

"Well, it just does.*"*

"But how?"

"I wish I knew. It must be kind of like what a basketball player feels when he tells you he was 'in the zone.' You know, he puts up an impossible shot but knows the minute the ball leaves his hands that it will go right in the basket. I just know it's going to go the way I want it to."

"But, how do you know when *it's going to work?"*

"That's the thing. I don't. It's not something I can control. I can't force things to break my way. But...not often, just once in a while, when the pressure's on, I know it's going to happen for me."

And then a twinkle came into his eye.

"Maybe there is a little real magic in the world after all."

Holli was looking at me expectantly. My hand was still folded over hers.

"Feel the coin in there?"

She nodded.

"We're going to count to three together. Ready?"

She nodded a third time, concentration wrinkling her freckled nose.

"One, two..."

Still holding her closed fist, I raised and lowered her hand on each count.

I had never successfully done this trick before, but as we counted together, a red-outlined Holli from somewhere behind the real one smoothly zoomed forward, like shirts on an automatic rack at the dry cleaners.

And, before Red Holli was subsumed into Holli-in-front-of-Trav, there was something else…

Not a memory flashback like I had just experienced, but…a flash, a glimpse, a…sound.

It was a piano playing. A tune I knew, but couldn't quite…

But then it was gone. And Holli was looking at me, a little impatiently.

"Three?"

The girl pursed her lips, looking at me like I was kind of slow.

"Three."

I took my hand away from hers and nodded at her to open it.

She opened her fist. It was empty.

Holli's mouth dropped.

"Where did it go?"

"Check your jacket pocket."

She did so, and gasped.

She slowly brought her hand out and showed the coin to Martin and me. One of the hookers even raised an eyebrow.

"Cool! How did you do that? Do it again!"

"Yeah, very nice." Martin's tone was still cold. "Holli, I need to talk to Trav. Your mom will be down soon, okay?"

"Okay."

Her shoulders heaved in the universal big sigh of kids everywhere who couldn't understand the misplaced priorities of grownups.

Suddenly, she leaped forward and wrapped her arms around my hips.

"Thanks, Trav."

"My pleasure, Ms. Benjamin."

I squeezed her back and gently disengaged her arms.

"See you later," I said with a breeziness I didn't feel, and let Martin continue guiding me to the door.

As we approached the doorway, he pulled me close and spoke softly so the little girl couldn't hear.

"I won't embarrass you in front of the kid by tossing you out like you deserve, but this is the last benefit you'll ever get from me."

The edge was back in captain's voice.

"Once upon a time you were a good cop. And because of that, I'm not going to ask how you got back into the office. Because I hope there is still a shred of decency in you someplace that maybe doesn't want to get another cop in trouble. But the free pass ends now. I ever catch you in my shop again, I'll book you like any other asshole and let the system deal with you. Am I clear?"

I nodded.

"Get out."

I avoided Martin's eyes as I turned and opened the door. Not for the reason the captain probably thought, but that didn't really matter.

Outside, I took one final look at the station house. I walked a few steps down the street to escape the casual view of anyone inside, leaned against the wall and let out the breath I hadn't even realized I'd been holding.

How had I screwed up my life so much here?

Even though my original memories from this stream were back in place, they seemed more like a bad dream than things I had actually done.

But make no mistake, I *had* done everything that had caused my life here to go awry. I'd lost my job, pissed off the captain to the extent he'd just as soon arrest me as look at me, let Mary get away…

Sam was right. I'd been given a second chance. A chance to get away from the mess I'd made of my life here.

Sam.

Thanks to Sam, I still had that second chance.

Looking up and down the street to make sure no one was near, I pulled out the smartphone. I hadn't looked at the app Sam had sent me, but hopefully there was a way to signal him that something had gone wrong. Then maybe he could either push me on to Stream Zero, my original destination, or at least back to Stream One, where we could try the original shift again.

I swiped my index finger across the screen to wake the device up.

Nothing.

I pressed the power button.

The screen remained inert.

I flipped it over and picked at the back cover.

With my regular phone, sometimes popping the battery out fixed it when it had locked up. After pulling on all four of the phone's edges for a minute, I finally was able to pry off the back cover, remove and re-seat the battery.

I pressed the power button again, pushing down the sick turbulence that was beginning to roil in my stomach.

Still nothing.

After several minutes of fiddling, ending with me finally standing there and shaking the thing, I gave up.

Either the device had been damaged in my shift between streams or it wouldn't work because I didn't own this kind of phone here. Regardless, it was now just a brick.

I knocked the back of my head on the wall behind me a few times.

Which helped about as much as shaking the phone.

What now? How the hell did this happen?

Obviously, something had gone wrong with Sam's math. Or maybe there was some attraction or affinity to my home stream that exerted a pull Sam didn't take into account.

Regardless, here I was.

I wondered how long it would take for my consciousness to "settle" here like it had done in the other streams I'd visited. Would my memories of the other stream fade away?

In a way that would probably be a blessing.

Maybe in time, as I tried to pick up the pieces of the life I had completely broken here, I would forget how I'd had a chance to escape to something better, but had managed to screw that up, too.

No.

Certainly my life here completely sucked, but maybe the real issue wasn't the circumstances. Maybe it was my reaction to them. Sure, I'd kind of given up for a while. But that didn't mean I had to keep rolling over. If there was anything the past day had taught me, it was that I had the power to change things for myself.

And looking at the bright side, Trav Four might not be the brightest bulb on the tree, but at least I hadn't gone nuts and started killing people.

And I wasn't dead, like Trav One. Best to try and keep it that way.

I had unfinished business on Stream Zero, not to mention Stream One.

Up to now, I'd let events control me. If these streams were in fact like flowing water, I'd been that twig floating along, letting the current push me wherever.

It was time to quit being a twig, and become a fish, swimming where he wanted to go, regardless of the direction the current.

Actually, a better analogy might be a frog, since we called it stream *jumping*.

But, I was going to need some help to jump in the correct direction.

I started toward the impound lot.

And finally, a lucky break. The Mustang was parked in its usual spot. I didn't stop to think that it was odd that it would be there, since Captain Martin had fired me hours ago on this stream.

I approached the car, rummaging in my pocket for the keys. Fishing them out, I was fumbling for the unlock remote when there was a shout behind me.

"Hey! What the hell are you doing?"

"It's okay," I called, not looking. "It's my car."

"The hell it is."

Footsteps crunched on the gravel behind me.

I turned and looked at the man who had come up behind me. Jeans, Cardinals jacket, dark hair poking out from under his ball cap.

He looked quite familiar.

"Shit," we said together.

We may have been the same person, but I have to say he had a much faster reaction time.

While I was gaping, he quickly closed the distance between us.

"I don't know how the hell you got here," he growled, "But this is *not* a good time."

Too late, I saw him bring his hand up, and I was treated to the sight of my own fist plunging toward my face.

It connected with a starburst, and then things went black.

Yup, yellow.

The color of pain was definitely yellow.

And my nose hurt like you would not believe.

I blinked a few times and peered fuzzily at my surroundings.

I was in my apartment, but not the tidy version I'd left a few hours ago. The pizza box on the coffee table, vodka bottle on the floor and general clutter told me that this was the place where I'd woken up what felt like days ago.

For a moment, I thought that maybe I had never left this spot. Could it all have been an alcohol-fueled dream? In addition to being a drunk, was I also delusional, spinning a fantasy story of dimension-hopping so I could escape from this life I had so thoroughly messed up?

But no, while my head hurt like a son of a bitch, it was definitely the result of blunt force trauma, not a hangover.

Plus, I was not in the lounge chair where I generally passed out, but in one of my straight-backed kitchen chairs. Furthermore, my wrists and ankles were firmly fastened.

If I had in fact dreamed the last day, it would appear that I had also zip-tied myself to a chair.

"Welcome home, sport," said a voice behind me.

And Trav Becker strode into my field of view.

I didn't say anything. Just watched as he grabbed another of our kitchen chairs and sat on it backwards, straddling the chair back.

We regarded each other in silence for a few moments.

"I have to admit, I'm surprised to see you here," he finally said.

"Why am I tied up?" I asked.

"You're kind of a troublemaker," he replied evenly. "I didn't want you to give me any problems when you woke up."

"What kind of problems?"

"Look, Junior," he glanced at his watch. "I'm on kind of a tight timetable here. I'd love to hang around and answer all your little questions, but I have work to do. Thanks to the warm welcome the captain gave me this morning, thinking I was you, I got delayed…"

Which explained Martin acting like he had seen me earlier. I wanted to think about that some more, but he was still talking.

"…I tried to take you out of the game, but then Kaaro's stooges picked you up. I figured they would keep you busy for a lot longer than they apparently did."

"You were there, watching Sam and me? So that *was* you who took the shot at us."

He shrugged.

"In the long run, you may end up wishing I'd hit you."

He stood up, pushing the chair away. But then a puzzled frown creased his face.

"What I don't get though, is, why did you come back here?"

Watching your own face make expressions that you don't control is very weird, by the way.

"You were out of this stream," he mused. "Way better situation there—Mary, Adam. There was no Trav on the premises to exercise his prior property rights, all you had to do was move in. Why?"

I didn't say anything.

"And for that matter, how the hell did you get here in the first place? It's obvious your talent isn't manifested." He stopped for a minute, and somehow I knew he was playing back the shooting in his mind.

"Well, fully manifested, anyway. How did you even get here?"

We stared at each other some more, and I could almost see the cogs and gears turning in his brain.

Suddenly, he smiled. "Ahh."

He wagged a finger at me. "Clever. Not at all what I was expecting."

He turned to the couch. Most of the contents of my pockets were spread out over the cushions. Both guns, car keys...

And *two* phones.

He picked up the smartphone and turned back to me.

"This is how Sam's been chasing me between the streams, isn't it?"

He took my continued silence for assent, and started examining the device. He went through the same routine I had, pressing the power button, removing and reinserting the battery, even shaking it.

He finally gave up.

"It doesn't work." I said.

He looked back down at the phone, then back at me, tossing it up and down in his hands.

"So, you didn't get here under your own power at all. Sam is still driving. Which means he sent you after me. But something went wrong." He looked at the phone again before tossing it back onto the couch.

"Sucks for you. You had things pretty good back there. Should have left well enough alone. But..."

He surveyed the dirty apartment with a critical eye.

"...there is a certain symmetry to you ending up back where you belong."

He made a dusting off motion with his hands. "Well, not that this hasn't been fun, but I gotta go."

"Just answer me one question," I asked.

He raised an eyebrow.

"Is it true what Sam told me? You've been going from stream to stream killing us off? Are you insane?"

His look turned hard.

"Look, Junior," he said tightly. "You have no idea what is really going on. With me, with Sam. And now you're out of it. Best to try to forget all this even happened. You've got enough to do trying to put your life here back together, after the mess you made of it. Consider yourself lucky."

"Lucky?"

"You're alive."

"Yeah," I replied. "Why is that?"

He shook his head. "Sorry, you had your one question. Time to go."

"You're going to leave me tied up?"

"I can't have you trying to chase after me." He shrugged. "I'm pretty sure you can't follow where I'm going, but no sense in taking any chances. I wouldn't waste time looking for something to cut yourself loose with. I put all the knives and scissors up out of your reach.

"Make some noise, eventually someone will find you. And by then I'll have finished what I need to do without having to worry about you showing up again and messing it all up."

"Wait! Why don't you tell me what you're trying to accomplish? Maybe I can help."

"Sorry, Junior. No time. Gotta funeral to go to."

He put on our Cardinals jacket and smiled.

"You'll like this next bit."

He stared off into the distance for minute, his gaze going out of focus.

And he vanished.

Whoa.

Of all the weird things I had seen over the past few hours, that pretty much topped it.

I stared at the blank space where Trav Zero had stood for a couple of minutes. Finally, I turned my attention back to my predicament.

I twisted my wrists and ankles against the zip ties, but with no result other than rubbing them raw.

"Well, this is perfect," I muttered.

Despite what Zero had said, it would be hours, maybe days before someone on this stream would wonder where I was and start to come looking for me. I had pretty much alienated everyone here who would take an interest.

Besides, that "now you're out of it" crack had kind of pissed me off.

After Sam had clued me in on what Zero was doing, I had wanted to get involved.

To save lives. Set the time line to rights.

You know, hero stuff.

However, now more than anything, I wanted to find the smug son of a bitch who had left me here and punch him in my face.

But in order to do that, I was going to have to follow him to whichever stream he had gone to.

Which brought me back to my first problem. Getting untied.

Zip ties are a cheap and very effective restraint. Cops in plainclothes used them almost exclusively in our shop these days.

They are lightweight, easy to apply, and fit in a pocket.

But they can be broken off, if you know how to hit them just right. It wasn't that hard, but you needed some pretty good leverage and force to bust the little bracket piece that holds the teeth in place. If your wrists were tied to each other, it could be done, but knowing I knew that little trick, Zero had fastened each wrist and ankle to a part of the chair, to deny me that chance.

Which left cutting myself free.

I believed Zero when he had said he made sure all the sharp and saw-ey stuff would be out of my reach, even if I could move into, say, the kitchen.

That was the problem with going up against yourself. He knew exactly how I thought, not to mention all of my best hiding places.

So, if I was going to get out of this, I was going to have rely on things that Zero wouldn't know about.

I looked over to the pile of my stuff over on the couch. There was a tiny Swiss Army pen knife in the collection, I was certain. I always carried it, but that would have been the first thing he would have gotten rid of. And he'd emptied everything else out of my pockets.

Wait.

Or had he?

My hands were fastened to the chair at about waist level, and there was enough play in the restraints that if I really stretched my fingers, I could reach into my jeans pockets.

Zero had been thorough in cleaning them out, but he hadn't bothered with the change in my left one.

And one of the pieces of change in that pocket was the silver dollar I had vanished for little Holli.

Until I had reached in and found it, I hadn't even realized I had taken it from my safe box. But it had been there when I needed it.

Had it always been there, or had I somehow "called" it, through this talent that Zero said hadn't fully manifested itself? Morgan Foster believed I had some special ability. I had seen the red shift, which had kept Sam and me from getting shot, and helped me finish the magic trick.

Or, that could have been my imagination and I had vanished the coin the normal way.

Unlike Zero, I still had no idea how to direct things or people. The red shift, when it was there, seemed to help, but it wasn't consistent. No red outlines anywhere in the room to help me now, for instance.

But I had also recalled that time with Dad, at the target range, when he confessed that sometimes a magic trick went right simply because he really, *really* wanted it to.

Could it be that easy?

I thought of the coin. What if it wasn't just *any* coin from that box in my bedroom, but one special coin in particular?

I closed my eyes and imagined that coin.

It was from the 1970s, the one with President Eisenhower on the front (a coin expert would call that the *obverse*), and the Apollo 11 insignia on the *reverse*, commemorating the moon landing.

But this particular coin was not actual U.S. currency.

It was a magician's tool.

There was a tiny catch on the side, barely perceptible unless you were looking specifically for it. Pressing the catch caused a small, but very sharp blade to spring out of the side.

Just the thing a magician doing an escape trick might need.

Of course, there was only a single coin like that in the collection of silver dollars I had inherited from Dad. It was possible I hadn't picked it up at all, in which case this whole train of thought was a waste of time.

I still had no idea how to control these abilities that Zero had mastered. But we were the same person, I had to have them as well, didn't I?

How had Morgan described it?

Steering toward a particular outcome.

Well...it was *possible* the coin I had in my pocket was the bladed one.

Maybe it was all about convincing myself.

I closed my eyes, and took some calm breaths. I've had a yoga class or two over the years, but never taken the mental aspects of it very seriously. However, taking a few moments to center myself right now seemed like the right way to start.

I mentally blocked out my surroundings, the ache in my head and face, the restraints scraping my skin and concentrated on the coin.

I recalled its weight in my hand, the fine ridges on the front and back.

Now, the striations on its edge. I mentally rubbed a finger along the side of it, feeling the uniform ridges all along it, except in that one tiny spot, where the catch was.

Had I felt that catch when I had fished it out of my pocket to perform the trick for Holli?

Of course I had.

Holding on to that confidence, I stretched the fingers of my left hand into my pocket, twisting in the chair as much as my bonds allowed, to get closer to the coins way down inside.

Sweat broke out on my forehead with the strain of holding my legs and hands in such an unnatural position. But finally the tip of my middle finger came into contact with one coin that I could feel was substantially larger than the ones surrounding it.

"Come to poppa," I whispered, making a *come hither* motion to drag the coin up toward the top of the pocket.

It seemed to take hours, but finally I was successful. A glint of silver peeked out. I worked it out into my palm. Finally I felt its reassuring weight in my hand.

Now, for the acid test.

I took a minute to recall the confidence, the surety I had felt a moment previous. I *would* feel the blade catch. That was the only possibility.

I ran my thumb along the edge of the coin for real this time.

Right *there*.

And the small blade sprung free.

I let out the breath I didn't realize I'd been holding and gripped the coin firmly. It would be a foolish waste to have gotten this far only to drop it.

Soon I discovered that making the correct coin appear in my pocket was actually the easy part.

Twisting my fingers around to get at the plastic binding my hands, all the while holding onto a blade whose shape was about style, not function, was not easy.

Sweat continued to drip down my face and neck as I sawed through the zip tie.

Finally, the plastic parted, causing me to almost drop the coin-knife again. I carefully set it on my thigh and flexed my stiff fingers.

When the strength came back into them, I went to work on my right hand. This went quicker, of course, and it wasn't long before I was standing, stretching out the kinks in my legs and back from sitting for so long.

I put my jacket on and refilled my pockets. The last item to go in was my car keys. I held them in my hand and looked at them thoughtfully.

I still didn't really know how the whole stream-jumping thing worked, but every time *I* had jumped, I'd changed streams but remained in the same physical location.

That meant, hopefully, that Zero had brought me here in the car, not through parallel universe magic.

And, since he had jumped out of the apartment, not left physically, the car should be parked outside.

I had a long walk ahead of me if it wasn't.

I tried to summon up the same confidence that had helped me summon the coin and headed out to the street.

10

FORTUNATELY, EITHER MY luck was holding out, or I had "steered" correctly, because outside the apartment building squatted the dusty and dented Stream Four version of the Mustang. I couldn't remember if the keys in my pocket had originated in this stream or not, but I was willing to bet they would start my beloved beast.

I was correct. Pulling out onto the street, I continued the journey I had started hours ago, when I had arrived back here, toward someone who I hoped could help me get back on track.

I pointed the car toward Building 231.

The car was too quiet. I stabbed at the power button a couple of times before I remembered that the car's radio was busted here.

But the stereo in my head was working just fine.

For some reason, the opening lines from an old Bruce Springsteen song popped into my head.

I like his early stuff best, although he had done much better than most at staying relevant through the years. But *Born to Run* would always be my favorite of his albums, and one of the few non-jazz records that warranted acquiring vinyl, CD, and digital versions.

Of course, when Mary and I had started dating, the significance of the record had increased tenfold.

Anyone familiar with Springsteen knows a character named Mary pops up in any number of his songs.

Must be a Catholic thing.

So, for anyone who liked Bruce and had a girl named Mary, not associating the two was impossible. Especially one particular night, not long after we'd first started going out, when I picked her up at her parents' place and watched in awe as she danced across the porch, dress shimmering in the moonlight, unknowingly acting out the opening lyrics to "Thunder Road."

But that was a long time ago, particularly in this stream. I pulled my head out of memory land and forced myself to focus back to the business at hand.

I pulled into the Campus Town lot across the alley from the physics building and made my way to Sam's office. I was taking a chance that Sam would still be here this time of night. But I was in luck. A sliver of light seeped out from under his cartoon-covered door.

"Hey, Trav," he said after I knocked. "Kinda late for you to be wandering around campus, isn't it?"

"Um..." I searched my memory. This morning had been a *long* time ago. But Sam had shown up at my apartment first thing, and...

"Is your car working?"

"Yeah. Why?"

"So you didn't need to catch a ride with me today?"

"Noooo," Sam said. He hesitated, obviously choosing his words carefully. "I haven't seen you since night before last. Remember? They cut you off at the bar and called me to come take you home?"

"Right."

"Trav, what's wrong? You're acting really funny. Have you been, uh...?" He made a tippling motion with his hand.

"Not a drop, Sam. Although after I get done telling you what's happened to me today, you're going to think I *have* been drinking. But maybe we should continue this in the Cat Box."

"The Cat Box? How do you know about the Cat Box?"

"You told me."

"No," Sam shook his head. "We've only had it live for a day or two, and frankly, you haven't really been interested, or even coherent enough for me to get into it with you."

161

"Sorry, Sam. I know I haven't been good company lately. And I know this is going to sound crazy to you. But I've seen the Cat Box because you showed it to me. This morning."

"This morning? We went over that. I haven't seen you today."

"Not on this stream."

Sam's eyes went wide. "Okay dude, now you're starting to freak me out. For one thing, we haven't had any conversations about the Cat Box. Or streams. Or anything not related to you apparently deciding to drink yourself to death. And if we *had* talked about it, you'd know that's not how streams work. Hopping from reality to reality is a sci-fi plot device. There are no b…"

"No backsies," I finished. "Yeah, I know. You told me that. Of course, later you told me you were all wrong."

"What? Trav, you are not making sense."

"I know."

Everything hinged on making *this* Sam believe me. I kept going, the words coming out in a rush.

"But isn't it a little strange that I know about the Cat Box, even though you don't remember talking to me about it?"

Sam shrugged. "I must have mentioned it to you and forgot about it. And the rest is a vodka-fueled delusion."

"Yep, that would be the logical answer. But I am telling you the truth, Sam. Since I woke up yesterday with a bottle in one hand and my weapon in the other, I have been bouncing from reality to reality. Apparently at your direction."

"Me? Why would I do that?"

"Let me start at the beginning."

Slowly, I worked my way through the entire unbelievable chain of events. I had to hold my hand up several times to keep Sam from erupting with questions.

But then when I finally finished, he was silent for quite a while, digesting what I'd told him.

"It's a little hard to believe," he finally said.

"You're telling me."

DENNIS W. GREEN

"Trav, I'd like to believe you. Frankly, this is the most coherent I've seen you in weeks. But..."

"I get it," I replied. Now it was my turn to be silent while I thought.

Then I had a little inspiration.

"You said your Cat Box has only been running a few days. But, you can measure the incoming...quanta, right?"

"Of course. That's the point of the whole exercise."

"Then, if you fire it up with me in the room, you should see the same thing Sam on Stream One saw—an explosion of incoming quanta centered on me."

"Maybe," Sam scratched his chin. "But I'm still not sure that would prove anything."

"Humor me."

It took some cajoling, but curiosity finally got the better of him and we headed to his lab.

A few minutes later, he was staring at the blue explosions on his computer screen just like Sam One had.

"You're right. That is pretty weird. It still doesn't completely prove you've been jumping back and forth between the streams. But..."

"But what?"

Sam screwed up his face. "Let's say I buy all this. Mainly because you don't have the imagination God gave a rabbit, and I don't see how you could have come up with any of it yourself. And you're...well, you're different than when I saw you last. It's like you woke up."

"I guess maybe I have."

"Anyway. You say that you're back here in, what'd you call it, Stream Four, by mistake?"

I shrugged. "I guess. I don't know if it's something the other Sam did that went wrong, or if there's some attraction to my own stream he wasn't counting on."

Sam scowled at his computer screen. "What I don't get is how this Sam Zero is so much farther ahead on the project than me. We aren't going to be set up to run even the most basic quanta examinations for a couple of weeks."

"He said streams are like tributaries of a river running parallel to each other. Events can flow at slightly different rates but they generally catch up to each other at some point."

"Whatever. It's all insane anyway. That's as good an explanation as any." He looked seriously at me. "So, where does that leave us? What do you want to do?"

I leaned back in my chair. "I know the logical thing for me to do would probably be to let it all go. I'm back where I started from. And even if things did go better for me in one of those other streams, I caused my own problems in this stream. I should have to live with them, just like everybody else."

"I sense a 'but' coming," replied Sam.

"Yeah. If what the other Sam said is true, Trav Zero, crazy Trav, isn't going to stop till he gets rid of anyone who has anything to do with moving between streams. I don't know why he didn't kill me while he had the chance. But I don't think it's smart to sit around here waiting for him to come back and finish the job. And..."

I looked away from Sam.

"And?"

"Well, by coming here, I've probably put you in danger, too."

"Hmm. I hadn't thought of that."

"So we can sit here and wait for him to show up and get rid of two loose ends, or we can be a little more proactive."

"How?"

"Stick to the original plan. Find him before he finishes whatever he intends to do. Try to convince him to quit."

"And if you can't?"

"You know, I had almost this exact conversation with Sam Zero, only then it was *me* asking what I'd do when I found him."

"And what'd he...what did I say?"

"Worry about it later."

"Sounds like me. Well, how are you going to go about it?"

"I need to get back to Stream One and check on Sam Zero. I have a feeling that was where Trav Zero was heading when he left me."

"Do you think that was what he meant by going to a funeral?"

"If I can get there in time, maybe I can prevent the funeral."

"How do you plan to do that?"

"With your help."

"My help? I told you, we're not even close to wherever Sam Zero's gotten with all this. And it's not like we can ask him."

"Maybe we can."

I dug the smartphone out of my pocket. "We don't have him, but we have this."

Sam grinned. "Reverse engineer my own work? That sounds like fun."

He held out his hand.

"Gimme."

As Sam worked, I wandered around the lab.

The Stream Four Cat Box was definitely a work in progress. The same computer workstation was near the door, but the particle-reading device sat on the floor amidst a tangle of wires, some of which led out the door and down the hall. The same two stools sat in front of the main computer.

Sam perched on one, intent on the monitor. Bored with looking over Sam's shoulder, I paced back and forth across the small space, stepping over the wires and equipment.

"Don't touch anything," Sam warned, not even taking his eyes from the screen.

"Or what?" I responded. "I might slip into another reality? Too late."

"Actually, I was thinking more along the lines of you tripping and breaking your arm. Although now that I think of it, that would at least provide a way for me to identify you if any other Travs come popping in."

"Funny."

"Ah HA!" Sam leaned back and rubbed his eyes, then motioned me over. A satisfied smile stretched across his narrow face. "We're in."

I came back over, pulling the other stool near to Sam and sitting back down. I looked at the monitor. "So, what am I seeing?"

"Well, I didn't have any more luck than you did getting your phone to power up. So I popped out the sim card and stuck it into *my* phone." He gestured toward the two phones, sitting side by side on the tabletop. A USB cable ran from one phone into a port in the side of the monitor.

"This," he pointed to a directory listing, "is all the apps loaded onto the phone. And this," he clicked on a folder icon, "is the app Sam Zero put on the phone."

Sam stared at the display, frowning.

"Huh."

"What?"

"Oh, nothing. It's weird, looking through all this code. I've never seen it before, but every time I page down, it's like I already know what the next bunch of lines are going to look like."

"Do you understand it?"

"Kind of. The only problem is that the program is calling out to IP addresses that don't exist."

"Is that why my phone doesn't work?"

"No, that's a separate issue. Somewhere in this stream, this phone," he held up my device, "already exists. And it's probably turned on and connected to the cell network. When an identical phone, right down to the serial number, also tries to log on, it can't."

A thought occurred to me. I pulled my old flip phone out of my pocket and held it up.

"But I was on Stream One for hours, using this phone and it worked fine. Shouldn't the same thing have happened to it?"

Sam shrugged. "Hard to say. More than likely, since the user agreement that came with that phone was *inscribed on stone tablets*, the Stream One analog of it had been trashed. Or maybe there's some sort of inter-dimensional hoodoo going on that I don't understand yet."

He frowned at the inert phone on his desk again.

"Anyway, we can't be surprised that it doesn't work. The only thing I can figure out is that Sam Zero was counting on there being an operational Cat Box in the stream where he was sending you, and that somehow that would be a bridge that would allow a linkup that would allow *this* phone to talk back to him on Stream One. But, since my Cat Box isn't fully operational yet, those connections don't exist."

He slumped back in the stool, staring at the screen. Folding his arms across his chest, he reached up with one hand to pull on his lower lip.

"So, the phone doesn't help us?" I tried to keep disappointment out of my voice.

"I didn't say that. This code tells me what connections the phone is looking for. If I can..."

"What?"

"Well," Sam looked uncertain. "Remember back in school, sometimes in math class you had a problem to solve and you could get the answer on your calculator, but that didn't really do you much good, because in order to get full credit, you had to show your work?"

"Sure."

"That's what I have here. I know the answers, but I have to work backwards to fill in the gap between what I've already been working on and what I now know is the finished product. I'm ahead of the game because I know what the end result is, but there's still a big gap between where I am now and where I need to be."

"But can you do it?"

Sam scowled at me.

"You wound me. Of course I can do it. This other Sam isn't any smarter than me, he's just ahead. If he did it, I can do it. But it could take a while."

"How long?"

Sam shrugged and squinted again at the screen. "Hmmm. I'd say it's at least a two-pizza problem."

In spite of myself, I chuckled. "Smells better than a pipe at least. All right, Sherlock. How about if I go get the pizza while you get started?"

"Sounds good."

"Your usual?"

"Hmm."

Sam was already punching keys and making notes on a pad next to his keyboard. I knew further communication from him at this point was unlikely. Might as well go get the pizza.

I attracted Sam's attention long enough to get the entry door code so I could let myself back in, then took off.

There was a convenience store near the lab that stayed open late, and fortunately for us, made passable pizza. I picked up two, along with some sodas, and made my way back to the Cat Box.

As I walked, I thought about Mary again.

In this stream, I'd succeeded in driving her away, the poison of my own inability to move on after Adam's death causing everything good in my life to wither and die. Unbidden, the opening piano lick to "Thunder Road" began running through my head again.

I was whistling a counterpoint to the melody as I pushed open the door of the Cat Box.

"Pizza's here, Sherlock."

But Sam didn't reply.

He lay on the floor, the two stools from the desk overturned on top of him as blood seeped onto the tangle of wiring around his computer.

I dropped the pizza and sodas and knelt beside him, frantically grabbing his wrist to check for a pulse.

As I bent close to Sam's face, I could hear shallow breathing. I gave a relieved sigh. And a minute later he moaned and his eyelids started to flutter.

"Don't move," I warned him.

"Trav?" whispered Sam.

"Yeah. Look, lay still. I want to check you over."

Sam started to raise his head and shoulders off the ground, then fell back.

"Ow. Don't worry. Christ, my head hurts."

"Open your eyes."

He did, and I was relieved that neither of his pupils were dilated.

"I don't think you have a concussion, but stay still, all right?"

Sam nodded weakly.

"I'll be right back."

There was a kitchenette a couple of doors down. I was able to find some dishcloths, which I soaked in warm water, and some ice. I returned and dabbed gently on what looked to be about a 2-inch gash at the base of Sam's skull. Fortunately, the flow of blood had nearly stopped. I carefully helped him to a sitting position.

"Take it slow, Sam."

"Shit! Is that mine?" He stared at the blood among the wires on the floor.

"I think it looks worse than it is," I said. "Scalp wounds bleed a lot, but your pupils aren't blown. We should take you to the emergency room." I wrapped some of the ice in a cloth and carefully held it on the back of Sam's head.

"No, I'll be fine. Ow."

"Sorry." I adjusted my hold on the ice pack and Sam's head. "At the least, you're going to have a hell of a bump there. Do you remember what happened?"

Sam tried to shake his head.

"Ow."

"Talk, don't move."

"Right. I dunno. You left to get the pizza. I was untangling the code. I was trying to figure out what IP address the software was written to access. It's funny, as I was looking at the numbers, the IP addresses looked really familiar. So, I was loading WHOIS..."

"WHOIS?"

"It's a database of IP addresses."

"Whoever."

"Right." He smiled, then winced. "Ow. Don't make me laugh. Anyway, the door opened. I told you to put the pizza on the table, and WHAM."

"Are you sure it was me?"

Sam shrugged. "My back was to the door. But whoever it was had the door code or they couldn't have gotten in. And we haven't seen anyone else here, right?"

"Yeah."

"Aw, crap."

Sam had taken over the job of holding the ice to his head and was peering at the desk.

"What?"

"The phone is gone." He tried to get to his feet.

"Ow."

"Geez, Sam, take it easy. Here." I got a hand under his elbow and helped him over to the desk, righting a stool so he could sit.

Sam immediately started punching keys and moving the mouse, a process hampered by the fact he was working with one hand still holding the ice pack.

After I had him situated, I got on my hands and knees and looked all around the computer and the floor, just in case the phone had fallen somewhere. But Sam was right, it was gone. I straightened, rocking back on my knees, looking up at him.

"Well, it had to be Trav Zero. I wonder what caused him to come back to this stream."

"Are you sure he left?"

"Yeah. I watched him disappear. And I don't think it was just for my benefit. He seemed in a hurry to leave. But he came back for the phone. The question is, why?"

I posed the question, but I really wasn't thinking about Trav Zero and the phone. I was more interested in his state of mind.

The rough edges of Sam's wound indicated he'd probably been pistol-whipped. More than likely with the same .22 I'd been chasing through all these streams. But if Zero had a gun and no one else was around, why hadn't he finished the job?

Hell, he could have taken care of Sam, then waited here for me to come back and tied up all the loose ends. Why hadn't he? This was the second time he'd had a chance to get rid of me, and he hadn't taken it. What was he here for, if not for killing anyone who knew about stream-jumping? And why take the phone and leave us alive? Trav Zero didn't need the phone because he could...

Sam, who had continued poking at the keyboard, interrupted my train of thought.

"But the good news is I think I got all the code copied over. Actually, I may not even need the phone at all now. I know what kind

170

of information the app is trying to send. I have to figure out where it's going. There isn't exactly an Internet naming protocol for IP addresses in other universes. That's why these IPs..."

He paused. "I feel like I should know...there's something about these numbers..." He shook his head. "Well, back to WHOIS."

"Okay, this is where I came in," I said. "Can I get you anything? Do you feel up to a piece of pizza?"

"Yeah, I think so."

I went over to the box, folding the lid underneath the box, and sat it next to Sam. I opened a Mountain Dew for him as well.

"Thanks." Sam moved the ice up and down on the back of his head. "Ow. Ow. I don't suppose you have about twenty ibuprofen?"

"No, I..."

Wait. It had worked with the coin, hadn't it?

"Maybe I do."

"What?"

I held up a hand, forestalling Sam's questions. I stared hard at my friend for a moment, then let my gaze go out of focus.

I imagined Sam dragging himself in to work one day, feeling out of sorts. I'd seen him sick, or hung over, dozens of times, and frankly he didn't look too healthy at the moment. So it was easy to overlay the mental story I was building onto the reality in front of me.

And it wouldn't be too unlikely, that on one of those days when he wasn't feeling great, that Sam had one day brought to work...

There.

"Look in your middle drawer."

Sam raised both eyebrows, but did as I asked. He reached his free hand into the drawer and drew out a small bottle of ibuprofen. His eyebrows shot up.

"You know, I was looking for this the other day at home," he murmured. "I didn't remember bringing it here. How the hell did you...that's some trick."

I smiled. "And you know how much I love magic tricks."

"So, how'd you do it?"

"Still figuring that out. And to be honest, all I have is these little parlor tricks right now. The big stuff, what Zero does? No idea. And I'm not sure I have time to wait for you to replicate the hardware solution."

"What are you going to do?"

I looked around the room at the stacks of computers and devices, tangle of wire, blinking monitors—all the trappings of modern science.

And the contrast between Sam Zero's painstaking, and occasional faulty, negotiation of the various planes of reality versus the smooth, effortless transitions of Trav Zero.

Maybe I had been looking for assistance in the wrong place.

Or, to put it in *Star Trek* parlance, maybe I needed a little less Spock and a little more McCoy.

I nodded to myself. Decision made, I turned back to Sam.

"I have another idea. If it works, though, it means I may jump streams again."

"I understand," Sam said. "Well, even if you don't get back here, you've given me a pretty interesting problem to work on."

"And a concussion."

Now Sam smiled. "I don't hold you responsible for that. Although if you find Trav Zero, smack him a good one for me."

"Done."

I turned to go.

"Wait."

"What?"

"Well, just in case you do get back here, maybe we should have some sort of signal so I know it's...well, *you.*"

"Not a bad idea. What do you have in mind?"

"Just a word or phrase that only these versions of us would know."

"A code word, huh?" I looked again at the mess that was the Stream Four Cat Box.

"Cat litter."

"I like it." Impulsively, Sam stuck out his hand.

"Be careful."

I shook Sam's hand and pulled him into a one-armed embrace.

"Thanks, man. And remember, if you see me, and I don't know the secret word..." I reached into my pocket.

"Maybe you should take this."

Gingerly, Sam took the .22. "You realize I'm just as likely to shoot myself?"

"You'll be fine. If nothing else, maybe it will make him pause long enough for you to scamper away."

"*That* I can do."

"See you."

"And Trav?"

"Yeah?"

Sam gestured to his monitor again. "You see Sam Zero, tell him this is good work."

"I will."

Outside, I pulled Morgan Foster's business card out of my pocket and took off for a session with my psychic.

11

MORGAN FOSTER LIVED in one of a group of row houses in what locals called Czech Town.

In the late 1800s, dozens of these little houses had been built for the influx of immigrant workers enticed from Europe by plentiful work in a packing house, long since shuttered.

The company had put up block after block of these places, which looked like a Beaver Cleaver-era dwelling, but at about three-quarters scale. Perfect today for a single person or couple, but you wondered how the original 19th century family with a half-dozen kids made it without killing each other.

Very cute, but to me they had always looked like oversized dollhouses.

Many of the houses were torn down, but the neighborhood eventually attracted buyers who liked the charm and history, so a couple of blocks were preserved.

Morgan's house was one of eight or so on the block. Each was brightly painted and nicely landscaped. Some even had little picket fences.

Hers was painted robin's-egg blue. The yard wasn't fenced, but there was a short flagstone walk going up to the porch, which was not much bigger than its welcome mat.

Two juniper bushes, the spiral kind, wound inside and through themselves on either side of the front steps. A gray sign with the words *Psychic Readings* printed on a background of stars and a crescent moon was stuck into the ground.

I looked at my watch. It was awfully late for a business call. I would have to hope she was a night owl.

More importantly, what was I going to say?

Having been through the whole "I've bounced through four parallel universes since yesterday" thing with Sam, I had no idea how I was going to convince Morgan I was legit, let alone get her to help me. It had been hard enough with Sam. Had it not been for the demonstration in the Cat Box, I might have still been there trying to get him to believe me.

On this stream, Morgan didn't know me, as I had not been at The Kremlin to meet her. So before I could ask for her help, I was going to have to convince her I wasn't one, stark raving nuts, or two, some weird stalker.

And no Red Trav to follow either. *Never a ghostly guide around when you need one.*

I got out of the car and started up the walk.

There was no doorbell. I raised my hand to knock, but before I could, the door opened.

"Took you long enough," she said.

I stood there, hand still raised to knock.

"What?"

"Well, you've been parked out there for a good ten minutes. I was starting to think you were going to sit there all night."

"Umm, well…"

I decided to start over. "Look, I'm…"

"I know," she interrupted.

"What…?" I repeated.

She rolled her eyes. "Are you coming in or not?"

"Uhhh. Sure."

So much for having to convince her to let me in.

She stood aside as I entered and shut the door behind me.

We regarded each other for a minute.

She was barefoot, wearing a man's flannel shirt and black yoga pants. Her blonde mane was tamed by one of those comb-clip things and pulled behind her in a rough pony tail.

She held a pair of black-framed cat's eye reading glasses in one hand. I couldn't see the other.

She cocked her head to one side. "Well, what can I do for you?"

I didn't know where to start. I had the "convince her I'm not a nut" speech all ready to go. Without that on-ramp, I had no idea where to begin.

"Do you...know why I'm here?"

She sighed in frustration and shook her head. "That's not the way it works. I'm psychic, not telepathic. I heard you pull up, it's a little late for any of my neighbors to be having company. Then you sat in the car for a long time, like you were getting up your courage to come in. Typical behavior for a lot of people, especially men, visiting a psychic for the first time. So, you're here for a reading."

"Do you always let anyone who shows up at your doorstep in the middle of the night inside?"

She shrugged.

"You're harmless."

"You don't know that."

"You're right. I don't. But I get a vibe about people."

"And you trust it totally?"

"Well... I'm a pretty good judge, but..." she chewed on her bottom lip.

"But?"

"Like they say, 'Trust but verify.'"

And she brought her other hand around from behind her back.

It held a freaking Desert Eagle.

The giant handgun looked enormous in her dainty palm. It was as long as her forearm. She carefully did not point it at me, but I could tell from the ease with which she held it that she was uite comfortable with its weight in her hand.

"Jesus Christ, you don't do things by halves, do you?"

She shrugged, lowered the gun and looked at me. This time, though, her eyes narrowed and she seemed to be intently studying a spot in the middle of my forehead.

Suddenly, her jaw dropped and her eyes went wide with shock.

"Oh, my God. You're a..."

"A traveler," I finished.

"I need to sit down," she said. She put the gun down (carefully, I noted with approval) and waved me to a seat. There were two pieces of furniture in the diminutive front room, a comfortable-looking upholstered chair and a small couch. I took the chair and she went to the couch. She tucked her legs under her and studied me some more.

"Wow," she whispered.

"What?"

"It's...well...you. Look at you."

I spread my hands. "Look at what?"

"I...don't know how to explain it. I mean, I've seen people now and then who I could tell didn't start out on this plane, but this? Your aura..." She stopped, looking for words to continue.

"My aura...?"

"It's a *mess*. Different colors, moving in and out of focus, it's like you're only partially *here*."

She looked into my eyes again. "How do you feel?"

"Feel?"

"Yes. I have to tell you, Mr...?"

"Becker. Trav Becker. Call me Trav."

"Trav. I'll be honest. I've had clients suffering from mental trauma that required hospitalization who were carrying around less psychic baggage than you. How do you function?"

"Um, in a state of confusion mostly."

She gave me a quizzical frown, then her eyes widened again.

"Wait. This isn't really news to you, is it? You knew I would see something. That's why you're here."

"You're right. I need your help."

"*My* help? You don't know me. Oh..."

Her hand flew to her mouth as the realization dawned. "You *do* know me! Oh my God. You've met me on another plane!"

"Yeah, kind of."

I produced the business card I had received from her on Stream One.

She took it. Her hand trembled and she stared at it in wonder.

"*I* didn't give you this. I am holding an object that originated on another plane of reality. Shit. Shit shit shit shit shit shit shit shit. I don't believe this. I don't even know where to start. What is it like? What was *I* like?"

"Uhhh, swore a little less?"

"Oh, geez, sorry."

She started to say something else, but her attention was suddenly distracted by something to my left. I turned my head to discover a black triangular face a few inches away from me, studying me intently.

The face was attached to a large black and white cat. It had leapt up to the window ledge directly behind my chair. Its tail swished from side to side as it regarded me and it tentatively put one forepaw on the back of my chair, then the other. Its head followed. I held still as it got closer and closer to me, finally nudging me in the forehead with its own.

"Noah!" Morgan cried.

"No, it's okay." I smiled and scratched it between the ears. It pushed against my hand and started to purr.

"Well, if there was any doubt about you, that takes care of it," she said. "Noah is the best judge of character I have ever seen."

"No kidding."

"Oh, yes. It's easy for him, of course. I may not be telepathic but he is. He reads minds."

"Reads minds."

"He only approaches people who are trustworthy. If there was something wrong, he'd be under the bed. I've seen it time and time again. I know it sounds crazy."

"Honestly? Today…not even in the top ten."

By now the cat had completed the transition from window ledge to chair and my hand had scratched its way along his back to the base of his tail. I applied firmer pressure as I rubbed the bundle of nerves there and his rear came up to make sure I didn't lose contact.

"Well, you've made a friend for life now," she said, laughing. "Here, let me get him out of your way."

She produced a catnip mouse and tossed it across the room. Noah's head swiveled and he bounded after it, leaping from the back of my chair to its arm, then to the floor. He snagged the mouse and batted it across the hardwood floor. It skittered down a short hallway across from where I sat and he launched himself after it.

A moment later, he returned with the mouse clamped in his jaws. To my surprise, he marched directly to me and laid the toy at my feet. I picked it up and threw it. He bounded after it again.

"Now that's unusual," Morgan said.

"What is?"

"That's really friendly, even for him. He generally only offers prey to me, or someone he knows really well."

"Maybe he thinks I look hungry. Although if he can read minds, he knows I prefer my catnip fresh."

She stared at me thoughtfully. "You know, some people think that cats can perceive multiple planes of reality. That's why they stare at blank walls and chase things we can't see. Could he remember you from the other plane?"

I shook my head. "We didn't meet on the other plane."

"Hmmm," she hmmed doubtfully. "I wonder what he sees when he looks at you."

"A soft touch." I tossed the mouse once again. "I didn't know cats played fetch."

"Cats do whatever they please."

"Good point."

"Mr. Becker." Her look turned serious.

"Trav."

"Trav. Why are you here? I don't think it's to play with my cat."

I tossed the toy one more time, leaned back and steepled my hands in front of my face.

"I don't know how to start."

"How about at the beginning?"

"That's not as easy as it sounds."

It took me a couple of false starts, but I gave her a slightly abridged version of the story. It was very weird, as she asked me almost exactly the same questions as she had back on Stream One. And when I got to the part about my encounter with Trav Zero, I received a now-familiar reaction.

"YOU MET YOURSELF?"

"Well, got kidnapped by myself, actually."

"Trav, don't joke. This is not good."

"I know. But I can't do anything about it till I can figure out how he travels to the other streams."

"And you think I can help you with that?"

"I sure hope so. Sam Zero tried to send me to his home stream, and I ended up here. The Sam here can't help me much—his research isn't far enough along. Not to mention Zero showing back up to grab the phone. I guess what I'm saying is, science doesn't seem to be working for me. Maybe I need to try some..."

"Magic?" she finished.

I chuckled ruefully. "Some magic would be good right now."

"All right," she said. "Where should we start?"

She tapped a finger against her lips. "Tell me again how you got out after the other Trav tied you up."

I explained again how I had mentally talked myself into finding the special coin in my pocket.

"So..." she mused, "focus and concentration are part of it. Magic practitioners like to use focus objects in their rituals. Something that represents the person or situation they're trying to manipulate."

"Like a voodoo doll?"

"That's one application. Trav Zero didn't have anything like that?"

I shook my head.

"He stared into space for a couple of seconds, then disappeared."

"God, that's strange." She shivered.

"Actually, having a voodoo doll would have made it even stranger."

"Don't joke. Here's what I think. We have everything we should need to know right here."

180

"What do you mean?"

"He's *you*. Whatever he has, whatever he knows, you do, too. And he's not using a focus object or a device. The talent is inside him. Like it must be inside you. You mentioned your dad seemed to have a bit of the talent. That agrees with what the old texts say. It's hereditary."

"If you say all this is because the Force is strong in my family, I might have to hit something."

She looked confused. "What? Oh wait, that's a *Star Wars* reference, right?"

"Yeah."

"I never saw *Star Wars,*" she mused.

"No sci-fi fans in the coven?"

"What?" A puzzled frown crinkled her face.

"Uhh, never mind."

She narrowed her eyes, but continued. "Anyway, he's using some mental image, some projection to guide him to where he needs to go."

I could almost see the light bulb go off over her as an idea occurred to her.

"How do you remember stuff?"

"What?"

"Everyone has mental tricks, mnemonics that help them recall names, things that help them concentrate. You know."

"Uhhh. Well..."

And the piano lick from "Thunder Road" wound through my head, bringing an image of Mary with it.

"My God," I muttered as realization dawned. "It's *music*. Tunes or song lyrics that I associate with certain people. That's how he does it."

Morgan nodded. "That could be it," she murmured. "People— conscious beings—are the one, true reality."

I stared. "You told me that before. That we create and redefine reality on a continual basis."

"That sounds like something I would say."

Her eyes twinkled and a smile tugged at her lips. "Just how well do you know me...over there?"

"Actually, we just met."

"Hmm, I wonder." She said speculatively. And the look she gave me was...well, appraising.

"Anyway," she continued. "I think that's it. He uses the mnemonic device to firmly fix a certain person in mind..."

"...and then lines up the surroundings and circumstances that match the particular stream he is trying to get to," I finished.

We looked at each other.

I thought it through—the mental steps I would have to go through to build up the image of a particular person close to me, what was unique or different about them on that stream, then use that as a beacon to guide me.

Yeah, I could do that.

I stood up.

"Thank you."

She nodded ruefully. "So, you show up on my doorstep in the middle of the night, completely rearrange how I perceive reality, and now you're going to leave me here while you go out to save the Multiverse?"

"Uhh...sorry?" I said tentatively.

She smiled. "Kidding. Do you think you'll be back? Here, I mean. This plane."

"I don't know. It's not looking too likely at this point."

"Yeah. Well, do me one favor, okay?"

She stood as she spoke, took my arm and walked me to the door.

"Anything. I owe you."

"You bump into me again, be extra nice, okay?"

I frowned. "Sure. Why wouldn't I?"

"God...you can manipulate reality, but you're totally clueless, aren't you?"

"What?"

"Never mind." She stood on tiptoe and kissed me on the cheek.

"Take care of yourself, Trav Becker."

I smiled at her and stepped out onto the porch.

I fished the car keys out of my pocket, got back into the car and drove across town to my focus object.

Outside Mary's building, I sat in the dark, trying to stay awake. Even though I was nervous about testing my stream-jumping theory, I couldn't remember when I had last slept. It was quite late, but I had driven past the concert hall on the way over and confirmed that Mary's car was still parked in her usual spot. Receptions and meet-and-greets after her shows typically went this late or longer.

Finally, the *click-click* sound of high heels drifted through the open window and soon a slim figure strode into the light pooling in front of the apartment building. I got out of the car. Mary turned at the sound of the car door and watched me approach.

She wore a pencil-thin black skirt that revealed several inches of smooth, tanned leg above her knees, slim zip-up jacket, and dangerous heels—the outfit she liked to call "Symphony Slut."

Mary disliked the conservative formals that were normal symphony wear, what she called "bridesmaids' dresses."

"Besides," she'd said to me once, "the banker's wife drags him to the symphony, the least he deserves is a little eye candy."

She certainly was that. And I learned early in our relationship that there were definitely some fringe benefits.

Because whether it was from feeling all those male (and probably a few female) eyes on her, or from being caught up in the emotions of playing music, Mary often came home from concerts feeling pretty randy.

Despite the situation, I found myself beginning to get aroused at the memory of one particularly creative post-concert episode that had begun with me receiving a text that read *Gotta problem. Pines of Rome makes me soooooo hot. Can u help?*

I could, and did.

Three times.

But the blood flowed away from my loins and up to my cheeks as I got close enough to see the cool, almost hostile, look in her eyes as she watched me approach.

Here there had been no reconciliation after our last fight. I had been particularly cruel in my choice of words, bound and determined to drive her away.

I had succeeded only too well.

"Good concert?"

She nodded. "Shostakovich."

"Russians put honesty into their music because they couldn't in their lives."

Mary smiled wanly at the phrase she had said to me so often, then her eyes turned hard.

"What are you doing here, Trav?"

I realized I hadn't exactly thought this through. On this stream, I had no reason to accost Mary outside of her apartment. In fact, she'd be within her rights to be frightened by my sudden appearance.

"I, uh..."

I'd originally come here to use the sight of Mary to jump, but jumping streams or not, I owed *this* Mary more than just using her to get where I wanted to go.

"I was thinking about the other night..."

"You mean a month ago?"

"Yeah. I know that we can't go back to where we were, but I don't want to leave things with you like that. What happened wasn't your fault. I couldn't get past what happened to Adam, and going with Gene would have felt like I was running away, and I took it all out on you. I wanted to tell you I'm sorry."

Mary shifted her violin case to the hand holding her apartment keys and touched my arm.

"I wish we could have had this conversation a month ago, Trav. I know this has been hard on you, but you've got to learn that you don't always have to do everything by yourself. You have friends, people who love you, who want to help."

I nodded.

"I..." Mary swallowed, her eyes moistening. "I wish I could tell you this changes things with us, but..."

"I know. Too much has happened. Too much time has gone by."

She nodded. "And you're looking better than the last time I saw you. I'm glad. But that doesn't mean..."

"I know. I'm not expecting to pick things up again. That wasn't why I came. It's...if things are going to end, I wanted them to end on a good note. So to speak."

I chanced a small smile, and was rewarded with one from her.

"Nice."

"Everything all right here?" said a male voice behind me.

Mary looked up, startled. "Oh, Jack. Yes, everything's fine. Trav, you know Jack Armstrong."

I turned and regarded the man who'd come up the street while Mary and I were talking. He was a little taller than me, well-built with short dark hair. He was the communications director for one of the hospitals, a big orchestra sponsor, so he ran into Mary often.

My face got hot, and I pushed down a surge of anger. On this stream, I couldn't blame him for taking advantage of her newly-single status.

"Jack." I offered my hand.

Armstrong shook it, a little warily. He looked away from me to Mary. "Are we still...?"

"Yes," said Mary quickly, she lifted the arm with the violin case slightly. "Just let me put this away." Then to me, "We can talk later, right?"

I smiled and shook my head. "No, I don't think we need to. We're okay. Right?"

She nodded, a little uncertainly.

"I'll see you around then."

I looked back at Armstrong.

"Jack."

He nodded, and put out his hand to hold Mary's instrument while she unlocked the door.

She turned back to me and gave me a small, uncertain smile. Then she and Jack went inside.

I didn't think I had to be in Mary's presence to use her to focus on my jump. But it seemed wrong to take off, maybe forever, without manning up and talking to her. This was "my" Mary, after all.

Oh, well. I gave a mental shrug. *I might end up staying here anyway if this doesn't work. Then, I'll have all kinds of time to apologize. And I'll get to watch her with her new boyfriend.*

And with that pleasant thought, I thrust the mental image of Mary and Jack Armstrong aside and took a few steps away from the door.

I stared intently, summoning up Mary as I remembered her from Stream One. That part was easy. The feel, the smell of her as I held her, aided by the faint trace of her perfume lingering in the air here and now. Then I added the other people of Stream One. My partner who was alive, Leon Martin who did not want to lock me up...

And the door in front of me suddenly split into dozens of blue-tinged shadows on either side.

And one door outlined in red.

As I looked at that one, the notes of Roy Bittan's piano welled up out of the turntable of my mind and blossomed into the melody of "Thunder Road."

I turned toward the door with the red shift. I didn't have to walk toward it, though. It zoomed toward *me*, careening to a halt in a *Looney Tunes* kind of way, replacing the door directly in front of me.

And when my vision cleared, there was Mary back on her front stoop, juggling purse and violin case in one hand while she fiddled with her keys in the other.

"Need a hand?"

She started slightly, then looked at me over her shoulder and smiled. "Here I was wishing for an extra set of hands and my favorite ones simply appear from nowhere."

"All part of the fast, fair, friendly service," I replied.

"Here, make yourself useful."

She handed me the keys. I quickly found the correct one and unlocked the door, holding it open for her.

We went up the stairs and repeated the process on her apartment door.

Inside, Mary put down her bag and violin and stepped out of her heels with a grateful sigh. She shrugged out of the jacket, revealing a white, thin-strapped camisole, padded barefoot over to me and flowed into my arms.

"Mmm," I murmured when we came up for air. "Shostakovich went well?"

She cocked her head and looked at me quizzically. "How'd you know what we were playing tonight?"

"Oh, I pay closer attention than you think sometimes."

She might have asked another question, but I smothered it with my lips.

She looked deep into my eyes as we finished, and put her hand on my cheek.

"You're beat, I can tell. Do you want to stay?"

I smiled, not believing the change in my fortune from Stream Four.

"Tempting, sweetheart, but I only stopped over because I wanted to see you for a minute before I went back to work."

"More of that thing you can't talk about?"

"Yeah. Sorry."

She shrugged. "I'm trying to be okay with you not being able to tell me what you're doing at work, but remember your promise."

"My promise?"

"That we'd go away for a nice long vacation after this...whatever it is."

"Right. I haven't forgotten."

Not knowing in the first place was not the same as forgetting, I figured.

"Anyway, like I said...I needed to see you for a few minutes."

She gave me a worried look. "Are you sure you're okay? You look like you could sleep for a week."

I smiled and started to tell her I would be fine. But then I realized I was being unfair to her.

The next time Zero and I bumped into each other, he wouldn't make the mistake of going easy on me again. And he was far enough ahead of me on the skill meter in all this that the chances of me surviving that next meeting weren't great.

Trav on this stream was already dead, and if I didn't make it back, this would be the last time Mary saw "me" alive.

Sam knew about my situation. Hell, Morgan Foster, who I had just met, was hip to the entire thing.

Keeping Mary in the dark was wrong.

I didn't have time to spin the entire fantastic story for her, but she deserved to at least have some idea of the stakes. And she knew me well enough to see the internal argument I was having.

"Trav, what's wrong?"

I took hold of her hands.

"Look. You said once it wasn't about the danger of the job, it was about me being honest if I was getting into something that had the potential to be hairy."

"I know," she said quietly.

"This might be one of those times."

She tightened her grip on my hands.

"Isn't there something you can do? Someone who can help you? Are you sure you have to do…whatever it is?"

"I'm the only one. You know I'll do everything I can to be safe."

That got me a skeptical look.

"I'm probably blowing it out of proportion. Chances are it will be another day at the office."

I was trying for a tone of breezy confidence, but neither of us was buying it.

She sniffed, and I could see the beginnings of tears in her eyes.

"Thanks for being honest with me."

She flung herself at me, arms wrapping tightly around my neck.

"You come back to me, Trav Becker, you hear?"

"I will," I whispered.

I kissed her again. "I'll call you tomorrow."

"You better."

188

I kissed her one final time on the forehead and slipped back out the door.

Back on the street, I took a deep breath and tried to get my head back in the game. Mary had been right about me needing about a week of sleep, but there wasn't much I could do about it at this point.

I needed to get to Sam's lab and bring him up to date. It was late enough that Sam One would have left, and Sam Zero would have taken over.

He had to be frantic, as whatever mishap had sent me to Stream Four instead of Stream Zero certainly would have caused him to lose track of me.

And, my car keys may have jumped with me, but the Mustang had not. I had a nice, long walk ahead. I turned toward downtown and started walking.

And was so wrapped up in thinking about what I needed to tell Sam, how I was going to use my new stream-jumping talent to get to Stream Zero and all the other sci-fi aspects of my life, that I totally forgot rule number one of being a cop:

Be aware of your surroundings.

So, I was totally oblivious to the person sneaking up behind me until I got whacked over the head and the lights went out again.

12

The good news, I guess, was that this time it was a blow to the *back* of my head, instead of the front. So now my head throbbed equally on both sides.

Symmetry is important to me.

As I slowly came to, I was aware of the vibrating hum of a car in motion, and voices.

So, I was being taken someplace. My first thought was Trav Zero, but even with my eyes closed, I could tell that the car I was in was not the Mustang. So, unless Zero had added car theft to his list, this was another player.

I tuned into the voices. I couldn't make out the words, but there was no mistaking the Eastern European accent of the speaker.

It was Bilol Grymzin.

Great.

Just great.

He was obviously watching me for any signs of movement, because at the same moment I became aware of him, he spoke.

"Ah, awake now. I told you I would be seeing you again soon."

"How did you find me?"

I opened my eyes. I was in the back seat of Grymzin's big car. I had it to myself this time, though. Grymzin was up front with Gay-org.

I started to sit up, but froze when Grymzin brought his hand up, resting his pistol on the back of the front seat.

"Do not move. And you will keep your hands where I can see them."

Which meant they hadn't disarmed me. Probably barely had time to toss me into the back of the car before someone noticed. That was a potential point in my favor.

"How did you find me?" I repeated.

He shrugged. "You left with the blonde woman, but Mr. Kaaro knew you were also seeing the violin player. We were there for her, but got lucky."

A chill went through me as I realized how close Mary had come to getting taken by these two. How the hell had Kaaro known she was my girlfriend?

No time to ponder that now. I needed to focus on the immediate issue. Getting out of this in one piece.

"Where are you taking me?"

He didn't answer, just smiled and kept the gun trained on me.

I closed my eyes, ignoring the pain in the back of my head, and tried to think.

Grymzin was either taking me to Kaaro, meaning something had happened to make Kaaro think I was no longer working for him...

In which case he would kill me.

Or, Grymzin was free-lancing and had grabbed me on his own initiative.

In which case he would kill me.

So, either way, staying in this car would result in me ending up dead. And so would moving in any way, as long as Grymzin kept his gun trained on me.

Moving *physically,* at least.

I had successfully moved myself to another plane of reality. Time to see if I could do it again.

I had come from Stream Four. Could there still be a "path" back there that I could take?

I closed my eyes and focused again on Mary. But this time, not the loving but worried woman I had just seen, but the guarded, harder version I had also talked to.

And just to torture myself, I added Jack Armstrong to the picture as well.

The melody of "Thunder Road" drifted through my mind again as I shut out the motion of the car, the knowledge that there was a gun pointed at me, everything but the image of Mary—not so near to me physically right now, but always near to my soul.

Got it. I opened my eyes

"So Bill," I said breezily, "you a *Doctor Who* fan at all?"

Grymzin's unibrow furrowed and his eyes narrowed. He brought the gun up so it was aimed squarely at my forehead.

"You'll like this next bit," I continued with a grin.

And disappeared.

Okay, so maybe I should have thought through hopping streams from a moving car. But I was still new at this, remember?

I appeared back in Stream Four, about two-and-a-half feet off the ground.

Moving sideways at thirty-five miles an hour.

I had enough time to wrap my arms around my head and curl into a ball before I hit the ground.

And I hit hard. Then rolled about a hundred times. I managed to keep my head from striking the ground, keeping the impact points on my shoulders and butt.

I angled my body, trying to steer toward the curb, barely missing the right front tire of a passing Prius.

Smack. The gutter stopped my forward progress, at the cost of only about eight more bruises on my back.

I laid there on my side for a second, taking stock. I felt like I had gone three rounds with an MMA champ, but my jacket and jeans had taken the worst of it. Nothing appeared to be bleeding or broken. So I rolled over onto my hands and knees, and slowly got to my feet.

A well-dressed couple approached, taking in the gravel and dirt ground into my clothes and my bruised face. Their pace quickened as they hurried to get past me.

Not that I could blame them. I brushed myself off as best I could, and started walking toward campus, limping pretty good as my joints continued to complain about the trauma I had put them through.

I wasn't sure where Bill and Gay-org had been taking me, but they had unwittingly done me a favor by driving in the general direction I wanted to go, so I was actually about two miles closer to Sam's lab than I had been.

As I walked, I began the process of hopping back to Stream One, summoning the mental picture and the focus tune. I wasn't as smooth as Zero, but it seemed to be getting easier. I had to stop walking to make the actual shift, but I did it, and about fifteen minutes later I was back in Building 231.

The door was ajar, so I walked right in.

"Shit!" screeched Sam.

He fumbled in his desk. To my shock, he produced a gun. "Don't move! How the hell did you get here?"

I raised my hands. "Take it easy, Sam." I kept my voice soft and level. "It's me. Uh, Trav Four."

Sam's eyes narrowed. "Trav Four is...well, I don't know where he is." He gestured to the computer.

"I know," I replied. "You sent me back to where I came from."

"You were on Four?"

I nodded.

"You look *awful,*" he said. "What the hell happened to you?"

"I hopped streams in a moving car."

"That's crazy," he said. "Do you have any idea how much momentum you'd have to shed?"

"I do now."

Sam was still pointing the gun at me. "Trav Four didn't know how to shift between streams this morning. Am I supposed to believe you just figured it out?"

"What can I say? I'm a quick study. Look Sam, I'd love to keep my hands over my head for you, but I'm still a little sore."

"Yeah, right. So you can go for your gun. How do I know you're really Trav Four?"

"Well, *Sam* Four says to tell you your phone app is pretty good work. I think he was a little jealous. But he at least had the presence of mind to suggest a code word so he wouldn't shoot me by accident."

That made Sam chuckle, and he put the gun down. "Okay. If you were Zero, I'd probably already be dead."

"Tell me about it. I ran into him."

Sam's jaw dropped. "You met Trav Zero? How...? Why...?"

"Why am I still alive? No idea."

I explained how Zero had left me tied up but alive, and my subsequent escape.

"Wait," Sam said. "If Zero tied you up in your apartment, where did the moving car part come in?"

"Different bunch of folks I pissed off."

"Wow. Well, you've always had a way with people."

"Right. Anyway, I hopped back to Stream Four to get away from them, then back here again."

"Impressive. So, how did you do it?"

I explained about using songs as focus objects and the red shift.

Sam started nodding almost immediately.

"Yeah, any mnemonic that helped you focus would probably work. I should have figured with you it would be those old tunes."

"There is one thing that is bothering me," I said. "Did I travel to a new stream where the coin I needed was in my pocket? Was a new Stream Four created, Stream Four-A? That's a pretty flimsy occurrence to base a new universe on."

"Which is a pretty common objection to the 'many worlds theory,'" Sam allowed. "How many infinite universes can be brought into existence by the trillions of mundane decisions people make every day? Try this. Remember when I described the streams as branches of a river?"

I nodded.

"Each decision you make creates...call it a branchlet. Like a tiny tributary of a stream. But because that sole decision isn't enough to sustain its own existence, it's absorbed back into the main channel."

That made sense. "So, what Zero—and I guess I—can do, is find one of these branchlets that matches what we want to have happen."

"And by focusing on it, somehow you're able to absorb it into *your* stream."

194

"Wow." I sat down heavily on one of the stools that were still scattered around the Cat Box. "And what you do is nothing like that?"

Sam shook his head and gestured to his computer screen. "I can track objects as they move between streams. That's what the Cat Box was originally designed to do. And once I realized that you...that Zero could move back and forth, I developed the tracers. Eventually, I was able to create a map of our little corner of the Multiverse." He turned the monitor screen toward me.

I studied the confusion of colors, lines, and polygons that were continuously erasing and re-writing each other. It reminded me of that old screensaver with the pipes that continuously built and rebuilt whenever your computer went to sleep.

"And you can move through the streams using *that?*"

Sam shrugged. "It does take a while to learn, but yeah." He pointed to one "pipe" completely indistinguishable from the rest. "You see, that's the stream we're on..."

"Never mind." I held up a hand. "I'll take your word for it."

"But," Sam continued, "to answer your original question, no. I can't see or move around the streams like you do. I need gigs and gigs of processor power to do what you apparently can do by humming a tune. I might have figured it out by now if Zero hadn't gone nuts, and if..."

His voice trailed off as he stared at the screen and chewed on his lower lip.

This was not good. Sam only chewed on his lip when he was under stress.

"What is it, Sam?"

"Well, that kind of brings us to the next problem," he said finally.

"We have a *next* problem? We haven't solved the first one yet."

He swiveled in his chair to face me.

"While you were gone, the Cat Box started giving me some really crazy readings, so I re-ran a bunch of the equations and simulations."

He pointed to a cluster of pipes on the screen. "This is the region where we have had the most travel in between the streams. And the walls in between each plane are starting to...I don't know. Soften, I guess is one way to put it."

"Soften? What do you mean?"

"It's hard to explain without the math, but if we go back to our water analogy—what happens if you drag a stick in between two adjacent rivulets in the mud?"

"The water flows from one to the other—creates one slightly bigger rivulet, I guess."

"And if you do that enough times, you don't have several different streams, you have one dammed-up puddle."

"So, you're saying that our stream-jumping is—what, weakening the fabric of reality?"

He spread his hands. "Not you, not me, I don't think. But wherever Trav Zero has been going, that's where it's the worst. I was actually looking at Stream Four when you got here, because it appeared to be an anomaly. I didn't think Zero had been there. But when you said you had met him there, it fit back into the pattern."

"Trav," he continued, his voice tight. "We've got to stop him. The universe is not set up to accommodate this kind of activity."

It was amazing how Sam and Morgan Foster had managed to reach such similar conclusions coming from such different places.

"So what's the bottom line, Sam? Worst case? Apocalypse?"

He shook his head. "I don't think so. There is no buildup of energy that could cause, like, mass destruction. We aren't talking a disaster movie. Things will get...well, like I said, dammed up. Instead of flowing forward, time will slow down and eventually, just...stop."

"And what happens to us? The people?"

"You don't get it, Trav. When I said *stop* I meant everything stops. Time itself. Everything just quits...being. There aren't any words for it, but trust me, I don't think we want it to happen."

I had never seen Sam like this before. His hands were actually trembling.

"Okay, then. Just another reason to find Zero and stop him."

Sam nodded. "What's the plan?"

"Our original one. Go back to Stream Zero and look for clues."

"That didn't work out so well last time."

"Last time I had to rely on your software to send me. I think I can drive now."

Sam frowned. "I don't know, Trav. I still don't know what went wrong last time. And besides, how are you going to identify Stream Zero? You've never been there. Now, I can show you here..."

He once again pointed to the incomprehensible maze of figures on the screen.

I shook my head. "No. I need to do this my way."

"And how are you going to do that? What are you going to focus on that is unique to that stream?"

I smiled, pleased for once to be ahead of Sam. "It's not what *is* there that I'm looking for. It's what *isn't*."

"I'm not following you."

"I'm going to focus on what's *missing* from Stream Zero. You."

"Me."

"Yeah, you're *here*. There's a Sam-sized hole in Stream Zero. I need to find it."

I rolled my shoulders and rotated my neck. Now that the adrenaline of the high-speed stream hop had faded, my muscles were really starting to get stiff and ache.

"But first, some ibuprofen, I think. Are there some in that drawer?" I asked, pointing.

Sam opened it. "Yeah, I guess so. How did you know?"

"Lucky guess." I held out my hand. "Gimme."

He tossed me the bottle. I snatched it out of the air and shook four tablets out.

"Be right back."

The drinking fountain was by the restroom down the hall, in the opposite direction of the kitchenette. I took a big drink, holding the water in my mouth, then popped the pills in and swallowed.

Turning back around, I saw Sam coming back down the hall from the other direction. He must have decided he needed a little something as well, as he was holding a cup of coffee from the kitchenette.

Not looking in my direction, he opened the door to the Cat Box lab. I started toward him, opening my mouth to tell him to hold the door.

But the words died away as I saw his jaw drop and heard him shout.

"What the hell?!"

And then I watched as he was driven back against the corridor wall by a hail of bullets.

INTERLUDE

*O*FFICER BRIAN LOWE *stood at the corner of Houston and Elm, shifting his weight from one foot to another.*

The special noontime duty meant he wasn't getting his lunch on time, and he tried to ignore the growling in his stomach while he waited for the presidential motorcade to approach his duty station.

His partner, Hopkins, was in their squad car a few dozen yards away. Hopkins' head was bent over the two-way as he tried to follow the day's action through the squawks and squelching of the extra-large duty shift overloading every frequency the department had.

"Couple of blocks," Hopkins called.

Lowe nodded, sweeping his eyes back and forth across the crowd. Not that there was anything threatening about the throng of secretaries and businessmen lining the street. It was a big crowd, enjoying the unseasonably warm November day while waiting to catch a glimpse of the president and his wife as they slowly proceeded to his luncheon speech at the Trade Mart.

"Big day," said a voice behind him.

Lowe turned to look into the smiling face of another patrolman.

"Lowe, right?" asked the newcomer, extending his hand.

Lowe took it automatically. "Yeah," he replied. He frowned, studying the other man. After ten years, he thought he knew everyone on the force, but although this guy looked familiar in some way, he certainly wasn't someone Lowe could recall seeing around the station.

"Charlie Powell," he supplied. "On loan from Austin for today. They, uh, told me to check in with you."

"Ah, I see," Lowe said. "Didn't know they'd brought in any ringers. Pleasedtameetcha."

"Likewise," Powell shrugged. "You know how it is with the brass and the feds. Better to pull fifty cops off the streets than to admit to J. Edgar you need help from the feebs."

"Ain't that the truth?" chuckled Lowe. "Austin, eh?"

Powell nodded.

"Ever work in Dallas before?"

Powell shook his head.

"That's funny, because when you introduced yourself, for a second I thought I knew you."

"Really?"

"Yeah." Lowe had turned back to face the street, but kept the conversation going. "Have we met?"

"Don't think so," Powell replied slowly. "You get to Austin much?"

"Nah, it's just that..." Lowe's voice trailed off.

"What?"

"Well, now that I think of it, there was a cadet named Powell, couple of classes behind me at the academy. He kinda looked like you."

"Huh," Powell said. "What happened to him?"

"Got shot on his first ride along, only time the force has ever lost a trainee. Stuck in my mind."

"Ouch. Tough break."

"Yeah."

"That wasn't me."

Lowe smiled. "Guess not." He swept the crowd again. "What's your beat today?" He inclined his head toward the car. "Hopkins and I got this corner covered."

"I drew the short straw," Powell said. "Shortest you could possibly imagine."

"What?"

Lowe wasn't really listening. His attention was distracted by the first motorcycles leading the parade, which had turned the corner a block away.

"Nothing," Powell replied. "Just...uh, crowd control. Wander around, show the badge. From that little hill over there, I think."

He pointed to a grassy spot where only a few people were gathered, despite a clear line of sight to the street. He turned to go.

"I better move on. Nice to meet ya."

Lowe grunted in agreement, focused now on the convertible coming around the corner.

"Because sometimes the only way to keep disaster from happening," Powell continued softly, "is to do the worst thing anyone can imagine."

His shoulders slumped as he trudged up the hill.

Had Lowe been paying attention, he might have wondered how the pleasant, talkative officer with whom he'd passed the time now looked old and weighed down with doubt as he made his way through the crowd.

The escort cycles had dropped back to either side of the president's limousine to keep the onlookers from crowding in the street. Four Secret Service agents perched on the running boards of the next car, joining Lowe in sweeping the crowd.

The president had passed Lowe's station and he was starting to relax when he heard the shots. Three soft pops. *Lowe's eyes flashed to the president's car, just in time to hear another* crack, *but this one came from nearby.*

That little hill, just on the other side of the concrete pedestal.

All hell was breaking loose. The Secret Service guys leapt from the car and ran toward the president, who was slumped next to the other guy in the car—Lowe couldn't remember which Texas politico it was. The first lady was screaming, blood all over her face and coat.

Lowe's eyes swept the crowd of onlookers, attracted by a dark shape whipping around. He squinted and clearly saw the guy who had called himself Charlie Powell atop the hill, holstering his weapon.

Keeping the man in site, Lowe tore across the street, waving frantically at Hopkins. "Tom!" he cried. "Get up here! The shooter's in the park!"

Hopkins waved him to silence as he ran up to the car, leaning down over the radio.

"...and it came from the Texas Book Depository..."

The rest of the message was lost in static as a half-dozen other radios all tried transmitting at once.

"No!" Lowe shouted. "There was a shot from over there!"

He pointed back toward the plaza. "There's a guy. He said he was a cop, but..."

"Shut up, Brian," Hopkins cut him off. "The shooter was in the book depository." He pointed at the radio. "You heard 'em."

"But..." Lowe looked back toward Powell, standing still as a stone as people rushed all around him, staring straight at Lowe.

"I'm telling you, Tom. Something's not right. We need to go up and get that guy before he takes off."

"Fine," Hopkins replied. "Where is he?"

"He's right..." Lowe began.

What the hell?

"Where?" Hopkins demanded.

But Lowe didn't answer.

In the chaos that followed, Tom Hopkins forgot all about this short exchange.

Lowe didn't. But fortunately, it was never brought up in the dozens of interviews he endured—first by the feds, later by writers and journalists. He was by now eyeing his pension, and he had witnessed more than one career destroyed by saying the wrong thing to one of the conspiracy nuts. No way he was going to go down that road.

By the end of his life, Brian Lowe had pretty much convinced even himself that Charlie Powell had simply been a badge imported for the day, even though there was no Powell on the Austin roster.

And he worked equally hard to erase his own memory of the other thing he saw, just as he was turning to charge back up into the plaza— the figure in a police uniform that seemed to shimmer in the sunlight.

What he chose to remember was the view of the grassy knoll a second later.

Safely empty of anything remotely resembling a man with a badge.

13

I RUSHED OVER to Sam, catching him as he slid down the wall.

A bloody froth bubbled out between his lips. He looked up at me, his mouth opening and closing.

"Wha...wha..."

"Don't try and talk, buddy. I'll get help."

His hand reached up and grabbed my jacket. He shook his head.

"Wh..."

And he died.

I drew my gun and threw open the door to the Cat Box, sweeping the room.

It was empty.

"*Goddamn* it."

I swept my gun arm across the room a couple of times and checked behind the door, but the shooter had disappeared.

And since there was only one door into the room, that pretty much told me who it had been.

I went back to Sam. I was sure he was gone, but I double checked. Protocol required me to start chest compressions until medical personnel could confirm his death, but the six bloody holes in his chest told me it would be a waste of time.

I closed his eyes and gently moved him out of the hallway and into the lab. I laid him in a corner and went back out into the hallway. I got some kitchen cleaner and paper towels out of the kitchenette and started cleaning the blood and spilled coffee from the space where he had fallen.

I'd like to say that it was the fumes from the cleaner that made my eyes sting but that would be a lie.

Ah, Sam.

I was destroying evidence, of course, but none of that mattered right now.

I knew who Sam's killer was, and no official investigation would find him.

Two different Sams had asked me what I would do when I found Trav Zero, and I hadn't had a good answer either time.

I knew now. Whatever had caused Zero to go around the bend was never going to get any better. He simply had to be stopped. You don't stop to reason with a rabid dog, you put it down.

After I cleaned up, I surveyed the hallway. There would be DNA all over the place, but it would pass a casual inspection. And all I needed was a few hours' head start, then I'd be back to take care of Sam. I didn't know what I would tell the Stream One authorities, but that could wait.

I turned away from Sam's body and stared at the opposite wall. I didn't think I could go through with this if I had to look at him.

I had been counting on visualizing the hop to Stream Zero using a mental device that seemed obvious. It was the one stream where there wasn't a Sam.

But now, there was no longer a Sam in this stream either, and for that matter, who knew how many other streams had something similar happen in them and would be Sam-less as well?

No, I'd been thinking of this all wrong. The stream hopping had worked fine when I had a particular version of Mary to think of—I'd been back and forth between One and Four quite easily.

I needed a really clear mental vision of the person at my goal. And that would be easy. I would never forget looking into the face that was exactly my own, but somehow was harder, more cynical.

No, I would never forget Trav Zero.

I smiled grimly. Getting to Stream Zero would be easy. Then all I would have to do was find him, wherever he was hiding.

Hiding.

That was it. That was how I could find Trav Zero. He was The Hidden Man, *El Hombre Escondido*.

"Gotcha," I whispered.

And searched mentally for a slightly more aloof version of myself that caused the Spanish guitar and mandolin from "Too Many Nights Too Long" to swell within my mind.

Everything was pitch black. I fought down a surge of fear, panicking at the thought that I had done it wrong.

Forcing myself to stay calm, I stood still and listened. After a minute, I could pick out the sound of CPU fans behind me and a trickle of light on the floor in front of me.

I was still in the Cat Box. The lights had been turned off. Carefully, I made my way across the dark room toward the light seeping in under the door. I tried to open it a crack, but there was something wrong with my hand. I couldn't grip the door handle.

I frowned and felt around the wall for the light switch with my other hand. As soon as I turned on the lights, I realized what the problem was.

I had tried to open the door with the hand that still held my gun.

Okay, that wasn't good. I holstered my weapon, and took stock.

The ibuprofen was beginning to take effect, but I still ached from head to toe.

And my mental state…what was it Morgan had said? That she had seen mental patients with a less troubling aura than me?

The fact was, I was mentally and physically exhausted.

And I was getting ready to go up against a well-rested, Trav-killing version of myself who had already bested multiple versions of us.

As much as I wanted to keep moving, get this over with, I knew the smart thing to do was get some rest.

I locked the door, turned the light back off. Chances were good no one would be trying to get in here in the middle of the night. This was Sam Zero's lab, and he was dead on Stream One.

"Just fifteen minutes," I promised myself. I took off my jacket and wadded it up for a pillow. I would just close my eyes for a few minutes. There was no way I could sleep.

Famous last words.

A cart or something clattering down the hall woke me with a start.

"Owww," I moaned softly. The two head injuries, plus the post-car roll in the street—not to mention sleeping on the floor—made the first thing I noticed upon waking the ache in every corner of my body.

I carefully lifted my arm and touched the light button on my watch.

8:10 a.m. *Crap.* So much for "no way I could sleep."

I laid there for another minute or two, thinking that on the whole, the hangover from the other morning hadn't hurt this much.

I finally struggled to my feet and did some gentle stretches to try and get the blood moving again. I went over to Sam's computer stand and opened the drawer.

No ibuprofen on Stream Zero.

I could have tried the summoning trick again, but didn't want to take the time.

I put my jacket back on, opened the door a crack, and looked up and down the hallway.

Empty. That was good. Sam never seemed to worry much about security, but trying to explain my presence here without him around might have been tricky.

I exited the room quickly and made my way out of the building without encountering anyone.

Central Station was only a few blocks away, so I stuck my hands in my jacket pockets and started walking. The walk finished warming up my muscles, and the aches and pains faded into a dull throb I could ignore.

As I made my way across Campus Town, I cataloged what little I knew about Stream Zero.

Sam's research had advanced a lot quicker here than anywhere else. The Sam on Stream Four had indicated this Sam was months, maybe years, ahead of where he himself was with the Cat Box project.

Something Sam had done had "woken up" in Trav Zero what now appeared to be a latent ability in all Travs to manipulate and then travel among the different parallel realities. And apparently, this wasn't anything new. Prophets, fortune tellers, and mages throughout history had also had it. Dad even seemed to have had a touch of it.

And something had happened to Trav Zero that had caused him to not only believe that this power was wrong, but to take it upon himself to make sure no other Trav gained it.

And it must have been something pretty dramatic, because I could not imagine *anything* that could cause *me* to go all vigilante on...

Well, me. Not to mention poor Sam.

I shook my head. Even factoring out the stream-jumping, none of this made sense.

Oh, and whatever Trav Zero was doing, it was causing the structure of all the streams he had been visiting to break down. If he wasn't stopped soon, time itself was going to...stop.

And it was up to little old me to fix it.

What a mess.

There was a convenience store on the way to the station, and as I approached it I realized I was thirsty. I bought a bottle of water and walked the final two blocks to the station. As I put my hand on the front door handle, I stopped and looked around, frowning.

Something was different, something wasn't right.

But I couldn't identify what it was. I swept my gaze up and down the street a couple more times, but couldn't puzzle out what was bothering me. Finally I shrugged and went on inside.

The desk sergeant gave me a nod and a small wave as I came in, which caused me to let out a breath I hadn't even realized I'd been holding. Nothing Sam said indicated I was *persona non grata* in this stream, but it was nice to be sure.

Upstairs in the office, there was a bustle of activity — unusual for how early in the morning it was. And something else.

Everyone present was in uniform. There were only two things that would cause everyone to dress up. An official ceremony, which were rarely held on Thursdays...

Or a funeral.

Trav Zero had mentioned that he had to go to a funeral. At the time, I had thought it was an oblique way of talking about killing Sam, but maybe it was something else entirely.

My hunch was confirmed as Leon Martin's office door opened and the captain swept out. He looked at me and frowned.

"Honor guard forms up in fifteen minutes, Trav."

"Uh…I know. I have to run home, but there's time."

I was getting pretty good at not letting on in conversation that I didn't know what the hell anyone was talking about.

"Don't be late. Today of all days, we have to be there for Adam."

Oh, God. The knot that had begun to form in my stomach doubled over on itself and tightened as I realized that Stream Zero and Stream Four obviously had one sickening thing on common.

Here also, I had failed to save Adam. I realized with a sinking feeling that I was going to have to experience his funeral and its aftermath all over again.

That is, until my partner walked around the corner.

Once again, Adam Yount had, to me at least, returned from the dead. Like the rest of the squad, he wore his dress uniform.

But my relief at seeing Adam alive (again) was short-lived.

Because he looked *awful*.

Like the Adam I had met the previous day on my first stream jump, Adam wore a sling on his left arm. This one was black to better blend in with his dress blues. But unlike the ruddy, cheerful kid I had taken to breakfast, this Adam looked haggard. His complexion was sallow, and there were dark circles under his eyes. He looked like he hadn't slept well in days. In fact, he looked like I had looked when I'd awakened after the bender on Stream Four where all this had begun.

I moved toward Adam, but was actually glad Martin got there ahead of me, as I was afraid saying anything would reveal my total lack of knowledge of the situation.

"Adam, are you sure you want to go through with this? You don't have to go."

"She asked me to," Adam said softly.

"I know," returned Martin soothingly, like he was talking to a child. "But she'll understand. We'll *all* understand if you don't go. Anne doesn't hold you responsible. It was an accident."

Anne? And my stomach wrenched all over again, as I now remembered what it was I had seen outside the station house that had bothered me.

A small white cross in a stand, with some tiny pink rosebuds entwined around it. The kind of thing you sometimes saw along streets and highways where someone had been killed in a traffic accident.

And that someone was almost always a child.

Oh, no.

Holli.

"Of course it was an *accident*," said Adam bitterly. "But maybe, if I'd had both arms..." He raised the arm in the sling slightly, "maybe I could have swerved out of her way, at least a little bit. I was too *slow*. I was thinking about getting here, first day back after my sick leave. I wasn't paying enough attention."

"Adam, we've been over and over this, and the red light camera backs it up," interrupted the captain. "You were *not* traveling at an excessive rate of speed. Holli darted out right in your blind spot. There was *nothing* you could have done. Tell him, Trav."

My own thoughts were whirring so fast I barely heard the captain, but I stepped forward and put a hand on Adam's shoulder. "Cap's right, buddy..."

I searched for something else to say.

"There wasn't anything you could have done. Nothing anyone could have done."

But with a chill, I realized there was something.

In this stream, like in Stream One, Trav had saved Adam's life in that apartment parking lot.

And in that instant, I knew what had driven Trav Zero mad.

Even though he couldn't possibly have known the consequences of his actions, how could Zero have not felt responsible? What good could this gift of being able to change your reality to suit you be if you had to choose between the life of your partner or a little girl?

No one should have that kind of power. And just because Holli was still alive on other streams didn't make the anguish of Adam and Holli's poor mother here any less real.

I staggered back from Adam a little as all these realizations sunk in. Fortunately, all eyes were on him, and no one noticed me.

Maybe it wasn't jealousy, or a desire to keep the power out of the hands of others that had affected Zero at all. Maybe in his own twisted way, he was trying to *save* his other selves from having to go through what he had—the second guessing, the knowledge that every action he took caused consequences that only he could truly appreciate.

Maybe Trav Zero wasn't trying to eliminate his twins.

Maybe he thought he was *saving* us.

But regardless of how Zero was justifying his actions to himself, my original mission was intact. No one else needed to die, no matter how much easier or more beneficial Zero thought that would make things.

And he still had to answer for Sam.

Trav Zero had been ten steps ahead of me through this entire mess. Even when I had decided to hop to Stream Zero, I still was pretty vague about how I was going to best use my only tool, the element of surprise.

But as I looked around the room at all my fellow officers one more time, I realized my task had actually gotten a little easier.

Zero might have been ahead of me up to now, but I could predict his movements over the next ninety minutes or so precisely.

It wasn't much of an advantage, but it would have to be enough.

14

I EXCUSED MYSELF and went to the restroom. The bottle of water I'd downed on the way over, combined with the stress of the last few minutes, was causing my bladder to send panicked signals to my brain.

And I needed a couple of minutes to pull myself together.

After communing with the urinal, I washed my hands and, while I was at it, splashed cold water on my face. My hands were still trembling a little, and I forced myself to calm down.

The fact that Holli was still alive on other streams did nothing to lessen the sick feeling in my stomach. Her lovely little face and voice were stilled in the here and now.

I dried my face and hands and opened the door. Someone passed by as I was doing so. I followed the other officer down the short hall back to the squad.

"Damn, that was fast!" I heard Capt. Martin say.

Something made me stop, and I carefully peeked around the corner.

And quickly ducked back, my heart pounding all over again.

I had damn near followed Trav Zero into the room.

"What do you mean?" I heard my own voice ask Martin.

"What are you, a quick-change artist? I thought you said your uniform was at home," the captain responded.

"I, uh…it was here after all," said Zero.

I recognized the same tone I'd used myself so often the last two days—the slow cadence of trying not to let on that I didn't know what the other person was talking about.

But Zero was operating from a much superior knowledge base than I ever had. He would quickly twig to the fact there was another Trav running around.

I hurriedly backed down the hallway, quietly trotted down the stairs and outside. They'd be heading down any minute now.

My mind raced. What now?

The Mustang sat not twenty feet from me, but I dared not take it. If Zero suspected I had jumped here, that would confirm his suspicion.

Better to keep open the possibility that the anomaly Zero had experienced was either his imagination or, failing that, that I was hiding somewhere in the building.

But that left just one way to stay close to him.

Heavy footsteps sounded from inside and upstairs. I was out of time.

Before I could ponder the stupidity of what I was about to do, I was in motion, dashing for the Mustang.

As I ran, I dug my key fob out of my pocket and hit the trunk release. The lid popped open and I rolled inside. As I pulled the lid closed, I caught a glimpse of Martin leading Monroe, Zero and the rest of the day watch out of the building. Adam brought up the rear, still moving slowly.

I latched the trunk lid and wriggled around, trying to get comfortable. Fortunately, we Travs keep our trunks clean. Lying on a bed of jumper cables, umbrellas, and the other detritus that built up in a car trunk would have really sucked.

The car shook as Zero opened the door and got in. I waited for a second thunk, indicating the entrance of a passenger, but none came. I sighed in relief. A second occupant would have complicated my plan, as cobbled-together as it was.

Presently the engine roared to life and I settled in for the ride.

I couldn't remember the squad ever providing an honor guard to a civilian before, let alone a child, but Holli was special, and I approved, even as I ached not only for Anne, but also for Adam. Intellectually, I was sure he knew it wasn't his fault, but that wouldn't make him feel any less responsible.

And what was Zero feeling as he wheeled toward the cemetery? Had he already known about the streams at the time he had saved Adam, thinking he had cheated fate? Or had it been after Holli's death that he had learned that by saving one friend he had doomed another?

And what did this mean for the other streams I had visited? Holli on Stream Four should be safe. Adam was dead there. But what about the other streams where Adam was alive? Sam's words echoed in my mind.

Events don't always play out in the exact same order, but tend to end up at the same place.

Was that what had driven Zero mad? Knowing that he could never save both Adam and Holli? And even if it was possible to cheat destiny for one or two lucky people on some individual stream, what would it matter when tragedy was guaranteed on so many others?

Well, with any kind of luck, I would soon have the chance to ask.

The car ride to the cemetery lasted about fifteen minutes. Whether the entire service was being held at graveside or if the other mourners were coming from a church or funeral home service, I didn't know, but the police detail was going directly to the gravesite. Finally, Zero pulled off the main road, making several turns before parking. The door slammed, and I heard the muffled thumps of car doors closing.

I waited five full minutes after the last noise to make sure everyone had arrived. Finally, I wriggled around in the tight quarters of the trunk so that I could get to my phone. I opened it, using the lighted screen as a flashlight.

This model of Mustang had one of those releases in the trunk that opened a pass-through into the back seat for easy storage and transport of long items like skis. I found the catch that released the seat, and pushed it open.

An opening about twenty-four inches tall and eighteen inches wide brought some daylight into the dark trunk.

It was a tight fit, but eventually I was able to twist and squirm my way into the passenger compartment. I carefully worked myself into a sitting position on the back seat.

This had been a particularly chancy aspect of an already weak plan. Had the pass-through been a little smaller, I could have been trapped in the trunk, but I'd once again been lucky. I found myself wondering how some Trav who maybe had been a little bit more diligent in the gym with the shoulder press might have fared.

I could see the rear end of a hearse parked on the hillside out the front windshield. That was obviously where the service was taking place, although any people surrounding the grave were hidden from my view. I looked out the side windows, finally satisfying myself that no one was nearby. The back windows of the Mustang were small, and tinted enough to make it a little difficult to see in, but I was still relieved that movement inside the car was unlikely to attract attention.

I might have been able to successfully hide in the back seat in the first place, but hadn't wanted to take the chance of Zero seeing me. Hence the opportunity to experience the Mustang's ride from the point of view of the spare tire.

Among the items tossed into the back seat was the Cardinals jacket Zero had been wearing when I last saw him, a twin to the one I wore. I placed it next to me and sat in the seat for nearly a half hour, slumped down so that I could just see over the front seat and dashboard, watching for people to start coming over the hill toward their cars.

The morning had started off cool, but it didn't take long for the interior of the car to grow uncomfortably warm. Again, despite stress and uncomfortable position, I found myself dozing.

A car door slam woke me up. I peeked over the seat. The service was over and people were starting to make their way in my direction. I took out my weapon and arranged myself in the footwells of the back seat, throwing Zero's jacket over my feet in the hope that its dark color would disguise the fact there was twice as much coat in the car as there had been before.

Soon the door opened and shut again, and I held my breath as Zero settled himself. I almost gave myself away when something landed on my back, before realizing it was the coat of Zero's dress uniform.

I waited until I heard the click of the seat belt fastening to make my move, reasoning that anything that might inhibit Zero's movement would be to my advantage. I slid my arm slowly up the back of the driver's seat and pressed the nose of my automatic against Zero's neck.

I then slowly raised myself high enough to meet Zero's eyes in the rearview mirror. If Zero was surprised at the bizarre experience of looking into the mirror and seeing his own face, he didn't show it.

"Both hands on the wheel, where I can see them," I ordered.

Zero complied, eyes never leaving mine.

"I thought you'd stayed back at the station," Zero said.

"That was what I was hoping you'd think."

We stared at each other for what seemed like a long time.

"Well, are you going to shoot me, or are you just fascinated by our good looks?" Zero finally asked.

"I probably should," I replied, "but I have some questions."

Zero shook his head. "No time."

"What?"

"We. Don't. Have. Time."

"Time for what?"

Zero shook his head. "Later. Either shoot me now or let me start the car."

"Not until you tell me what the hurry is."

"The hurry is to save Rob Lennox."

Of all the insane things my twin could have said, I had not expected this. I slumped back in the seat, but made sure I kept the gun pointed forward.

"Rob Lennox? The witness against Kaaro? Our CI?"

Zero nodded.

"Out of all the crap that's going on, *that* is what this is all about?"

"Of course not," Zero snorted. "It's the least part of all this."

"Then why the hurry?"

"Because I am sick and tired of letting that kid die." Zero took his right hand off the steering wheel. I had let the gun drop a little and this caused me to bring the nose back up.

Zero shrugged. "So, what's it going to be? I'm starting the car, so if you're going to shoot, do it now."

"Go ahead. On one condition."

Zero's lips twitched in the beginning of a smile. "I know what the condition is. Tell you what, we rescue Lennox and I'll answer any question you can think of. But we have to leave *now*. I took a big chance even going to the funeral, but I couldn't let Adam go through it alone."

He started the car, and when I didn't pull the trigger, put the car into reverse and backed out.

I stayed slumped in the back seat, out of sight of the mourners we passed on the way to their own cars. Wouldn't want anyone to think they were seeing double.

As we pulled onto the freeway that formed a beltway around town, I sat fully up.

"Okay, but answer me one question at least. For a guy who's been going stream to stream killing people, why are you so concerned about one guy?"

"*That's* what you think?" Zero asked in disbelief. "How did you even get here, when you obviously have no fucking idea what's going on?" He shook his head. "Yeah, we definitely do not have time to get into that now. We need to think about how we're going to get into the Siemans building without us both getting shot."

"The Siemans building?"

I tried to think. Where had that come up?

"Wait," I said, remembering. "That's where Monroe said they found Lennox's body. But that was on my stream. How'd you know about it?"

"Why do you think I was on Stream Four in the first place, Junior? It wasn't to hang out with you. I was too late to save him there, but I was counting on being able to pick up enough information to help me save him *here*. You aren't the only one who picks up stuff hiding in the bathroom."

"If you've been following me around, why am I still alive?"

"I told you, later. After we find Lennox. Now what do you know about the Siemans building?"

"Not much. I don't think I've been there since I, uh…we picked up that sofa with Dad for Christmas that year."

"You weren't there with Kaaro?" Zero stopped himself. "Oh, wait. You're from the stream where you so thoroughly fucked things up you never got the undercover assignment at all."

"Well, at least on my stream I didn't become a complete asshole, as is obviously the case here."

Zero sighed. "All right, I'm sorry. That was out of line. We've all had our crosses to bear on each stream."

"What's yours, then?"

Zero shook his head. "Not germane. We're just about there."

"This is not over. Don't think you're going to get away with this madness."

"Fine," he replied flatly. "I'll do whatever you want. *After* we rescue Rob."

"I am starting to understand how our unwillingness to communicate can piss people off," I mused.

Zero, perhaps characteristically, did not reply.

While we had been talking, or rather while Zero had been stonewalling, we had entered the warehouse district. The Siemans building was only a few blocks from The Kremlin as the crow flies, but the rehabbing hadn't reached this far yet.

None of the buildings had received any attention in years. A few were skeletons from past fires and interrupted demolitions. Broken windows gaped like missing teeth in the ones that stood more or less intact. The buildings that weren't locked up tight provided shelter to high school drinking parties, raves, and of course drugs, both consumption and manufacture.

Zero stopped the Mustang about a block away from our destination.

We climbed out. It was at this moment I realized a hitherto unknown weakness in my original plan. I was glad I didn't have to keep my gun trained on Zero as I extricated myself from the cramped back seat of my two-door car.

"How do you want to play this?" I asked, trying to look dignified after my clown-car exit. I tossed Zero the Cards jacket.

"Depends on what our lookout has come up with," he said shortly.

"Our lookout?"

Zero jerked his head about halfway up the block, where I could see a figure disengage itself from an overflowing dumpster and slowly, haltingly make its way toward us, as if each movement hurt.

As the figure grew closer, I could make out a strikingly familiar, if much dirtier Cards jacket and hat, and for the second time in an hour, found myself looking at my own face from the outside.

But there were differences.

In addition to the dirt, this Trav's complexion was gray, and dark circles rimmed the underside of his eyes. He looked tired, and I had been correct—he was hiding a wince every time he moved. Now that I was closer, I could see that Hurt Trav was cradling his left arm.

He was looking me up and down in return, but carefully, as the movement obviously was painful.

"Where did you find *him?*"

"He found me," Zero responded. He jerked his head toward a narrow alley that stood between the two buildings facing us. "Over there. Bad enough to have three white guys standing around in broad daylight here, let alone all three with the same face."

"So, which stream?" Hurt Trav asked.

"Sam calls it Four," I replied.

"The fuckup?" Hurt Trav looked at Zero. "He's kidding, right?"

Zero shrugged. "He made it here under his own steam. That says something."

"Can we quit talking about me like I'm not here?" I asked, fed up. I turned to Hurt Trav. "What the hell happened to you?"

Hurt Trav didn't reply, just looked at Zero with a raised eyebrow.

"He's not saying," Zero said. "I found him bleeding on my couch a couple of days ago when I jumped home."

"Which stream I'm from isn't important," Hurt Trav said. "Suffice it to say I needed someplace quiet to recuperate and, as long as I'm here, I might as well help where I can."

"This is a quiet place?" I asked in disbelief. "What the hell is going on in your stream, World War Three?"

"Doesn't pertain to the business at hand," he said simply. "Now, are we going to do this or what?"

"Anything happen while I was gone?" Zero asked.

"Kaaro showed up a few minutes ago, with Bilol." Hurt Trav gestured toward the black car. "Driver's watching the street. Probably Gay-org."

Zero nodded.

"Will someone please explain to me what we're doing here?" I asked. Zero and Hurt Trav exchanged an inscrutable look.

"Well, if you wouldn't have been so preoccupied with getting your ass fired, Junior," Zero said acidly, "you might have heard Monroe talking about how they had a hell of a time ID'ing the body because of the fire."

"Fire?"

"Yeah, the whole building went up. Not sure if the point was to hide the body, or something exploded."

"Exploded. This just gets better and better."

Zero turned to Hurt Trav. "You up to getting Gay-org out of the way?"

He nodded. "Just give me time to get into position." He looked around, and picked up a rag laying in a corner of the alley. Then he slowly crossed back across the street and reached into the car, pulling out the blanket from the back seat.

Zero watched our injured double (or would that be triple?) slowly make his way up the street.

"There is something else going on here," he mused, eyes following Hurt Trav's progress. "I get the feeling he is involved in a completely different battle, and this is just a pleasant diversion till he heads back to the real fight."

"What?" I asked. "Like he's in the Inter-Dimensional Army? You think there's some sort of Seal Team Six that goes around fixing streams?"

"No idea," he shook his head. "Doesn't matter. Not our problem. C'mon. We're running out of time."

He squatted down and, using his finger and a pile of fine dirt that had blown into a corner of the alley, drew a large square.

"The warehouse is pretty much open space on the first floor. Front door on the north side, you have to go up maybe a half-dozen steps to get to the main floor. West side is mostly taken up by the loading docks, right here. There's a catwalk that goes around the outside at about the second floor level, from when it was a foundry. Two small offices on that level, connected to the main floor by a metal stairway, and the cash railway, of course."

I had forgotten about the building's most unique feature.

The original Siemans department store had introduced a unique money handling system.

There were no cash registers anywhere in the store. A customer's money or check was put into a latched metal container, about the size of a soup can. The container was then clipped to a fast moving belt, which was surrounded by a narrow wire enclosure, not much wider around than the container itself. The store's ceiling was covered with a complex spider web of the tracks, like a tiny monorail system, which zipped the little box to the cashier's office, where the purchase was recorded and change made, then sent back.

Most cash railways like this were eventually replaced by pneumatic tubes—the kind still in use by bank drive-ups—before they were wiped out by the parallel evolutionary line of cash registers.

When Siemans made the switch, the cash railway was moved to the warehouse, allowing for paperwork and pickup receipts to be stored in the second floor office, but still easily accessed.

I was too young to remember the setup in the store, but vividly recalled Dad handing a pickup receipt to the warehouse manager, who put it into the cash car and sent it screaming along its little railway. The small box shot straight up and to a junction which switched its path to horizontal and disappeared into a small window in the upper office, to be duly authorized and begin its clickety return journey moments later.

Zero was pointing to his crude drawing.

"They probably have Lennox stashed in the southeast corner, as far away from the doors as possible. I figure we go in and split up. First one who finds him, signals the other, who creates a diversion so we can all get out."

I looked at my doppelgänger doubtfully. "Just the two of us? And until I showed up you were going to do this with our brain-injured brother? Did it ever occur to you to get some backup?"

"What was I supposed to say?" Zero mimed holding a phone to his ear. "'I know where Kaaro's got my CI stashed, Captain Martin, because I heard another version of you say so. Can you send the squad down to help me and my twin from a parallel universe get him out of there?'"

I continued to stare at him. I had a feeling there was something he wasn't telling me.

Finally, he sighed.

"Okay," he said reluctantly, "Do you think I'm stupid? I made a call before I got in the car, but it will be a while before they get here."

He rubbed the drawing out of the dirt. "But we can't wait for them. Let's go. If Kaaro's here, that means Lennox is running out of time."

He started to stand, but I grabbed his wrist.

"Ok, fine. I'll go with you. But answer me one question first. Then, I'll wait patiently until you feel like telling me the whole story."

At first, I thought Zero would refuse again, but he finally nodded.

"Go ahead."

"*Why?*"

"Why what?"

"Why risk your life—all our lives—for one confidential informant? Who knows what the consequences are? Holli died here because Adam lived. Because you saved him. Lennox is already dead on at least one other stream. What does it matter if he lives on this one?"

"It matters," Zero said quietly. He sighed again, this time with the weight of someone who simply knew too much.

"I know, I went through the same thing. Drove me more than a little crazy for a while. What right do I have to interfere? But I finally realized you have to do what you think is right, and live with the consequences. The thing it took me a long time to realize is that the real burden of being able to travel and manipulate the streams isn't being able to change things. It's being able to truly *understand* the consequences of your actions in a way no normal person ever can.

"I don't have to wonder what the unseen ramifications of my saving Adam were. I just helped bury one. But I made the best decision I could at the time with the information I had."

"What about the others?"

He didn't ask me what others. He knew exactly what I was talking about.

"Them or me, Junior."

I studied his drawn, tight face for a long time. Finally, I asked the other question that had been burning inside me ever since I had arrived in this stream.

"Would you do it again?"

"What?"

"Save Adam. Knowing what you know now."

He sighed, rubbing the dust from his hands off on his jeans.

"I don't know, man. I ask myself that question a hundred times a day. But I can't change it. And the good news is, I'm the only one who has to live with the knowledge. Sometimes all the choices suck. But that doesn't mean you still don't have to make one."

"That's a heavy burden."

"Comes with the job, I guess." He stood up. "But you know what? Rob Lennox doesn't have to die today. And I for one would like to keep it that way. I've seen that kid die too many times. It's not happening on *my* stream. Satisfied?"

"What about Sam? And the other Travs?"

"Later." Obviously, his store of conversation was now depleted. "You ready?"

I nodded.

"Then let's roll."

15

WE PICKED OUR way through a connecting back alley to the Siemans building, making sure we stayed out of Gay-org's line of sight.

A chunk of two-by-four lay on the ground near the building. Zero picked it up and prepared to break one of the basement windows at our feet.

"Wait," I interrupted, pointing up. A rusting fire escape hugged the side of the building, starting five feet or so above our heads. About three flights up a broken window gaped.

Zero nodded. "Good idea. Quieter. Plus, they won't be expecting anyone to come in from up top. I'll need a boost up."

We stared at each other for a second, then despite everything, I started to chuckle. After a beat, Zero did too.

Normally, it's the lighter partner who received the boost. In this situation, though, it would take a pretty sophisticated digital scale to figure out who should give whom the lift up.

"I'll go around front and wait for him to do his thing," I offered when the moment had passed. "Think you can figure out a way to distract them so I can get inside?"

"I'll think of something," Zero replied, as he stepped into the cradle I had made with my hands. A moment later, I straightened as Zero pushed off with his free leg and stretched to grip the lowest rung of the fire escape. He pulled himself up the rest of the way and crouched, nodding at me before starting to pick his way quietly up the metal stairway.

Staying close to the side of the building, I made my way toward the street side. I looked over at Gay-org's car in time to see a figure shambling slowly from the general direction of the Mustang.

Hurt Trav had wrapped the blanket around him and pulled his ball cap low over his eyes. With a slow, halting gait which I knew could only partly be an act, he looked exactly like the average homeless person this section of the warehouse district attracted.

Hurt Trav finally reached Gay-org's car. Approaching the driver's side from behind, he pulled the rag out of his pocket and began wiping it back and forth across the windshield.

I smiled. Even from across the street I could see the look of horror on Gay-org's face as a bum smeared dust, grease, and God-knew-what all over Anton Kaaro's pristine windshield. He leaned out of the open window and began shouting and gesturing at Hurt Trav, who completely ignored him and continued his "cleaning," apparently confident his fine work would earn a nice tip.

I waited till Gay-org's attention was completely focused on Hurt Trav, and then slipped quickly around the corner of the building, hoping Kaaro and Bill hadn't locked the door behind them.

The door was full-length glass, like you'd find in a storefront, although both the upper and lower halves were covered with bars, a nod to security even in the era when Siemans had been a going concern. As I approached the door, an old friend got there ahead of me.

Red Trav confidently reached for the door handle, and a red-tinged version of the door opened for him. I followed suit, and breathed a quiet sigh of relief when it opened for me just as easily.

I slid inside quickly, then looked back out through the upper set of bars to see that Gay-org had now gotten out of the car and rounded on Hurt Trav, who was cowering back like a dog about to be whipped. I wasn't sure what his next move was going to be, but I'd have to trust that he knew what he was doing.

In the meantime, the little drama Hurt Trav had created meant I had gotten in without being seen. I directed my attention to my surroundings.

I was on a small landing, and seven or eight stairs led up to the main floor of the warehouse.

Red Trav had already started creeping up the stairs, and was now crouching so that his eyes were barely clearing the top level. I climbed up as well, trying to move as quietly as my shadow. I crouched low as I approached the top of the stairs and peeked over the last one.

As Zero had indicated, the warehouse was one large, open room.

But it wasn't an empty room. Remnants of the building's former use were everywhere. Big appliance boxes and furniture pallets were scattered haphazardly here and there. But there was also a surprising amount of new and intact furniture. Obviously, when Kaaro had purchased the warehouse he'd also gotten the building's contents.

Mattresses, desks, chairs, and bookcases were visible, but by far the largest, and most surprising item in the room was an enormous, white, submarine-shaped tank that squatted next to three cherry-finish dining room tables which had been pushed together to create a work area.

The ornate, carved legs of the tables provided a stark contrast to a collection of glass beakers, propane torches, measuring spoons, and plastic bags that littered the top of each.

I immediately recognized the instruments of a meth lab. Kaaro had obviously found a unique solution to the problem of acquiring anhydrous ammonia to use in the cooking process.

He had bought himself his own tankful of the stuff.

Behind the tables and to the left of the anhydrous tank, I could see that some furniture had been pressed into service by Kaaro and his men. Two recliners and a large sectional sofa had been arranged in a bizarre parody of a conversational grouping.

Bizarre because the focal point of the grouping was not a work of art, or even a big screen TV, but a kitchen chair containing the bound figure of Rob Lennox.

Even from a distance, I could see the bruises on Lennox's face, and blood crusted over one eye and his lower lip. But other than that, he was conscious and seemed to be aware of his surroundings.

Completing the weird tableau was a group of people reclining in the furniture surrounding Lennox, sucking on bottles of beer like a group of buddies gathered in the man cave for some football. From my vantage point, I could see Kaaro, along with Grymzin and the backs of at least three other heads.

I slid my weapon out of the shoulder rig and waited for Zero to make his move.

I didn't have to wait long. A clattering and humming sound suddenly filled the room as the old Siemans cash railway system shuddered to life.

Every eye in the place watched as one of the small cash cars popped out of a window in the upper floor where the offices had been. It popped and clanked its way along the ceiling, then down a rail which paralleled the staircase before coming to rest in a basket resting on a counter. As the car dropped into the basket, it popped open and a folded piece of paper fell out.

While everyone was focused on the basket and the paper, I began quietly picking my way across the room.

Kaaro inclined his head, and Bill walked over to the basket and fished the paper out. He unfolded it and turned toward Kaaro.

There were two words written in big block letters on it. Even across the room, I could clearly read the lettering.

METH -

REALLY?

"I'm disappointed, Kaaro," a voice called from above.

Everyone looked up. Zero stood in the doorway of the upper office, shaking his head in mock disbelief. Grymzin was the only one of the seated group I could see clearly, and I could see him start to go for his own weapon, then stop when he realized Zero had his own gun out and trained on Kaaro.

"I mean, meth? You couldn't have been into something with a little more style? I would have figured you more for a coke guy. Maybe even heroin, but not meth. Really classy, Anton."

"I'm a businessman, Travis," Kaaro shrugged. "So, is this where I react in shock to discover that your coming to my employ was all an act, an undercover assignment? You are a little late." He gestured to Lennox. "Your friend Robert has already told me everything."

"I'm surprised you bought it as long as you did," Zero said.

"Who said I bought anything?" demanded Kaaro. "I could see that the information you brought me was either unimportant or plain wrong. Exactly what I would expect from someone only trying to *appear* useful. I suspected you were not what you claimed to be, so I cultivated an alternate source of information."

"An alternate source?" Zero asked.

"Yeah," said a voice from a darkened area of the warehouse from our left.

Amy Harper strode into view. She was still wearing the leather jacket I'd seen her in at the station, but had traded the ripped jeans for indigo ones, tight enough to show nary a crease, tucked into high-heeled boots that went past her knees.

Oh, and a gun, of course, trained on Zero.

"Amy?" Zero said.

"What, you're surprised?" she asked. "Do you know how long I've been in the uniform division in Leon Martin's little boys club? Eight years. While I got to watch you, and that drip Adam, get promoted over me. Nothing else for me but to go into business for myself."

"Thank you, darling," Kaaro slid an arm around her waist. "What did your captain want?"

Her free hand held her phone. "Just to tell me the rest of the squad is having lunch after the funeral if I wanted to join them," she reported. "All but Trav. He zipped out of there right after the burial. Alone."

She pressed her lips together and gave a comical frown. "You come here without backup, Trav?" she said with a mocking tone. "Real smart."

"Hmm. Not so smart after all." Kaaro looked up at Zero. "I think you will drop *your* weapon. You can't cover all of us."

"Don't be ridiculous," Zero said. "Do you think I would show up here without backup?"

"Then where is it?" Kaaro asked mockingly.

That was an entrance line if I ever head one.

"Right here," I said, standing up and striding past the cooking tables.

Kaaro, Amy and the other men swiveled. Five jaws dropped in unison. Six, if you counted Lennox, who was squinting blearily, trying to follow what was going on.

Kaaro looked at me, then looked back up at Zero, who was now slowly descending the stairs, keeping his weapon trained on Kaaro and Amy.

"What...?" Kaaro began.

Give credit to Bilol Grymzin. Rather than get stuck thinking about the impossibility of a second Trav appearing from nowhere, he accepted me as simply another target and did what came naturally.

The big Uzbek swung his pistol toward me and fired.

But I hadn't waited for Grymzin to move. I fired my own gun as I dove to one side.

Despite what you see in the movies, firing in motion like that broke most every rule about safely discharging your weapon. In firearms training, the move would have gained me a reprimand.

In practice, it didn't gain me any style points, but it did the job.

The bullet caught the Uzbek in the chest, pulling him off center. Grymzin's round whizzed past my head, and I heard a ping as the bullet caromed off something on the table behind me.

Out of the corner of one eye, I saw one of the other thugs go down, thanks to Zero.

But Kaaro was almost as quick as Grymzin. As Zero fired at him, he grabbed Amy Harper by the arm and swung her in front of him. Zero's bullet caught her in the chest.

Kaaro neatly plucked her gun from her nerveless hand and shot Zero.

Zero clutched his stomach, tumbling head first down the remainder of the stairs. He lay crumpled at the bottom and didn't move.

I got another round off as I dove behind the sectional, and the fourth man toppled over a recliner. I popped back up, firing at Kaaro, who tossed Amy aside with no more thought than a used Kleenex. He ducked behind Lennox.

I watched as Kaaro's gun came around from behind the chair and pointed at Lennox's temple. He and I both straightened.

"That is some trick," Kaaro said, nodding at Zero's still form. "Mind telling me how you did it?"

"You wouldn't believe me if I told you."

"Suit yourself," he replied with a shrug. "Now put down your gun, or I shoot."

"You'll shoot him anyway. And me, if I do."

"I will certainly shoot him if you don't."

"And then I shoot you."

Kaaro smiled. "Then we are at something of an impasse. Or not."

And quick as a snake, he shifted his aim from Lennox to me and pulled the trigger.

16

THE IMPACT KNOCKED me back into one of the tables piled high with drug paraphernalia. I slid to the ground, feeling like I'd been kicked by a horse.

There wasn't any pain, but for some reason, none of my muscles seemed to want to obey the instructions my brain was trying to send. Warmth began to spread across my chest, while at the same time, my arms and legs started to feel cold.

I watched as Kaaro returned the gun to Lennox's temple. I knew there was some reason this should concern me, but for the life of me, I couldn't figure out why.

Kaaro's gaze slid off me as if I were no longer worth his notice, and his finger tightened on the trigger.

The snap of the gunshot reverberated up to the rafters.

Kaaro's smile turned to a look of surprise, and he moved his free hand toward his back. The momentum of the half-turn caused him to twist as he slowly crumpled into a heap.

"I told you. I am not watching that kid die again," said Trav Zero.

Zero had pushed himself up on one elbow, resting his gun on his own shoulder to steady his shot. The effort had obviously taken whatever energy he had left. He watched expressionlessly as Kaaro dropped, and then he sagged back to the floor again himself, his face white.

My right side still refused to obey, but I discovered I could move my left arm and hip after a fashion. I put my hand on the ground a few inches away from my body, and shifted my legs to meet it.

I succeeded in pulling myself forward a few inches. Encouraged, I repeated the maneuver, and managed to lurch and drag myself across the floor, finally reaching Zero.

He opened one eye as my shadow fell on his face. "Had to go and get yourself shot," he rasped.

"Look who's talking."

I coughed, trying to ignore the ache that my journey across the room had now woken up in my chest. It felt like there were steel bands surrounding my lungs. I couldn't seem to catch my breath.

I wiped my mouth on my sleeve. It came away red.

"Help me up," Zero commanded.

Somehow, with the three functioning limbs we had between us, we were able to get Zero into a half-sitting, half-reclining position against the stairs he'd tumbled down.

I eyed the other stairs, the ones that led down to the door, about ten miles away.

"Maybe I can get over there and attract somebody's attention," I ventured.

Zero chuckled, which brought on a coughing fit.

"Right," he rumbled when his hacking had past. "Both of us would bleed out before you got past him." He jerked his head at Lennox.

I had completely forgotten about the bound man, who was watching us uncertainly. His gag kept him from speaking, so whether he was wondering if the pounding he'd taken was causing him to see double or what, I didn't know.

I took a deep breath, preparing to drag myself over to Lennox. Maybe I could get him untied before I passed out.

"Wait." I felt Zero's hand tighten on his arm.

"What?"

"I think I can help."

"Help?" Now it was my turn to give a phlegmy chuckle. "What can you do?"

"This." Zero's eyes went out of focus.

For a second, I thought he had passed out. Or maybe died. But then, I felt...

What?

I couldn't explain it. It was like a hot wind blew through the warehouse, but it didn't disturb anything in the room. And there might have been fog, but nothing was really obscured.

But as I followed the direction of Zero's fixed, blank stare, I could suddenly see dozens, no, hundreds of red and blue-tinged figures cavorting in and out of my field of vision.

Some were me, some were Zero. I could pick out Grymzin, Amy, Kaaro, and the other thugs as well. In the next few seconds, I watched the entire gun battle re-enacted a dozen times.

Most of the time, the scenario ended with two bloody Travs leaning against the stairs, Kaaro and Amy's bodies crumpled nearby. But I watched Kaaro dispatch both Zero and me, along with Lennox, at least twice.

And then, out of the corner of my eye, I caught a glimpse of a red-tinged figure, one of the very few actually standing upright. Well, more or less upright.

It was me, leaning heavily against the table I had hit on my way down. This Trav was wounded, but not as badly. On that branchlet, Kaaro's shot must have gone a little wide, grazing Red Trav instead of lodging in his chest.

"Yessss," Zero hissed. Now he closed his eyes and I could feel the ghostly wind increase its velocity, still without disturbing anything in the physical world.

But it affected Red Trav. He was coming closer and closer. Or maybe it was me who was moving. Regardless, the red figure suddenly loomed large in front of me, obscuring more and more of the room behind it.

"What are you do-" I began.

"Shhh!" Zero commanded. "Come to Poppa," he whispered.

And suddenly the pressure on my chest was gone. The bloody froth on my lips disappeared. I was still crouched over Zero, but my right hand, operational once again, now cradled Zero's head. My left side burned like hell, but the sucking chest wound was gone. Now there was only a bleeding crease.

Zero was watching me, and a faint smile touched his lips. "How was that?"

"What the hell?" I began, then winced. "Actually, it hurt less to be fatally shot."

"Ingrate."

"What did you do?"

Zero managed a shrug. "Found a more agreeable reality. Didn't think you'd object."

"Well, spill! Tell me how you did it. I can return the favor."

Zero shook his head. "It's a small window of opportunity. Only enough time to make it happen for one of us."

"But..."

Before I could continue, Zero raised a hand weakly. He had another spasm of coughing.

"...known for a while something like this was going to happen," he continued when his coughing subsided. "Fewer and fewer reds and blues chasing me around. Look."

The maelstrom of figures were still gamboling around us, acting out the events in the warehouse in what seemed like random order.

But in all of the dozens—hell, hundreds—of different versions of the fight in the warehouse playing out around them, none showed Trav Zero upright.

As I watched, the figures disappeared group by group. Some faded from view, as whatever magic Zero had used to bring them into being wore off. The others zoomed in close to Zero, Lennox and me, subsuming into us, but this time without the shocking effect of the Red Trav that Zero had summoned.

A few seconds later, all the outlined figures were gone, leaving only the three of us, and the bodies of Amy, Kaaro, and his men.

"And, reality finds an equilibrium it can live with," Zero pronounced.

He chuckled at the stricken expression on my face.

"I thought this might be coming. Over the last couple of days it seemed like I was seeing few and fewer choices."

Zero's voice got a little stronger as he warmed to his tale. "But when I saw you, I could see you had the nearly infinite choices coming out of your past and present just like I used to."

Another coughing fit, as if the effort of saying so much had cost him.

"...anyway, thought it would be me, but I guess it's you. Sorry to leave you with the mess Sam and I created. And you better get your ass moving, since you were so clumsy."

"What?"

Zero shook his head at my bewildered tone, inclining it toward the table where Red Trav had first made his appearance.

As I followed Zero's gaze, I once again felt the disturbing sensation of another set of memories coming into being side by side with my own remembrances of the last few minutes, and then begin to over-write my own mental files.

I twisted out of the way as Kaaro took the shot, but not quite quickly enough. A lance of white-hot pain shot through my side as the bullet creased the side of my chest. But there was enough momentum to cause me to spin around, one arm flying across the table...

...knocking a heating element into a pile of paper used to wrap the final product up for delivery...

And while we had been lying there, the fire had spread across the table and onto a pile of cardboard packing materials. With this ready source of fuel, the flames now leapt high into the air and had spread to discarded fast food sacks and wrappers and more cardboard packing that stretched across the room.

In other words, a trail of combustibles that led right to the anhydrous tank.

"Shit!" I turned to Zero, starting to slide the arm that still cradled his head underneath his shoulders to lift him up. But Zero, with a sudden surge of strength, pushed away from me.

"Go. Take care of...both of them, and..." Zero swallowed, now having trouble catching his breath. But he managed to point to Lennox.

"Get the kid out of here. If he dies, I will come back and haunt you, I swear."

I looked across the room again. Lennox was smack in the middle of the trail of cardboard and papers catching fire, hopping in his chair almost comically while he struggled against his bonds.

"Fuck that," I snarled. "Don't move. I'll be right back."

Gently laying Zero's head on the ground, I stood up as quickly as I could, then had to steady myself against the stairway's handrail. Even though I wasn't dying anymore, I'd still lost a lot of blood. I had to stand still a second while the room stopped spinning.

I looked over at Amy Harper. She lay crumpled in a twisted pile next to Kaaro, her eyes blank and staring.

Then I started coughing, the smoke making it even more difficult to get my breath.

I lurched across the room, squinting and hacking, finally bumping into Lennox almost by accident. I whipped out the coin knife and sawed at the zip ties holding him to the chair as the smoke got thicker and thicker around us.

Finally, Lennox was free. He shook the circulation back into his arms and legs while I leaned on the chair back, one arm in front of my mouth, trying to use my sleeve as an air filter.

Lennox shot to his feet, turning back to reach for me. Holding each other upright, we stumbled across the room and pulled Zero to his feet. We staggered toward the door, coughing and nearly tripping each other as we headed down the stairs.

We hit the crash bars of the door, tumbling onto the sidewalk. Through tearing eyes I could make out a figure slowly moving toward us.

I reached for my weapon but my holster was empty. I'd dropped it somewhere along the line. I disengaged myself from Zero and put myself between the still-hacking Lennox and whatever was coming.

"Easy!" exclaimed Hurt Trav, showing two empty palms. He took me by the shoulders, just in time for me to cough up what felt like another quart of smoke.

"Geez, I was about to come in and get you guys."

"Never mind me," I choked, then was caught by another round of hacking. I motioned to Lennox, who was gently letting Zero down to the ground.

Zero wasn't breathing.

"Oh, no you don't," I growled.

I arranged him on his back, pressed the heel of my hand into his breastbone and pressed. Hard and fast.

"One and two and one and two and one and two."

I went as fast as I could, but the smoke and loss of blood soon had me out of breath. My lungs felt like they were on fire.

"Can you take over?" I gasped.

Hurt Trav nodded. As he took over the chest compressions, I slid one hand under Zero's neck to straighten his airway. Taking a deep breath, I pinched his nose and blew air into his mouth.

Just when I thought the day couldn't get any weirder.

Wide-eyed, Lennox watched me give the kiss of life to myself while another version of me gave me CPR.

We worked in silence for what seemed like hours. Zero remained still and unresponsive.

Finally, I rocked back on my heels, dizzy from the smoke and deep breathing.

I put a hand on Hurt Trav's shoulder. "That's enough. He's gon-"

And of course, that was the moment Zero coughed.

Weakly, but it was definitely a cough. Then a huge inhale and his eyelids fluttered as he coughed again.

A crash sounded from the warehouse.

Clothes on fire, Bilol Grymzin lurched through the door.

An agonized scream tore through his blackened lips.

He had a gun in each hand.

I again reached for my weapon, forgetting in my panic I didn't have it. But again, my hand closed on empty air.

I watched helplessly. Time seemed to slow down as Grymzin raised his hands to fire.

BLAM BLAM BLAM BLAM.

Bullets tore into the Uzbek, driving him back into the burning doorway. A beam fell across him and he disappeared in a shower of sparks.

I turned around.

Morgan Foster gripped her Desert Eagle in a two-handed stance, smoke curling out of its barrel.

And behind her, holding the just-slightly-shorter-than-legal barrel of his favorite shotgun stood a lean, grizzled figure. His jaw was clenched, his mouth a tight, narrow line. Piercing blue eyes calmly anticipated any more threats that might issue from the burning structure.

Mike Becker.

Dad.

"Backup," Zero rumbled. Which triggered another coughing fit.

"Trav!"

Morgan threw her gun aside and dropped to her knees beside me. She cradled Zero's head in her hands.

"Ohh, you stupid, stupid man! What did you think you were doing?"

Her tone was harsh, but her touch was tender. She ran her hands over his hair and face, as if reassuring herself he was really there.

"Don't you *ever* worry me like that again. I was frantic trying to get over here in time. If I would have been two seconds later finding your dad…"

Her voice trailed off as she noticed Hurt Trav and me for the first time.

"You…and you…" she stuttered

"Morgan, I think you know Trav. And Trav," grunted Zero.

She looked at me, eyes wide, then at Hurt Trav. Then at Zero, then back again.

"Unbelievable," she murmured. "You think you understand. That you're ready. But until you actually see it…"

A high-pitched squeal sounded from inside the burning building.

"Ah, geez," I wheezed, pulling myself to my feet. "C'mon. We gotta move…anhydrous tank…"

Morgan and I pulled Zero to his feet, Dad and Hurt Trav grabbed Lennox. Holding each other upright, we hobbled across the street as a deep rumble erupted from the warehouse.

The ground shook as we collapsed against the side of Gay-org's car, just as an enormous plume of smoke burped out of the warehouse. Fresh air flowed into the vacuum created by the explosion, providing an inexhaustible source of fuel, and the windows glowed as tongues of fire spat through any available opening.

When I had caught my breath, I realized whose car we were leaned up against. I looked around, then at Hurt Trav, who answered even before I could ask the question.

"Back seat. He won't wake up for a while."

"Jesus Christ," exclaimed a hoarse voice. "How many of you are there?"

Rob Lennox stared incredulously at the three of us.

"I thought it was the smoke, or oxygen deprivation. What the hell?"

"Long story," I said.

Another *whump* emanated from the warehouse, and for a few minutes we watched the building burn.

Zero finally broke the silence.

"Well, I guess our work here is done. *Ow*."

We all looked at him. Like the rest of us, he was propped up against the car, but he was holding his abdomen. In all the chaos, I hadn't really checked what his actual injury was.

Morgan gently pulled his hands away from his stomach while I pushed his shirt out of the way.

There wasn't as much blood as you would think, but his abdomen was a mess of blood and torn skin.

Sirens began to sound in the distance.

"There will be an ambulance here soon," I said.

Zero nodded. Now that the excitement was over, his complexion was gray, skin stretched tightly across his face.

"Here, rest against me," Morgan said. She pulled his arm up and draped it over her shoulder. "Easy," she said tenderly, "you've had a busy day."

She giggled and touched her forehead to his.

I stared at them.

"You've seen *Star Wars.*"

She looked at me, then at Zero. "Of course."

"Let me get this straight," I said. "You...two?"

"Of course," Morgan repeated, frowning.

"Go easy on him," Zero said. "He's from the Mary-verse."

Morgan looked at me then ducked her gaze, her cheeks coloring. "Sorry."

"Uh, it's okay," I said.

"Seems to me I promised you I'd answer your questions," Zero said, changing the subject.

"I'm good," I replied. "I think I know what's going on."

"Yeah?"

I nodded. "Somewhere between getting shot and almost burned to death, I figured it out. I'll take care of it. You won't have to worry about any crap coming back on you. Or this stream."

"Thanks."

"Anyway," I pointed to his stomach. "You'll get that sewed up and be back tying me to a chair in no time."

"I don't think so." Another cough. "I told you something was changing with me. I'm not seeing the streams anymore."

"You're wounded. It'll be back once you're on the mend."

"Maybe, but it's up to you. For now, at least. Good luck."

I nodded.

"And Trav?"

"Yeah?"

"Don't fuck it up this time."

"Right."

"Will somebody tell me what the *hell* is going on?" demanded Rob Lennox.

"What do we do about him?" I asked Zero. "We don't want him going around talking about getting rescued by three Trav Beckers."

Lennox held up his hands. "Hey, I don't care how many of you there are, I'll stay shut. Besides, once I get into Witness Protection, I won't even have to see *one* of you, right?"

"Don't worry about it," Zero reassured me. "After you're gone, this will all start to fade, and pretty soon he'll only remember getting pulled out of there by Trav Becker. *One* Trav Becker. And I...OUCH!"

He held his stomach again. Morgan gave him a worried look.

Which reminded me. I looked around. Our merry little band was one short. Hurt Trav was nowhere to be seen.

"Someone's missing," I said to Zero.

He nodded. "Pulled a fade right after I started breathing again. Probably figured it was getting a little crowded."

"Think we'll ever know what his deal was?"

Zero shrugged. "Like I said, not our problem. He didn't want to get us involved, I figure he knows what he's doing."

"Be pretty sad if we couldn't trust *him*," I said. We both smiled.

The sirens were getting closer.

Zero stuck out his hand. "Sorry to leave you to clean the mess up over there."

I gripped it. "I made enough of a mess of my own the first time around. Never imagined I'd get a second chance." I paused. "You're sure you'll be okay? We're leaving a pretty good mess right here. They're gonna chew your ass for going in there without backup."

"Better to get it chewed than have to explain it was my twins from parallel universes who saved it. We'll be fine. Right, Rob?"

Zero slapped Lennox on the shoulder. He'd been looking from Zero to me and back again while we carried on our shorthand conversation. His eyes still looked a little glazed.

"Do you need anything?" Zero asked.

"I'd take a weapon, I guess," I said. "Mine must be still..." I gestured toward the warehouse.

Zero nodded and reached into his pocket, pulling his service weapon out and handing it to me. "Yours will turn up in the debris, I'm sure. Anything else?"

I shook my head, and turned to Morgan.

"Take care of him."

She bobbed her head, squeezing closer to him.

"Ow," Zero complained.

"Tough it out, you big baby," she whispered. "You are not getting away from me again."

I turned away, and found myself facing my dad. He grinned ruefully at Zero and me, shaking his head.

"I can't even tell you how strange this is."

"You weren't giving him mouth-to-mouth."

"True."

We stared at each other for a moment.

"Thanks for showing up," I said finally.

"My pleasure, pal." He clapped me on the shoulder.

I put my hand over his.

"It's good to see you."

He nodded. "Trav...that one," he inclined his head toward Zero, "told me I wasn't around several of the places he'd been. That the case where you are?"

I nodded.

"How long?"

"A year."

"Wow. That's more than a little strange, too. I'm sorry, Son."

"It's not your fault."

"Still, I hate to think of your mom alone."

"She misses you every day."

"Like I would if it was the other way around."

"I'm sure it is. Somewhere."

"Good point."

The sirens were getting closer. Dad cocked his head at the sound.

"You better go. Going to be tough enough explaining all this to Leon without two of you being around."

"Yeah."

I couldn't bring myself to turn away from him. "Dad, I..."

"C'mere, Son." He opened his arms, and I went into them. For a second, I was six again, sheltered from everything that was scary in the world.

"Dad, I wasn't there, when you...you know, on my stream."

He pushed away from me, just a little, so he could look me in the face.

"Son, it's okay. I've had a good life. Married a wonderful woman, got to watch you grow up. On the whole, I'm glad to still be here. But if it ended tomorrow, or had ended a year ago? No regrets. And you shouldn't have any either. Tell you what..."

"What?"

He dug into his pocket, producing an oversize coin.

"Did you end up with this?"

It was the "special" silver dollar.

"Yeah. Saved my ass," I replied, producing my version and showing it to him.

"Trade me."

I frowned, but handed mine over. He dropped his in my palm, then looked at the one I'd given him.

"I'm sorry I can't be there for you every day like I can for him." Another nod toward Zero. "But whenever I touch this, I'll think of you over there, taking care of your mom, and being strong for her."

My throat was threatening to squeeze shut entirely, and it had nothing to do with the smoke I'd inhaled.

"And I'll think of you over *here,* keeping him out of trouble." My turn to nod toward Zero.

He smiled and nodded ruefully. "I'll try."

I hugged him again.

"Thanks," I whispered hoarsely.

"The least I could do."

Finally, I turned back to Zero, sketching a two-fingered salute to him. He nodded in return. I inclined my head to Morgan and Dad.

"Have they ever seen...?"

He shook his head.

"Oh. Well, then." I grinned at him.

"You'll like this next bit," I said.

And disappeared.

17

"What the hell is going on over on Stream Zero?" Sam Zero asked.

Dead Sam, lying in the corner of the Cat Box, did not answer.

"Last time I saw a mess like that," he continued, frowning, "it was that little bit of time here on One when the two of *us* were both running around."

He peered at his computer screen. "Damn. That's worse than before, almost like there are more than two convergences..."

There was an explosion of white, then the screen settled down to its normal display.

"Crap. Looks like Zero took out another one. Told you," he said to the corpse. "You owe me ten bucks."

"You were betting against me, Sam?" I said, "I'm disappointed."

He whirled around, grabbing for the .22, which rested by his mouse pad.

"Don't."

I showed him the barrel of my own weapon.

"How long have you been standing there?"

"Long enough."

"Trav, I..."

I shook my head. "I don't want to hear it. What I want to know is how many?"

"How many what?"

"How many of us you sent after Trav Zero."

"Where is he?"

"He won't be joining us."

"Wow. I'm impressed." He visibly relaxed. "When I brought you up, I didn't think your chances were better than any of the others."

"How many, Sam?"

"It's not important."

"The hell it isn't. You found a stream where I was just broken and messed up enough to listen to you, then you aimed me at Trav Zero. And I wasn't the first. I heard you. *'Zero took out another one.'* What I want to know is how many?"

"Trav..."

"How many?"

He sighed. "Nineteen."

"Oh, God. Nineteen, and they're all dead?"

"Not *all* of them," he said quickly. "The ability didn't manifest itself in all of them. There was one who did himself before I could get to him..."

"And what about Trav One? Where did he fit in?"

Sam looked uncomfortable. "I couldn't offer to let you stay here on this stream as long as he was around. It was a necessary sacrifice."

"A necessary sacrifice? Sam, listen to yourself!"

"I did what I had to do!" he hissed. "It was Zero who ran off in the first place. I had no choice but try to bring him back in. He was *dangerous*. He wouldn't listen."

"So you kept throwing Travs at him, hoping one of us would get lucky."

He shrugged. "Who better to send after him than the person who knew him best? A pretty elegant solution, if I do say so myself."

"Elegant. Christ, Sam..."

"What was I supposed to do, Trav? I had to protect myself, protect the project!"

"And what about Sam One?" I said softly.

Sam looked over at the body in the corner, then shrugged. "That was *your* fault."

"My fault?"

He nodded. "You were getting too powerful. I never expected you to develop the same abilities as Trav Zero so fast. I tried to slow you down by sending you to Stream Four, but you got out of that and found your way back here. You needed to be removed from the equation.

When the door opened, I just shot. It should have been you. See? Your fault."

I didn't even try to follow him down that twisted path of self-delusion.

"You were pulling the strings all along, Sam. But *why?* Why go to all this trouble? What was so important about Zero that you sent us out to kill him?"

"I told you. He was dangerous. Uncontrollable."

"You keep saying that. What needed to be controlled?"

Sam's eyes widened, as if he couldn't believe what he was hearing.

"What needed to be controlled? How can you even ask me that? You can choose and mold the very fabric of reality itself. Do you have any idea of the power you have?"

"That's not how it works," I said. "It's not about power. If there's anything I've learned from all of this, it's that thinking you can fix what is wrong with the world, or even your own life, is the first step to screwing everything up. Zero figured it out. All we get is the knowledge of consequences. It's not about fixing things. It's about living with the fact that only you get to fully understand the ramifications of your decisions."

Sam snorted. "That's a limiting view. You can't accomplish anything worthwhile without..."

"...sending nineteen versions of your best friend off to get killed?"

"It's not too late, Trav," Sam begged. He gestured to the computer screen. "I've been working for weeks on an algorithm that would let me manage all the permutations of a given situation on the nearby streams, and output the best possible outcome."

"Best for who?"

Sam shook his head. "You're not seeing the big picture. We can't afford to worry about small effects on individuals. I'm talking about being able to fix what's wrong with our country, our society, our history!"

"Wait a minute. What happened to 'all this stream hopping is breaking down the structure of the streams' you were so worried about yesterday?"

"Just a bump in the road. What I've been working on the last couple of days will allow us to judiciously...help things along, without causing damage."

"And if they don't, you can hop to a new stream, leaving this one in whatever shambles you create?"

"Can't make an omelet without breaking a few eggs, Trav."

"Well, speaking as one of the eggs, Sam, I say it's time for you to get away from the stove."

He sighed. "Sorry you feel that way." He shook his head sadly. "I think we would have made a good team. But I can't let you stand in the way of my work."

I realized I had let him distract me. I'd been so focused on keeping Sam's hands away from the computer keyboard I hadn't noticed one hand slipping toward the gun.

I hardly had time to rue this rookie mistake before Sam snatched up the gun and pointed it at me.

"Put it down, Sam."

"Sorry, Trav."

"Will you really shoot me just because I'm not going to go along with your nutty idea to take control of history?"

"It's not nutty. I'll do what I have to do. Again. The question is, will *you* really shoot *me*?"

"Won't have to."

"No?"

My gaze flickered to a spot behind him. Too late, Sam saw movement out of the corner of his eye and half-turned, but was unable to avoid the two-handed blow that slammed into the back of his skull.

Sam's eyes rolled up into the back of his head and he slid bonelessly out of his chair to the floor.

"Geez," said the version of Sam that had popped into existence a couple of minutes before, "if I ever get that whacked out, promise that *you'll* clobber *me* if I'm not around to do the job."

"Count on it. Boy, am I glad to see you."

I bent to examine the unconscious Sam.

"Will he be okay?" asked Awake Sam.

"Yeah," I replied. "He'll have a headache."

"Been there."

Ahh, a clue.

"Well, you probably now have your revenge for getting conked yourself. That is you, right? Sam Four?"

Sam nodded. "Uhh, cat litter."

"Right," I chuckled. "Gonna tell me how you appeared just in the nick of time?"

He shrugged. "I told you I thought I would be able to sideload the OS from the phone that got stolen, but it took a lot of time to get it perfectly configured. I only finished a few minutes ago. The settings from the original were preserved. It was still set to keep tabs on you. So I pushed the button, and *voila,* got here just in time to listen to Dr. Evil explain his plan for world domination."

"You heard that, huh?"

"Most of it. Am I eight cups of crazy everywhere else you've been?"

"Don't know. I've only really met you and him. Well, and Sam One, before this one shot him." I raised an eyebrow. "So, it's pretty much fifty-fifty at this point."

"Funny. And he did that?" He looked over at Dead Sam, shuddered and turned away.

"Yeah. He said it was an accident, and it might have been. He could have killed you, but he just knocked you out."

"So he was the one who stole the phone from me? Not Trav Zero?"

I shrugged. "Zero and I didn't discuss it, but he had no reason to. He was after Sam, not me. Sam Zero here made up the whole story to get me, and other Travs before me, to go after him. Trav Zero *was* hunting, but not other Travs. He was hunting *this* Sam, to stop him."

"So Zero didn't kill the other Travs?"

"Not all of them. Sam Zero sent so many of us at Trav Zero, he had to defend himself. It made him…"

"Made him what?"

"Hard. Jaded. Cynical." I recalled the bleak look in Zero's eyes as he had remembered the matching faces of those he'd killed.

Them or me, Junior.

Sam couldn't stop staring. First, at his own unconscious body, then the dead one.

"I can't get over how he could end up so completely, totally nuts. Could you believe all that crap he was spouting off about fixing history?"

"I don't blame you for being freaked out," I replied. "But..."

I searched for the right words.

"They're us, but they're also not us. That's the thing about the streams, each represents another set of possibilities. You *could* end up like him, but you don't have to."

"I hope not," Sam said with a shiver. He glanced at Conked Sam once again.

"So, what do we do with him?"

I thought for a minute. "Actually, I have an idea. I'll need your help, though."

"Absolutely." Sam examined the phone he'd smacked his twin with. "I'm going to need to...er, bum a ride home to Stream Four from you anyway. It appears I have voided the manufacturer's warranty on this device."

I smiled mysteriously. "Actually, we should talk about that."

"What do you mean?"

Sam's eyes got wide as I explained.

"Wake up."

I nudged Sam Zero with the toe of my shoe.

He squinted as he tried to bring his surroundings into focus.

"What happened?"

He frowned as he tried to summon up his last conscious memories, finally landing on the last thing he recalled.

"Who hit me?"

"That would be me."

Sam Zero frowned again as he tried to identify the familiar voice, then winced as Sam Four peeked around me.

"Oh, crap. Look Trav, it's not like you think…"

"It's exactly like I think," I interrupted. "You were trying to use…me…mes, meses…us. The Travs. You were using us as your tool to remake the world. And not only that, we were disposable. If one Trav didn't work out, you just plucked out another one and started all over again."

Avoiding my gaze, Sam Zero sought out his own double.

"It wasn't like that. C'mon, you know," he pleaded. "Tell him."

"Tell him what?" Sam Four scoffed. "That I'm batshit crazy? Nope, just you. I have no desire to remake the universe, and I'll bet Sam One didn't either. You didn't even think twice before you skragged the poor son of a bitch. He just happened along at an inconvenient time."

"You don't understand," Sam Zero muttered. "I should have given you the same treatment."

"Yeah, well—woulda, coulda, shoulda."

Sam Zero sat up and peered blearily around, finally getting a mental lock as he identified his surroundings as my apartment.

The cluttered, grimy, Stream Four version of my apartment.

This familiarity seemed to give Sam Zero a new-found energy. He folded his arms and looked at Sam Four and me, jaw set.

"So, what do we do now?" he asked

"You get what you deserve," I replied.

"Really?" A smile tugged at the corner of Sam Zero's face. "Who's gonna give it to me? You?"

Then he turned to Sam Four.

"You? Neither of you have the stones."

"How would you know?" Sam retorted. "Maybe I got just enough crazy in me to do the job. It obviously comes naturally to me."

He started toward Sam Zero, but I grabbed his arm.

"Don't let him get to you, Sam. That's not what we're here for."

"What *are* we here for?" demanded Sam Zero. "You planning to dump me here on this backwater stream? That won't stop me."

He tapped his temple. "I have everything I need up here to start again. I'll be back up and running in a matter of days, no matter where I am."

"Not from here, I don't think."

As I spoke, I was pulling out my phone and pressing buttons.

"Whatever," Sam Zero started to stand. "I'm out of here."

Sam Four produced the .22.

"Sit down, asshole."

Zero appeared ready to escalate the conversation and see if he could further rattle Sam Four, but then his attention was directed back to me.

"Unknown subject with a gun outside my residence," I said softly, but with the right amount of urgency in my voice. "Please dispatch a unit, *now!*"

Sam Zero looked at Sam Four.

"What the hell are you doing?"

I pointed the phone at Sam Four. "Giving you what you deserve," he said a little too loudly.

"No!" I cried, just as loud. I nodded at Sam Four.

The color drained from Zero's face as Sam brought the pistol up. He pointed it right at Zero's face for a second, smiling tightly at the panic in his twin's face.

Then he shifted the muzzle of the gun a few inches to the left and put a round into the couch.

As soon as the gun was fired, I disconnected the call.

"How much time do we have?" Sam Four asked.

"Maybe two minutes," I said. "My phone is registered with the department as belonging to an officer. When I dialed 911, my name and GPS location popped up on the screen. Second shift just came on duty and at least four black-and-whites have to pass right by this building when they head out."

"What...?" Sam Zero began.

"You're right," I interrupted. "You could start right up again from just about any place you could imagine. Except possibly a jail cell."

"A jail cell?" A little bravado started to creep back into Sam Zero's voice. "What are you going to charge me with? Nineteen counts of killing the same guy?"

I shook my head sadly.

"No. I think one will do."

I could hear sirens begin to sound, the dopplered wailing quite close.

I turned to Sam and extended my hand.

"Time to go."

Sam Four tossed the gun at Sam Zero, who caught it by reflex. And for the first time, he could now see the body of Dead Trav, sprawled out on the floor, gunshot wound to the head, looking as if he had been shot moments instead of hours previously.

We shimmered out of existence, leaving Sam Zero standing over the body, murder weapon in hand, as the door crashed open.

—

18

"So, that's it then?" Sam blew on his coffee, then took a sip. We were sitting in his office.

"Yeah, pretty cut and dried, I think," I replied. "The forensics will be a little screwy, because that Trav has actually been dead well over a day. But the recording of my call combined with the eyewitness evidence of the responding officers should be enough to make the inconsistencies go away. It's an officer-involved shooting, bail will be high. And with any kind of luck, he'll be spouting enough crazy talk that he might even be committed until the trial. But even if he makes bail, we trashed his lab…"

"My lab."

"Right. Sorry again we had to do that."

Sam waved a hand. "S'all right. And, uh, thanks for…"

"Getting rid of Sam One's body?"

He nodded.

"Hey, after having to move *my* own corpse, I wouldn't wish that on anyone else."

"What'd you do with him?"

"Took him to Stream Zero. They're a Sam short over there. I left him in the lab, with some drug paraphernalia nearby. I talked to Trav Zero. He'll spin a story that Sam had been acting strange, but the Rob Lennox situation happened before he could look into it. He'll make it convincing. And he's got plenty of help."

"What do you mean by that?" Sam asked.

"Never mind."

Sam was quiet for a moment. "He deserved better."

"Yeah."

"Look, not to change the subject…" he began.

"Actually, please change the subject. If I ever have to see your dead body again, I want it to be old."

"Me, too. Anyway, I was going over the stuff in Sam One's lab…"

"Was he further along than you?"

"Oh, yeah. Another couple of weeks and he would have been right there with Sam Zero. That's probably why he picked this stream in the first place. He didn't have to re-create as much from scratch. But that wasn't what I was going to say."

"Oh?"

"I, uh, think I figured out what Sam Zero was trying to do. You know, that 'new algorithm' he was talking about?"

I nodded.

"Apparently, he had come up with a way to…well, disassociate a stream from the causality matrix it had come out of."

"Okaaayyyy…"

Sam could tell he had lost me.

"He was trying to create…well, a pocket universe that Trav Zero couldn't get to."

"And what about everyone else in his little pocket universe?"

Sam's lips tightened. "Well, that stuff he was saying about being able to predict and direct outcomes?"

"Yeah."

"It would have been a lot easier without other streams nearby. Remember, stuff and people shift around all the time. That creates some pressure within nearby streams to conform to each other. Remember, we're all headed to the same future…"

"…we just take different ways to get there," I finished.

"Anyway," he continued, "he might actually have been able to set himself up as king once he spun this stream off from the others."

"Wow."

"Yeah."

We were silent again.

"So, what now?" Sam finally asked.

"Well-come to Stream One!" I replied, in my best Ricardo Montalban voice. "It's where all the cool stream hoppers go to retire."

"Retire? Is that what we're doing?"

"Definitely." I said firmly. "I don't think it's healthy for you to go mucking around in any more of this."

"Hey, you're not getting any argument from me," he shot back, a little defensively. "Sam Zero is the one with the God complex, not me. I'm shutting the Cat Box down. I'm thinking I'll rejoin the physics establishment and write a grant to get in on some Higgs-Boson research. That's pretty safe, and should keep me occupied for a long time. Maybe the rest of my career."

"Whatever you say, but I hope you don't mind if I keep an eye on you. We both have an investment in you not going down Zero's path."

"I'd be upset if you didn't," he said with a slight shudder. "I would like to say that if I end up like him, shoot me. But that's probably what will actually happen, isn't it?"

"We won't let it get that far, I promise."

"I hope so. And what about you? You're quitting, too?"

I nodded. "I'm not the quantum police. The Multiverse is going to have to take care of itself."

"You can quit?" he asked. "Just like that?"

"Just like that."

Of course, Sam couldn't see what I could see behind him. A line of Sams stretching into the distance. All outlined in blue.

Except for one in red.

"What?" Sam turned around to look over his shoulder. "What are you looking at?"

I forced my glance away. Not my problem.

"Nothing."

"So, what do we do now?"

I smiled. "Like a wise man once told me, 'Go, explore your new world.'"

"Do I know this wise man?"

"Very well."

We shook hands. I checked my watch.

"I need to get to work."

Sam nodded. "Me, too. Lotta files to organize. You sure you're not gonna…you know…"

"Positive."

I wasn't exactly lying to Sam. I would be happy to walk away. Just not quite yet.

I pulled out my phone as I got into the car and sat there for a long minute, staring at it. I had been putting off making this call ever since I had woken up. I couldn't really articulate why, but I felt…well, guilty about calling my mom.

After all, I'd gotten to see her husband last night while she never would get to hold him again.

Finally, I pushed the speed dial button.

"Hello?"

"Hi, Mom."

"Good morning. It's early. Is everything all right?"

"Fine. Just wanted to check in."

"This wouldn't have anything to do with the fact that you know your mother worries whenever a big police raid leads the morning news, does it?"

"Ah, you see right through me," I said, a smile tugging at my lips. "Can't talk about it, but I knew you'd be wondering."

"Well, it was nice of you to call."

"Mom…"

"What is it, Trav? What's the matter?"

I opened and closed my mouth a couple of times, my careful rehearsal failing me totally.

"Uh, well, I was thinking about Dad…"

There was a short pause. "I know, Son. I miss him too, especially this week. It being the anniversary and all."

"Yeah, me too," I cleared my throat, trying hard to clear the lump that had formed there. The silver dollar was in my free hand, and I rubbed it between my thumb and forefinger.

"Anyway, I thought I'd come over for a while tonight. Catch up with you."

"That would be nice."

We agreed on a time, and I snapped the phone shut. I sat there for a couple of minutes more, rubbing the coin. Finally, I started the engine and headed for the station.

The staff lot was full, so I found a parking spot on the street. As I got out of the car, my phone started to vibrate. The soft rumble was followed a second later by the opening notes to "Thunder Road," and I smiled. A weight lifted from my shoulders as I opened it back up.

"Hey."

"Hey yourself," said Mary. "Where were you last night? I tried to call."

"Uh…kind of a stakeout. No calls."

"A likely story. You were probably shacked up with some floozy."

I pushed the memory of Trav Zero and Morgan Foster embracing out my head.

"No way. You're the only floozy for me."

"Careful. Compliments like that will go to my head."

"I'll take my chances."

"Busy tonight?"

"Well, I want to stop over and see my mom for a while. I didn't really talk to her…you know, the other day."

"She'll like that."

"But then…I haven't forgotten my promise. I'm putting in for some vacation. Take a week off, maybe three. Can you get away?"

"Time off?" Mary's tone got suspicious. "Who are you and what have you done with Trav Becker?"

"That's actually kind of an interesting story."

"Maybe you can tell me all about it. On a beach someplace?"

"I like the way you think."

Ahead of me, near the front door of the station, some movement caught my eye. Holli Benjamin let the door whisper shut behind her. Her bright pink top made a sharp contrast against the dull red brick exterior of the building. A colorful backpack nearly as big as she was made her look like a fluorescent turtle.

I started to walk a little faster.

"Hey, gotta go. I'll call you after I see Mom."

257

"I'll be waiting."

"Love you."

"Love you, too. Bye."

I looked back over my shoulder and could make out a familiar vehicle heading up the street in my direction, maybe a half block away.

I broke into a jog, and intercepted Holli as she got to the curb.

"Morning."

Holli squinted up at me. "Hi, Trav."

I glanced at the street, where Holli had been about to cross in between two parked cars, then at the little girl.

"Didn't your mom tell you never to cross in the middle of the street?"

"I wasn't going to!"

I looked at her skeptically.

"Well, maybe just this once. But I'm gonna be late."

She looked around, obviously trying to distract my attention from her transgression.

"Oh look, there's Adam! Hi, Adam!"

Holli waved as Adam cruised past. I watched as his head turned in our direction. Adam looked a little startled, then beeped his horn.

I didn't let the little girl see me release the breath I'd been holding.

"Yeah, there's Adam. And he's a great driver. But even he can't always see someone darting out into the middle of the street in front of him. You have to be more careful."

"Are you going to tell my mom?"

"I won't if you promise me you'll always walk down to the light from now on."

"I promise. If *you* promise to show me a magic trick after school?"

"Blackmailer. Okay. You got it."

"Awesome! Bye, Trav!"

She skipped down to the corner, looking back at me as she pressed the walk button on the traffic light pole. The light changed, and she waved. I waved back.

I was opening the door to head into the station when I heard a voice behind me.

"Glad you were standing there, man," Adam said. "I might not have seen her." He shuddered. "Can't even imagine what might have happened."

"You can't get caught up in what might have been, Adam. Take my word for it. It'll drive you crazy."

He clapped me on the shoulder. "I'm surprised you even came in this morning, hero. How late were you up processing Kaaro and his crew?"

"Late enough," I yawned. "But I needed to see it through till the end."

The raid on the Siemans warehouse on this stream had not been nearly as exciting as the one on Stream Zero, but there had been a couple of hairy moments, especially knowing that Kaaro had a mole in the department.

"And, I still can't believe that about Amy," Adam continued, almost as if he had read my mind. "There's only one person less likely to go over to the Dark Side."

"Who's that?" I asked absently.

"You, dummy." He shook his head. "Still hard to believe you pulled off that undercover assignment in the first place. Kaaro can't possibly be as smart as everyone says if he believed a straight arrow like you would ever turn."

"You'd be surprised what people are capable of."

I opened the door for him. "Tell you what. Let me put at least a small dent in whatever paperwork is left over from last night, then we'll head out for an early lunch."

"Okay. Where?"

I looked out at the row of Adams stretching beyond my partner, finally locating the one I wanted. A red-lined image of him with one arm draped affectionately around Kim the waitress zipped into my field of vision.

"The diner. Definitely the diner. I think you'll like today's special."

POSTSCRIPT

"*S*O, THAT'S IT *then?*"

"*That's it.*"

"*He said he's done. That he wasn't going to become a quantum cop.*"

"*He saved the girl.*"

"*We all have a soft spot for the girl. I still think all he learned from this was that he* shouldn't *interfere.*"

"*He took an oath. To serve and protect. If we need him, he'll be there.*"

"*Well, I guess you'd know.*"

"*I would.*"

PRISONER

"*THEY'RE COMING.*"

Bright, arterial blood spurted from the shoulder of the man standing at my door. It contrasted with a darker stain that soaked his abdomen. The arm that wasn't gushing blood was wrapped around his stomach, trying to hold his guts in.

He swayed a couple of times and crumpled to the ground.

I managed to catch him before he hit, lowering him to the floor as gently as I could. I cradled his head as his mouth worked, but all that came out was a rusty wheeze.

"Don't try to talk," I said. "I'll get help."

He focused on me with some difficulty, reaching for the collar of my shirt with a bloody hand. He pulled me close to his face.

"They're *coming*," he whispered again.

And died.

I gently laid his head back and placed the hand that had grabbed my shirt on his chest. I laid two fingers on his neck to verify there was no pulse, but I knew there was no life remaining in his now-blank, staring eyes.

I rocked back on my haunches and regarded the dead man on my living room floor.

I knew him. His name was Trav Becker. Thirty-two, eleven year veteran of our town's PD, last four of those a detective. Single, but with a girlfriend totally out of his league. He was thinking of asking her to tie the knot.

I knew he'd broken his elbow jumping off a play set at his eighth birthday party.

I knew that he was still coming to terms with the death of his dad, even though it had been more than two years.

And that he was now strictly a beer drinker because of some very unpleasant memories involving vodka.

I knew a lot more about him than that.

In fact, I knew everything about him.

Because Trav Becker is also my name.

And this was not the first time I had found myself staring my own dead body. In fact, it wasn't even the first time in this room.

It is not something you get used to.

PRISONER
By
Dennis W. Green
Now Available

AUTHOR'S NOTE

A COUPLE OF YEARS prior to the publication of *Traveler*, I began meeting regularly with two friends, Rob Cline and Lennox Randon, in a writers group to complete novels we all had on the shelf.

Randon (he goes by his last name) was at the time in remission from stomach cancer, and publishing a book was on a bucket list he was no longer putting off. He recruited Rob first, who then got me involved.

When the guy with cancer says he is going to make writing a priority, it's hard to make excuses for not also doing the work.

This association has resulted in all three of us publishing books, a better average than most writing groups, I think.

At the time of this writing, Randon's cancer has returned. But he is working on his second book, a little weaker perhaps, but staying positive and being an inspiration to Rob, me, and everyone who meets him.

There would be no *Traveler* without Lennox Randon.

If you enjoyed *Traveler*, please check out Randon's *Friends Dogs Bullets Lovers* and Rob's *Murder by the Slice*, both available in the usual formats online at Amazon and Barnes & Noble.

Honest feedback and reviews are always welcome, on book review sites as well as my own web page, www.denniswgreen.com.

THE MUSIC OF TRAVELER

MUSIC IS IMPORTANT to Trav Becker, and to me. Each of us has a personal soundtrack of songs that conjure up a certain feeling, or time in our lives. Part of the fun of writing this novel was thinking about songs that have been important to me, and weaving them into Trav's story.

Here is the music mentioned in *Traveler:*

- "Freddie the Freeloader," from *Kind of Blue* - Miles Davis
- "I Shot the Sheriff," from *461 Ocean Boulevard* - Eric Clapton
- "Too Many Nights Too Long" from *Rose of Cimarron_*- Poco
- "Buffalo River Home," from *Perfectly Good Guitar* - John Hiatt.
- "Birdland," from *Heavy Weather* - Weather Report
- "In the Court of the Crimson King," from *In The Court of the Crimson King* - King Crimson
- "Thunder Road," from *Born To Run* - Bruce Springsteen

If you purchase any of the songs or albums from the links on my website, a few shekels will go to KCCK-FM, the public radio station where I work. It's a little payback for the time I spent thinking about the book when I should have been working. Oh, and if you like jazz and blues, check it out.

I've posted a playlist of these and some of Trav's other favorite songs at http://denniswgreen.com/the-music-of-traveler/

ABOUT THE AUTHOR

DENNIS W. GREEN is a writer, radio personality, actor, college administrator, sports announcer, tech geek, husband, and dad who lives his life by Robert Heinlein's admonition: Specialization is for insects.

As a DJ, his adventures were covered by newspapers from Anchorage to Los Angeles. As a writer, his work has been published in the small press and broadcast trades. He is the editor of the triathlon news site, www.heartofamericatri.com, and also muses on his own blog, www.denniswgreen.com.

By day, he is the general manager of Iowa's only jazz radio station, KCCK-FM. And if it's 5:30 a.m., you can probably find him in the pool, working out with the Milky Way Masters swim club.

Follow Dennis on Twitter, *@dgreencr*, or email *D@denniswgreen.com*.

Made in the USA
Lexington, KY
29 October 2019

56270311R00151